THE VILLAGE GREEN BOOKSHOP

Rachael Lucas writes novels for adults and teenagers, including the Carnegie-nominated *The State of Grace*, which was selected as an Outstanding Book for Young People with Disabilities by IBBY. She lives by the seaside in the north west of England with her family. She is the author of *The Telephone Box Library*, *Finding Hope at Hillside Farm*, *Wildflower Bay*, *Coming Up Roses*, *Sealed with a Kiss*, *The State of Grace* and *My Box-Shaped Heart*.

You can follow Rachael on Twitter @karamina and on Instagram @rachaellucas.

Also by Rachael Lucas

The Telephone Box Library
Finding Hope at Hillside Farm
Wildflower Bay
Coming Up Roses
Sealed with a Kiss

The State of Grace
My Box-Shaped Heart

e-novella
Sealed with a Christmas Kiss

The Village Green Bookshop

Rachael Lucas

PAN BOOKS

First published 2021 by Macmillan

First published in paperback 2021 by Pan Books
an imprint of Pan Macmillan
The Smithson, 6 Briset Street, London EC1M 5NR
EU representative: Macmillan Publishers Ireland Ltd, Mallard Lodge,
Lansdowne Village, Dublin 4
Associated companies throughout the world
www.panmacmillan.com

ISBN 978-1-5290-5873-4

1 3 5 7 9 8 6 4 2

A CIP catalogue record for this book is available from the British Library.

Typeset by Palimpsest Book Production Ltd, Falkirk, Stirlingshire
Printed and bound by CPI Group (UK) Ltd, Croydon, CR0 4YY

To James, with all the loves

Chapter One

'I can't believe you've been left in the lurch to go on your own.'

Hannah Reynolds took the opportunity that a queue of traffic offered to look fleetingly at her own expression in the rear-view mirror of her untidy car. At thirty-five, she still managed to look like a schoolgirl who'd been told off – again – for talking in class. She rolled her eyes. Somehow the girl she'd been, though, had been replaced with a pretty-ish (her own estimation – trying to embrace the whole *love yourself* movement on Instagram) woman with a tangle of dark brown curls (and a sprinkling of sneaky greys).

Traffic began to shift, slowly, and she waved with gratitude as a lorry driver held back, giving her space to move left into the lane that fed into the Oxford turn-off. Meanwhile, her friend Katie was still grumbling her disapproval through the hands-free phone.

'You're too bloody soft, that's your problem.'

'I know,' Hannah said patiently. She didn't really think she was. If you asked her – which the loving but strident Katie didn't, very often – she'd admit that she could be a bit of a pushover, but that she stood up for what mattered. And if that meant that Phil, her salesman husband who worked increasingly ridiculous hours, couldn't make it to her Aunt Jess's funeral and she had to go alone, well, that was just what happened in modern families. Or that's what she told herself, at least.

'But Phil had work. Ben has an exam. The last thing he needs is any more trouble at school.'

A picture of Ben earlier this morning – rucksack slung casually over his shoulder, the mop of dark curls he'd inherited from her hanging over his eyes – popped into her head. It was a source of constant amazement to her that she had a fifteen-year-old son, when she still didn't feel like a proper grown-up herself. But somehow the little boy had grown into a hulking six-foot teenager with a fine line in sarcastic humour and an increasing propensity for getting into trouble, both in and out of school.

'I'm just saying that if someone in Phil's family had died, you'd have been there no matter what.'

Hannah rolled her eyes again. Katie was right. Of course she was right.

'Yes, I would. *I'm the sucker, he's an idiot*, that's the end of it.'

She knew precisely how the conversation was going to go – and Katie, who was like a dog with a bone about these things, wasn't going to give up.

'Oh come on, don't get arsey.' Katie's tone softened slightly.

'I'm not. Bloody hell!' She swore as a motorcyclist swerved suddenly in front of her, so she had to slam on the brakes. 'Not you, a maniac on a bike.'

'I did wonder.' Katie laughed. 'Look, I love Phil. I think he's a perfectly nice husband and father, and all that stuff. I just love you more, and it makes me cross that you've somehow made a career out of being the easy-going one.'

Don't come round here with your undeniable logic, Hannah thought, shaking her head.

'Just maybe for once think about putting yourself first? For me?'

'Deal.' Even as she said it, she knew that the chances of that happening were vanishingly small. Katie knew exactly the same – after all, they'd all been friends since secondary school, growing up together in the Manchester suburbs. The difference was that while Katie had made something of her life, Hannah had somehow ended up pretty much where they'd started off, with only the stretch marks and frown lines of motherhood to show for it.

'Right. Got to go. Speak later. Love you!'

It was easy for Katie, Hannah reflected, turning off the motorway and watching as the green of the countryside was replaced with the sprawling outskirts of Oxford. She was on her own, no children, had a brilliant job as head of research at a huge multinational company, and didn't take any shit. She'd been working on not taking any shit since she left university, graduating with a first (of course) and climbing the ladder with a dogged determination to succeed.

It wasn't quite so easy to start not taking any shit at the age of thirty-five, when you'd had a lifetime of being the lovely, obliging one. Hannah ran through the mental list of things she'd put aside for one reason or another. Oxford always brought this hankering out in her. Years ago, when she'd found out she was pregnant at nineteen – in the first term of her degree – she'd put aside her ambition to be a professor of literature among the dreaming spires and instead married Phil, her sixth-form sweetheart, who'd been slogging away at a business studies degree at a red-brick uni in Lancashire. He had carried on his studies while she got a job working part-time at a nursery school, and when Ben was born she'd taken him to work, popped him in the baby room and fed him on her breaks. Logical, methodical, reliable. These were the words people used to describe her. They weren't bad things, though. That was what she consoled herself with.

The grey sky split apart and the city was lit with a shaft of bright, pale sunlight as she drove down the road, the golden stone soaking up the light as if it was the least it deserved. The hotel was situated down a pretty tree-lined driveway – an old manor house that looked over a meadow full of cows grazing incongruously opposite a row of tattered shops and student houses. She parked the car, hauled her overnight bag out of the boot and headed inside to check in.

If there was one thing the Reynolds family did well – excelled at, in fact – it was funerals. In the foyer of the hotel, she could see an assortment of distant friends and relations – most of whom she hadn't seen since her mother's funeral two years before. They looked up on seeing her, greeting her with warm smiles of welcome.

'No Phil today?'

'Is he following on?' Her cousin Andy lifted his chin and looked at her over the top of his pint of Guinness.

'He's working. Can't get away. Last-minute thing.' She pressed her lips together and waited.

'Oh, what a shame. And Ben?'

'School. An exam.' I'm going to have this conversation about eighteen times before the service, Hannah thought to herself, smiling politely and pointing in the direction of the reception desk. 'Just going to check in.'

'Hannah Reynolds,' she said, taking out a credit card and handing it across to the girl behind the desk.

'And will Mr Reynolds be joining you later?'

She suppressed a small roar of fury.

'Not today,' she said politely. 'Not this time.'

The funeral was just as moving as she expected. Tears – because Aunt Jess, Hannah's mother's sister, was only seventy-eight, no age at all, as everyone was telling themselves. Laughter – because her daughter Beth, who was as exuberant, loud and chatty as ever – had put together a photo montage set to music which made everyone snort with amusement at the things Jess had got up to. Hannah had swallowed back the enormous lump in her throat that formed the moment she saw a picture of Jess standing arm in arm with her sister, Hannah's mum. They'd been best friends. Being an only child meant Hannah had missed out on that kind of bond herself.

Washing her hands in the bathroom before the buffet,

she thought about Ben and the troubles he'd been having at school. If he'd had a sibling, would things have been different? If they hadn't been shuttled from London to Inverness, and then to Manchester, would he have been more settled? If she'd tried harder to find out why she couldn't get pregnant again – well – no. That wasn't really her fault. She'd tried. She'd taken the vitamins and eaten all the things they'd recommended and bloody Phil had taken it into his head that it couldn't possibly be his fault because somehow it had to be her problem, not his, but . . .

'You okay? Look like you're miles away.'

Hannah looked up, seeing her cousin Beth's reflection in the mirror. She shook her head. She was lost in her own self-absorbed thoughts, and here was Beth, who'd just lost her mum, asking if *she* was all right.

She turned, reaching out to give Beth a hug. 'I'm fine. How are you? It was a lovely service, wasn't it?'

Beth gave an irreverent snort, which made Hannah laugh. 'Everyone always says that, don't they? Imagine if we did a TripAdvisor for funerals. 1/10 – terrible boring ceremony, shit food. 4/10 – sandwiches delicious, guests mind-numbing.'

Hannah giggled. 'You know what I mean.'

'I do. Phil didn't decide to drop everything at the last minute and make a surprise appearance, I see.'

'Don't you start.' Hannah shook her head.

'He doesn't deserve you, you know.'

'That's what I'm always telling him.' She wasn't, actually. She followed Beth back to the function room, where everyone was milling about drinking slightly warm white wine and eating sandwiches. Beth had a word with the woman behind the bar and returned with a chilled bottle of Pinot Grigio.

'Let's sneak off outside. I can't do any more of this polite conversation. I want to hear everything that's going on.' She tipped an unwise amount of wine into Hannah's glass. 'Shame Ben couldn't have made it – he and Lauren haven't seen each other in years . . . What?'

Hannah indicated the glass with a nod of her head. 'I'm going to be over the limit tomorrow at this rate.'

'Bollocks.' Beth poured herself a similarly huge glass. 'So, little cousin, what's going on in your world?'

'You've just lost your mum,' Hannah began. 'We shouldn't be talking about me.'

It was lovely to spend some time with Beth. Growing up without siblings, the two of them had developed a close bond despite their apparent differences. She and Beth were opposites in so many ways – Beth had always been a magnet for gossip, bold as brass, not afraid to say what she thought and upset people. Hannah, on the other hand, had done pretty much anything she could for an easy life.

'I'm not being funny, but I've been losing her for a year and a half. Cancer is evil. Honestly, by the end, it was like waiting for a bloody train that's hours late. She hated it, I hated it. I lost her ages ago, not last month.' Beth shook her head in a gesture of frustration.

'I know, but . . .'

'Honestly, it's a relief to talk about something other than funeral arrangements, medication deliveries and Macmillan nurses, amazing though they are. I feel like my life's been completely subsumed by cancer for the last eighteen months.'

'Okay.' Hannah took a large mouthful of wine and looked out across the terrace. 'So weird that there are cows just there in the middle of the city.'

'I know. It's like being back in the village, except with all the glorious advantages of actual civilization.'

'I thought you loved living in Little Maudley?'

'I do.' Beth looked thoughtful. 'Well, I did. But I've been back and forth so much, and – I dunno, it's just all this has made me realize I want something more.' She gazed out of the window again, looking out at the city that stretched into the distance.

'What about Lauren?'

'Even more so her.'

As if she'd heard her name, Lauren appeared – tall, willowy, impossibly glamorous in a short black form-fitting dress, her hair tumbling down her back in perfectly coiffed curls.

'Do you mind if me and Ellie go into town?' She gave Hannah a brief smile. They'd kissed hello before the service, Hannah marvelling at how tall and assured her niece seemed. It was a far cry from the childhood days when Lauren and Ben would run around the garden in their waterproofs, covered in mud.

'I think that's fair enough.' Beth reached for her phone and tapped on the screen. 'There, I've transferred some money to your account. Go and get a Wagamama's or something.'

'Thanks, Mum.' Lauren's face brightened. 'You're a star.'

'I'm a sucker, is what I am.' Beth blew her daughter a kiss and she and Hannah watched as Lauren headed back inside and linked arms with her identically glamorous friend. They sashayed off across the room and headed into the city centre.

'God, we weren't that self-assured when we were eighteen, were we?'

'No chance.' Beth chuckled. 'But that's partly why I've decided I'm moving through here. She needs something more than the village has to offer.'

'Moving to Oxford? What about the shop?'

'I just need to find someone to take it over. It's not exactly rocket science.' Beth rubbed her ear thoughtfully and then pulled off her earrings, shoving them into the pocket of her bag. 'I hate being dressed up for things like this.'

'You two are like chalk and cheese.' Hannah tipped her head in the direction of the door where Lauren had just been, wafting expensive-smelling perfume.

'You're not joking. How did I give birth to someone who looks like she should be on *Love Island*, when I'm happiest in a pair of jeans and Converse?'

'How did I give birth to a football genius, when neither I nor Phil can figure out the offside rule and grass pitches give me raging hay fever?'

'Being a parent is weird.'

'It definitely is.' Hannah tipped her glass forward and chinked it against the edge of her cousin's in a toast of agreement.

'Mum was saying a while back that you'd been having some trouble with Ben?'

Hannah ran a hand through her hair, pushing it back off her face in the gesture she always used when she was stressed or thinking. She'd been doing it so much of late, she half expected to find long strands of it coming away in her hand.

'He's just fifteen. Very fifteen.'

Beth nodded in the way that only another parent, or a teacher, could. 'I get it.'

'There's a group of lads that live near us – he hangs around with them after school – they're not exactly focused on their education. In fact, they seem to be more focused on what mischief they can get up to, if you know what I mean.'

'Drugs?' Beth widened her eyes in horror.

'No.' Hannah shook her head vehemently. 'But we've had a bit of under-age drinking, and . . .'

'Do you remember getting plastered at Grandma and Grandpa Miller's silver wedding?' Beth interrupted, to Hannah's relief. The catalogue of Ben's misdemeanours was growing weekly, and driving down the motorway with only the radio for company had given her time to think about what was going on.

Hannah laughed. 'Yes I do.'

'A bit of drinking isn't the end of the world – even if he is under age.' Beth raised an eyebrow. 'I've had all sorts of nonsense with Lauren. It's what they do.'

'No, I know. But getting picked up by the police for shoplifting with the same gang of lads is more of a problem.' Hannah's shoulders dropped slightly. The relief of saying it out loud, when until now she'd been keeping it secret from absolutely everyone, was huge.

'Ohhh.' Beth made a face. 'He did not?'

'Oh, he did.' Hannah shook her head. 'And worse still, because he's got as much nous as me when it comes to stuff like that, the others got away and it was all pinned on him.'

'My God.'

'I know. So the school got involved, and social services came to visit to make sure I was doing a good enough job of parenting—'

'Er, hello – what about Phil?'

'Oh yeah, him too – only he was working as usual, so it all sort of fell down to me.'

'Of course. Honestly, Han, you're like a single parent with none of the advantages.'

'There are advantages?'

'Course there bloody are. Nobody hogging the duvet, nobody farts in bed after they've eaten parsnips with Sunday dinner, I get the remote to myself, and—'

'You wouldn't like to meet someone?'

Beth poured them both another – equally huge – glass of wine. 'Course I would. Don't think it hasn't crossed my mind when I think about moving through here.' She waggled her eyebrows. 'Online dating in Little Maudley isn't exactly up to much. I reckon there's a far better chance of finding someone gorgeous and rich and charming in the middle of the city, don't you?'

'Well, that's the theory, anyway. Can't say it's worked that well for half my friends back home – they're always complaining that everyone on the dating sites is either married or commitment-phobic.'

'I'll take my chances. A bit of action wouldn't go amiss,' said Beth, making them both giggle.

'So how exactly are you planning this escape from country life?'

'Oh, it's simple,' Beth said, pulling a face. 'All I have to do is find someone to take over the village shop, move our stuff to Mum's place, and we're sorted.'

'Surely it's not that hard to find someone to take over the shop?' Hannah followed the Facebook page for Beth's shop. It seemed like the hub of the little village community, and her cousin clearly ran it with military efficiency.

'You'd think.' Beth shook her head. 'But Little Maudley is a bit – well . . .'

'Stuck up?' Hannah hadn't visited for years, but what she remembered of the village was a picture-postcard community with not a single stem of lavender out of place.

Beth snorted and shook her head. '*Particular* is the word I was going to use. They have a lot of opinions about everything.'

'But it is lovely.'

'It is. But there's a weird arrangement where I've got

the lease on the post office building, but the shop sort of belongs to the village.'

'How does that work?'

'It's a co-op. Long, very complicated story. Anyway, Flo runs the cafe – so that bit is fine – and I run the shop. We've even got an author-in-residence.'

'Very posh. How come?'

'She moved to the village a couple of years ago after she got divorced – fell in love with it after reading about the telephone box library. Anyway, she's got two kids at secondary school and can't get any work done at home, so she comes and sits at the table in the corner of the cafe and writes.'

'That's so gorgeous.' Hannah rested her chin in her hands and – definitely feeling the effect of the wine – closed her eyes. It sounded like the life she'd always dreamed of, and yet somehow she was stuck in a semi-detached 1930s house in suburban Manchester with a husband who hadn't even texted to see how the funeral had gone, and . . .

'You could always come and run it.'

Hannah's eyes snapped open.

'What?'

'Oh my God.' Beth sat up and clapped her hands together, excitedly. 'I was joking, but – actually, it'd be perfect. You want to get Ben away from those dodgy lads. There's nothing like that goes on in Little Maudley.'

'From what you've said, there's nothing goes on in Little Maudley full stop,' Hannah teased.

13

'Well yes, that's true as well, but – oh, this is a genius idea – Phil travels for work, right?'

'He does.' The tiniest glimmer of excitement was kindling somewhere deep in Hannah's stomach. She could feel it warming her – or was that the wine?

'So,' Beth said, building on her idea, 'it doesn't actually matter *where* he lives, because he doesn't have an office to commute to, does he?'

'Well, no . . .' Hannah said slowly. 'No. He doesn't.'

'Come and see the shop tomorrow on the way home.' Beth looked about fourteen again, her face lit up with excitement. 'Will you?'

The thought of escaping to an idyllic Cotswolds village was heavenly. Hannah visualized the rolling fields and a blue sky studded with fluffy white clouds, and the warm honey stone of the cottages that nestled into the hill surrounding the beautiful old church in Little Maudley. Living there would be like living in an episode of some heartwarming Sunday-night TV drama.

And then she shook herself, and reality asserted itself once again. That sort of thing didn't happen to her.

'I can't just turn our lives upside down and move us to a village in the Cotswolds on a whim.'

'Why not? Life's short,' Beth said, shaking her head. 'Seriously. Look at our family history. Both our mothers died young. We could have popped our clogs by the time we're seventy. Do you want to spend the rest of it wondering what might have been?'

Hannah exhaled, slowly. For another moment, she let

herself imagine how it would feel if, for once in their lives, she and Phil did something because *she* wanted to, not because it was good for his career, or because they were doing the right thing. There was absolutely no way she could just up sticks and move to another part of the country. Or was there? They'd done it lots of times in the past. Yes, she had friends in Manchester, but it wasn't like emigrating to Australia or something.

'Fine.' She put her glass down on the table and crossed her arms decidedly. 'I'll come tomorrow and have a look. But just a look.'

Beth did a fist pump of delight. 'Yes.'

'Just a look!'

'I reckon our mums would be impressed.' Beth raised a glass and chinked the edge of Hannah's almost empty one.

'Maybe.' Hannah chewed her lip, thoughtfully. She was already thinking of all the reasons it couldn't possibly work. By tomorrow, she'd have managed to convince herself it was just a pipe dream – but for now, she decided, she'd go with it. If nothing else, it had made Beth happy, and that mattered most of all, today of all days.

Chapter Two

There were two phones on the kitchen table and both were buzzing insistently. Jake picked them up, switched them both to silent and tossed them back onto the scrubbed oak where they slid like bobsleighs, colliding as they crashed into a glass bowl full of gleaming red apples.

The kitchen was spotless – thanks to Jenna, his cleaner – which meant there was absolutely nothing to do. He picked up an apple and bit into it, gazing at the view of rolling Cotswold countryside that stretched out before him. It was a far cry from a council estate in Manchester, where he'd spent his childhood kicking a ball about in the narrow close between the rows of red-brick houses after school. Or – he gave a rueful smile, thinking of his attendance record – instead of school, sometimes. Most of the time he'd dodged class, preferring to hang out with the older lads from the estate who'd finished at sixteen and were supposed to be on youth training schemes. That had mainly meant hanging around, drinking rank-tasting cheap cider and catcalling any girls who happened to pass by the scruffy patch of grass where they all congregated.

Imagine if Tommo could see him now. He hitched a hip up onto the kitchen counter and surveyed the room. There was – as was de rigueur in the Home Counties –

an Aga, a massive lump of steel that made the room unbearably baking hot in summer and somehow managed to be completely unreliable when it came to cooking anything. Two shiny white Belfast sinks, complete with expensive satin chrome accessories. An island, shelves stacked with tasteful white crockery. Diana, his most recent ex-girlfriend, had spent months getting the place sorted to her taste – which suited Jake, who didn't really have any opinions on which tiles they should use as a splashback or whether they should go chunky or smooth for the glassware. He'd gone along with it, because he was still reeling from the shock of walking away from the game.

Lots of players approached their career as a pyramid: they started at the bottom, climbed their way to the peak and then headed back down through smaller teams, not caring about the money or the plaudits but just wanting the chance to do what they loved. But Jake's shock injury had put paid to that. He reached down, absent-mindedly rubbing the side of his shin. The freak accident in a game against Manchester United had made front-page news – the internet devouring the hideous, sickening moment when two players collided with him at the same time in a sliding tackle that ended everything. Months of physio had made it clear he would never make it back to the top of his game, and so he made the executive decision to walk away, let his team find another defender and retire gracefully.

'I've met someone else' wasn't really part of the deal.

He'd loved Diana, almost. She was pretty and efficient, even if she did have a steely determination that made him feel slightly odd. She was the perfect woman for a player to have on his arm – sleek blonde hair, tall, leggy, always immaculately dressed. The sort of woman that twelve-year-old Jake would have had eyes on stalks for.

'Someone else where?'

'Does that matter?' She'd popped a cherry in her mouth and smiled beguilingly, which made him feel uncomfortable.

'I don't suppose so.' He'd shrugged. 'I just – I thought we were a thing?'

'We were,' she said, ruefully. 'But I met Adam, and . . .'

Adam Leyland was captain of another Premier League team. Tall, with close-cropped black hair and a slightly menacing air (he'd been red-carded on more occasions than his manager cared to recall), there'd been no love lost between him and Jake. One night at a sponsors' dinner he'd made a beeline for Diana and made it pretty clear that he'd set her in his sights. She'd feigned innocent obliviousness, but he'd noticed that after that she'd started keeping a close watch on her phone and her nights out with the girls had increased twofold. And then the accident had happened, and when he was rushed into surgery she'd been nowhere to be seen. His agent had promised – as he was wheeled away, blanching with pain and yet completely out of it on gas and air – that he'd get hold of her while Jake was under.

'I'm sorry, mate,' Max had said later, pushing a hand

through his slicked-back pale blond hair. 'Tried every-where, couldn't get an answer. I spoke to Charlotte and she said she thought she was off on some silent retreat.'

Jake had closed his eyes, still nauseous from the anaes-thetic, and slipped back into unconsciousness.

You'd have thought that losing your career would be enough to contend with – that, and the stuff from his past that was always lurking at the edges, waiting to pop up and ruin everything – but no. The next day, Diana had appeared at the private hospital on the edge of Oxford where he was recuperating in a room that would put a five-star hotel to shame. She'd blushed prettily and placed a hand-tied bunch of flowers on the side table, fiddling with the ribbon that held them together, then turned to face him.

'Sorry, honey, I was—'

And in that split second he knew. '. . . With Adam Leyland?'

'On a mindfulness retreat,' she finished, lamely. She tucked a strand of hair behind her ear in a way that reminded him of when they'd first met, and he felt a knot tighten in his gut.

He raised an eyebrow. He was propped up on a stack of pillows, his knackered leg still raised and pinned in three places. He felt puffy and agitated and desperate for a workout to help clear his head, but of course the chances of that were non-existent.

And then it had all spilled out. The thing about Diana was, she was an uncomplicated soul – what his friend

Gerry, who worked in the city and had a mind like a sly, calculating ferret, would have called *more beauty than brains*. So it seemed perfectly logical to her that she'd met someone else and now was the time to pursue it, even if it was right in the middle of Jake's entire life falling apart.

So here he was now, looking around the kitchen that was decorated to her specification, wondering if he should rip the whole lot out and start again. It wasn't as if he couldn't afford it; even now, when the sponsorship deals and the exciting evening invitations had dried up, he still had enough money in the bank, not to mention tied up in wisely chosen investments, not to have to worry about being skint ever again. It was a strange feeling. But even so, there was always a nagging fear that something might go wrong. Every time he picked up his wallet and pulled out his card to pay for something, a fleeting reminder of how it had felt growing up would rise, the feelings starting in his gut and filling him with a gnawing discomfort that maybe all this was ephemeral, and one day he'd end up back in Manchester in the tiny boxroom where he'd started.

Football was a fickle game, and he'd had enough of it. Eighteen months on, he'd recovered to what any normal man would consider full fitness – but to an ex-pro footballer, he was still constantly irritated by what he couldn't do rather than satisfied with what he could. Talking of which – he checked his watch – it was time to get out for a run.

He pulled on his trainers and headed out down the

long, tree-lined drive. Thick post-and-rail fencing had replaced the rusting iron that had been there when he bought the house three years ago, and behind it grazed a flock of sheep belonging to Jack, the farmer who rented the fifty acres that had come along with the house. Back in the past, the house had boasted a stable yard, a working dairy farm and a collection of farm workers' cottages where the employees all lived. Those had dwindled away over the years following the war, but Greenhowes was still known as the Big House to the residents of Little Maudley, the nearest village.

During the Second World War the house had been requisitioned and used as a hospital for injured servicemen, with its owners happily mucking in and doing their bit to help men who'd been broken apart in ways that made Jake's double break and countless pins look like a walk in the park. But after that, the family who owned it had fallen victim to death duties and crippling maintenance bills. Eventually, when the heir of the estate had been faced with a bill for a new roof that would have completely cleaned him out, he'd simply walked away, claiming bankruptcy. After that, the place had stood empty for almost ten years.

There was something about the dilapidated, filthy, totally unloved manor house which had appealed to Jake. He'd been advised to invest in property – and his last contract had seen him earning more money per day than anyone in his family had ever known in a year. Even if he'd known where she was, it was too late to help his mother – nobody could do that, it seemed. But he'd already set his aunty Jane up in a villa in Spain where she lived quite contentedly with Shaun, her second husband, and an assortment of sleek vizslas who lay about by the side of the pool with their tails wagging contentedly. She wanted for nothing, which after the years she'd spent working as a cleaner to pay for his football boots and his game subs was the least Jake could do.

His cousin Lisa was living in an expensive detached house on an estate in Cheshire, where she was experiencing the whole WAG lifestyle by proxy. She'd featured in *The Real Housewives of Cheshire* and ran an exclusive and high-class beauty therapy clinic as her business, with not a perfectly smooth and beautifully coloured hair out of place. Her forehead, Jake reflected with a smile, was also perfectly smooth, thanks to an overly enthusiastic Botox administration by a new nurse at the clinic. She'd come on FaceTime the other day and it had been a good five minutes before he'd been able to stop crying with laughter at her frozen expression.

He took a left at the top of the drive, heading up the hill towards the far edge of the village. It was the edge of summer – just at that point in July where the leaves hadn't yet begun to fade and curl at the tips, and the sunlight was bright and yellow and clear. Stepping away from the game had given him time to notice things he'd never had a chance to before, and he revelled in it.

He'd fallen for the character of the old place and chosen the workmen who were charged with renovating it accordingly. He didn't want the cheapest or the fastest – he wanted people who could see the bones of the house and wanted to restore her (in his head, somehow, he knew that Greenhowes was female) back to her former glory. And so it had happened, piece by piece: ancient wooden balustrades polished with loving hands back to a soft gleam, the wooden fire surrounds and their tiled mantels glowing in winter as logs crackled in the grate. It was almost there, now – the perfect combination of comfortable old house style and all mod cons.

It had been almost perfect, until that night. Then he'd broken his leg, lost his job, lost his contract, lost his girlfriend. And now here he was, living mortgage-free in a house big enough for a family of ten, all by himself. Or he had been, until—

As if he'd summoned her, the phone rang again.

'Where are you?'

Sarah's voice came through his airpods. He kept a steady pace, running up the hill towards the village, determined that he wasn't going to be interrupted this time.

'Just out for a run.'

'I'm feeling a bit – stressy.'

He puffed out a breath and tried to keep his pace. But he could already feel the tug of responsibility pulling him back towards the house and a moment later he paused, putting fisted hands to his eyes in frustration, and turned on his heel.

'I'll be there in five.'

'Thank you,' said a whispered voice.

Chapter Three

It wasn't often that Hannah had a night of uninterrupted sleep in a hotel room – in fact, she reflected, sitting in the hotel restaurant looking out over the terrace and the ever-present cows, she couldn't remember it ever happening before. She and Phil had been together since their teens, and then Ben had come along. Despite their closeness, her mum hadn't been one to offer much in the way of childcare – always busy with work or socializing – and so they'd tended to operate as a fairly tight-knit band of three.

So last night she'd lain starfish-shaped and luxuriating in the middle of the huge king-size bed and then woken in her own time at eight thirty this morning, not wondering about school runs or PE kit or lunch money. She didn't even have a headache, which was miraculous given how much wine she and Beth had put away.

See you at the shop whenever.

The message from Beth was waiting on her phone. She felt a bit uncomfortable. There was no way of getting out of it, not without hurting her cousin's feelings. But the truth was that she'd woken up knowing that last night's conversation had been one of those ridiculous 'what if we won the lottery?' chats that you know will never lead to anything. She had a home in Manchester – Ben had school. Phil wouldn't contemplate a move, not even for a second. There was no way she could expect the whole world of their little family to revolve around one of her whims, no matter how amazing it would be to live in a picture-perfect village and run a little shop.

Now, though, eating her bacon and eggs, she felt the possibilities stir in her head. She'd never asked for anything in the course of their fifteen years together. She'd been pliant and easy-going, dealt with Phil's moves and coped admirably with everything life had thrown at them. Maybe it was her time now, with Ben aged fifteen and on the verge of growing up. Maybe she'd have a look and allow herself the luxury of imagining what it would feel like to live another life. It couldn't do any harm, could it?

She checked out and drove north up the A34. This whole area was such a contrast to the uniformity of the 1930s streets where she lived. The fields were busy with tractors chugging away, and the landscape was rolling and bucolic – like something from a poem. She followed the instructions of her satnav and shortly afterwards found herself on the road leading to Little Maudley. It curved around, wending its way over a river. She crossed a bridge, drove up the hill, dipped back down into the valley and waited at one side of another pretty stone bridge as yet another tractor trundled across, the farmer in the cab giving her a wave of acknowledgement. It felt as far removed from Manchester life as it was possible to get.

And then she passed the sign that welcomed *careful*

drivers to Little Maudley, and squeezed her foot on the brake in an involuntary motion. A man walking two shaggy-looking red setters gave her a knowing smile and she drove on. Two neat rows of honey-coloured terraced houses lined the street. A discreet sign etched on a window indicated that a beauty therapist worked there, behind the shaded glass. It was almost impossibly tasteful, and so clean that she felt as if her slightly scruffy Ford Focus was going to lower the tone as she drove over the river bridge and up the narrow hill towards the main street. Here, more terraces were interspersed with the occasional chocolate-box white thatched cottage. And there was a signpost, hung with a basket of newly planted geraniums, pointing towards the local shop and post office.

Up the hill and over, where a huge, solid church of blonde stone stood behind a wall festooned with colourful bunting. The trees were hung with coloured flags. There must have been some kind of village fête going on – the thought of it made Hannah fizz with excitement and then laugh at herself. Maybe if they moved here, she could become the sort of person who went to WI meetings and made jam and owned a pair of green wellies. She could imagine Ben's scornful face.

And there on the green was the famous telephone box library – decorated, too, with bunting, and stuffed full of books. She pulled up alongside it and wound down the window, intrigued by the sign stuck on the outside of the door exhorting villagers to *please* not add books to the shelves without asking permission.

On the street opposite sat a white thatched cottage, window boxes stuffed full of flowers, looking ridiculously picturesque. All the doors and woodwork in the village had been painted the same colour, Hannah noticed. She drove again, turning left and feeling a jolt of excitement as she saw the sign for the village shop.

She pulled up outside it and looked out of the window. A postman was loading sacks of mail into the back of his van. It was like stepping into an episode of *Postman Pat*; she half-expected a black-and-white cat to appear, wending between her ankles as she made her way inside. But instead, there was Beth, bursting out of the door with her make-up-free face wreathed in smiles. She was back in her usual outfit of a loose shirt and jeans, hair tied back from her face in a workmanlike ponytail. She dusted her hands off on a black apron that had 'The Old Post Office' embroidered on it in a modern, stylish font.

'Oh my God, you made it. I honestly wondered if it was one of those things you say when you're a bit pissed and regret the next morning.'

Hannah shook her head. 'No, I'm definitely here.' A knot of apprehension made its presence felt in her stomach. The shop was even prettier than she remembered, and the village was almost too perfect to be real.

'Come on then, let's show you round.'

Inside, the place looked immaculate. Fresh bread and newly laid local eggs stood under a prettily hand-chalked sign, and the shelves were laden with expensive-looking deli products as well as the usual washing powder, tins of baked beans and emergency candles. But alongside the emergency in-case-of-power-outage six-pack of table candles, there was a collection of expensive hand-poured, essential oil and soy wax candles in tins.

'Made by Helen Bromsgrove, who lives in the village. It's her new thing. Not that she needs a thing, considering she never stops, but – anyway. It's a fundraising project.'

There was a noticeboard studded with neatly laid out signs and posters for village events, and a reminder that the WI meeting would be taking place a week late this month owing to unexpected events.

Hannah had taken a peek at the Little Maudley village Facebook group while eating her breakfast. It was clear that being a good villager was a fairly high priority on everyone's list, which was ironic given the number of mildly catty posts objecting to over-full bins the day before collection day or the untidiness of houses where the gardens weren't up to scratch. There had been several names that kept popping up and if Hannah remembered correctly, Helen Bromsgrove was one of them. Not only did she make candles, but she seemed to be very much involved in every aspect of village life.

There was a jingling of bells as the shop door opened and a slim, neatly dressed woman with expensively high-lighted hair walked in. She glanced from Beth to Hannah and gave a confident smile. 'Hello,' she said, reaching for one of the wicker shopping baskets stacked just inside the front door.

'Talk of the devil,' said Beth, under her breath. And

then she said in her normal tone, 'How funny, Helen – we were just talking about your candles.'

'Oh, really?' Helen looked pleased with herself.

'Yes,' Hannah said, picking one up and inhaling the scent of lavender and jasmine. 'They're lovely.'

Helen softened slightly. 'Do you think?'

'They're selling like hot cakes,' Beth said, adding, 'or hot candles,' as an afterthought.

'Good, good.' Helen put a box of eggs and a loaf of freshly baked bread into her basket. 'That's what I like to hear.' She made her way around the shop, checking a neatly written list, then placed her basket on the counter. Hannah, meanwhile, had been standing still, trying to imagine what it would be like if this were her life. It was so peaceful and small and lovely. No sirens were blaring outside, and the only traffic that passed by as she looked out the window was a tractor rattling a trailer laden with bales of hay.

'I must have a word with George about the next parish council meeting,' Helen said, pulling out a red spotted Cath Kidston purse from her handbag as she waited for Beth to ring everything through the till. 'We're still using far too many plastic bags in the village. I've been seeing people coming out of the shop with them all month.'

'I've been selling lots of these,' Beth said, pointing to a display of tote bags hanging behind the counter. They were stamped with an image of the village shop and the words 'Little Maudley Loves the Environment'.

'Oh, yes, I know. But people just don't make enough

effort.' Helen tutted, looking disapproving. 'You need to try and push them a bit more or we're never going to raise the money we need for the village hall kitchen.' She glanced at Hannah and held out her hand in greeting.

Hannah shook it. 'Hello, I'm Hannah Reynolds, Beth's cousin.'

'Goodness, you don't look at all alike.' Helen looked at them both in surprise.

'Well, no.' Beth looked nonplussed.

'Well, lovely to meet you, Hannah. Perhaps I'll see you again sometime.'

Beth shot Hannah a sly look and nudged her. 'Sooner than you might think,' she said, making Helen frown slightly. 'It's a long story.'

Beth waited until the door had clicked shut before snorting with laughter. 'Oh God, Helen's a perfect example of why I'm desperate to escape this bloody place.'

'She seems quite nice to me,' Hannah said, watching as Helen crossed the village green and stopped outside the telephone box library. A moment later, she'd straightened a sign that was taped inside and stood for a moment with her arms crossed, admiring her handiwork. 'Very . . . community-minded.'

'That's one word for her. She's such a queen bee.' Beth leaned forward on the counter, resting her chin in her hands. 'I mean, her heart's in the right place, but she's one of those people that has to be involved in *every*thing, if you know what I mean?'

'What's the deal with the village hall kitchen?'

'Well, funnily enough, I don't think we're going to make enough money selling tote bags and Helen's scented candles to rip out the old one and put in a new one, but that's the aim. We're getting a grant – they're going to match whatever we make by the end of the year – but . . .' She stopped herself. 'I have no idea why I'm telling you all this stuff. It's hardly going to persuade you to come and live here, is it?'

Hannah didn't say anything. She was thinking that it sounded as if everything Beth had had enough of about village life seemed pretty much perfect to her. Maybe it was just about perspective . . .

The door jingled again as a woman with long dark hair tied back in a ponytail backed into the shop, staggering under the weight of a huge box of books.

'Can I just put these with the others in the store room?' She balanced the edge of the box on the counter and looked beseechingly at Beth, who tutted, half-joking.

'Oh my God, Lucy, we've got millions in there already.'

'I don't know what else to do with them. We've got doubles of doubles, and most of them are almost new.'

Beth reached over and peered at the books that were visible on the top of the box, flicking through a hardback about gardens. 'This one doesn't even look like it's been read. Lucy, this is my cousin Hannah. Lucy's another incomer – she's from Brighton. She came here to visit and never left. She's with Sam, the guy I was telling you about last night who makes the treehouses?' Beth rattled on, seemingly unaware that Lucy seemed more than a little uncomfortable about being the topic of discussion. Picking up her box of books, she headed across the shop to a little window alcove where several other boxes were already stacked up.

'Can I just shove these here for now?'

'You'll need to get your Sam to come and make a shelf for them at this rate.'

Hannah looked at the alcove. It was a pretty arched shape, and the window overlooked the village green. If this was her place, she'd . . . Well, there was no point thinking about that. Last night's conversation had been lovely, and being here felt like stepping into an old-fashioned novel, but back home she knew she had a mountain of washing to catch up on, a house that would probably look like a bomb site and a son who was up to goodness knows what.

'It all started with the telephone box library,' Lucy explained, after she'd put the box down and straightened up again. 'Only we can't keep up with the donations, and we're running out of places to put all the books.'

'So somehow, muggins here has ended up as a sort of book depository.' Beth shook her head.

'We keep trying to tell people to cool it a bit, hand them on to the charity shops or something instead; but nobody seems to get the hint.'

'You should sell them second-hand,' said Hannah, almost without thinking. 'You said you're trying to raise money for the village hall?'

'Uh-oh,' said Beth. 'Helen's got to you already.'

'Hardly,' Hannah laughed. 'It just seems like a logical thing to do.'

Lucy and Beth exchanged glances.

'She's got a point,' said Lucy. 'A village bookshelf to go with the library?'

'Hello?' A voice came from the far end of the shop. 'I'm trying to reach the top shelf, and I can't quite manage it.'

'Two secs,' said Beth, leaving Hannah standing with Lucy.

'It's mad, isn't it?' Lucy picked up a brand new book, still with the supermarket sticker on it. 'Can you imagine giving away books?'

Hannah shook her head. 'Not really one of my problems. I've got bookshelves in every room, and I keep promising I'll hand some on to the charity shop, but they're like old friends.'

'Exactly.' Lucy smiled. 'I've still got loads of the books I read when I was young.'

'Me too. I thought I'd pass them on to my son, but he's not exactly a massive fan of books.'

'Nor is my partner. He's dyslexic, and he's never really got over how shitty they were about it at school. Thank goodness things are different now.' She paused. 'I'm a teacher – we've got so many ways to help dyslexic kids who are struggling with reading.'

'My son isn't dyslexic – he's just not very keen on reading.'

'No, not everyone is. It's hard to get them to focus,

isn't it, when there's the lure of social media and all that stuff?'

'Exactly.'

Hannah had spent years trying to find the perfect book that might lure Phil or Ben in – sports biographies for Ben, interesting books on personal development or business stuff for Phil. All of them sat untouched on the bookshelf in the hall at home.

'So,' Beth returned. 'Hannah's full of ideas for the shop, aren't you?'

'It was just a thought.' Hannah felt slightly uncomfortable with the attention.

'A good one,' said Lucy. 'Anyway, I need to go. We've got Bunty coming for a visit later on.'

'Ahh,' said Beth. 'Give her my love. I haven't seen her for ages.'

'She's doing much better after her op.' Lucy pulled the door open and paused for a moment. 'Nice to meet you.' She smiled at Hannah.

'You too.'

'See,' said Beth, triumphantly. 'You're a hit with the locals, too.'

'Yeah.' Hannah fiddled with her sleeve, picking at a loose thread. 'But I can't just give up everything and come and live here and run your shop.'

'Why not?'

'I've got responsibilities.'

'You can bring them with you.'

'It's not that simple.'

'It is,' Beth said, crossing her arms. 'It is, if you want it to be. Seriously, Han, you need to think about it. You can't spend your whole life pleasing other people and not yourself.'

'I'll think about it,' she said, mainly to get Beth off her back.

'Right. That's a deal. Now, I'm going to hand over to this afternoon's volunteer and then make you some lunch. How does that sound?'

'Perfect.'

Beth led Hannah through the little passageway that linked the shop with her cottage. Tiny and almost ridiculously quaint, it had been built at the same time as The Old Post Office where the shop now stood. The sitting room was low-beamed and dark, with two deep-silled windows that looked out over the village green and down the street. A brick fireplace took up most of the side wall and a huge, sagging sofa was stuffed with pillows. Beth motioned for Hannah to sit down.

'I'll get us some lunch. Are you in a rush to get back?'

Ben was playing football, and she'd had a brief text from Phil to say he was working and not to rush home. She shook her head. 'I'm fine.'

'Good. That gives me time to work on you.' Beth gave a cackle and disappeared into the kitchen. 'You sit there and imagine what it'd be like to live here.'

Hannah didn't sit down. Instead, she went over to the bookshelf, which was filled with an odd jumble of some of Lauren's schoolbooks and the sort of celebrity

35

biographies people give for Christmas when they're not sure what else to give. Houses without books always seemed weird to her – and the idea of all those boxes of books in the shop was nagging at her. It wouldn't take much to turn that little alcove into a mini bookshop. For a moment, she let herself daydream about mornings spent running the shop and afternoons sorting through secondhand books. Phil would be off working, and Ben happy at school. The village was probably full of people who loved books and she could chat away to them, comparing notes on which Jane Austen novel was the best (*Pride and Prejudice*, of course, although she still had a soft spot for Mr Knightley in *Emma*).

'What are you up to?' Beth called through from the kitchen, a few moments later.

'Just looking at your bookshelf.'

'You won't find much there; I've never been much of a reader. Hang on, I've got something to show you.'

Beth came back into the sitting room and clicked on the mouse beside her computer. A moment later she was scrolling through a complicated-looking Excel spreadsheet, which was colour-coded and had a list of names running down the side. Hannah tried to focus on it, but spreadsheets had always been a mystery to her.

'I just needed to double-check something, but actually, it's a good thing for you to see. Basically we have one person that manages the place – that would be you –' Beth gave her a meaningful look – 'and the rest are volunteers.' She tapped the end of a biro against her teeth, then pulled a slightly battered Post-it note off the side of the monitor and crumpled it up in her hand. 'All you have to do is turn up, do your bit, and then let the others get on with it.'

Hannah looked sideways at her. 'And everyone just turns up?'

'Well, that's the theory.' Beth rolled her eyes. 'I mean, sometimes someone doesn't turn up, and you've got to chase them a bit . . .'

That sounded more like it. Hannah looked around the little sitting room again, taking in the possibilities. She could imagine standing behind a counter with an apron on, chatting to the locals, feeling like part of a community. It was exactly what Ben needed. If she could get him down here and away from the bad influences in Manchester, maybe things could go back to the way they'd been before hormones and teenage grumpiness had hit. And a bookshop . . . it was as if someone was offering her a dream come true on a silver platter.

There was absolutely no way she could do it. That was the only minor detail.

Chapter Four

The whole way home, the idea went round and round in her head. How the hell had she ended up being such a wet blanket? Beth *and* Katie had pointed out to her in the space of a couple of days just how much of a yes-woman she was. She went back and forth on the idea – chugging up the motorway, trapped in a sea of cones between huge HGV lorries, musing on what sort of person would uproot everyone in their family just on the basis of a whim.

Her music was interrupted by a call.

'How did it go?'

It was Katie, ringing from a hotel room in London.

'Okay. Sad, nice. Weird. You know how funerals are.'

'Yeah. Just thought I'd check up on you. Any other interesting news?'

'Well . . .' She opened her mouth and paused. 'Nothing, really.'

She wasn't sure why she didn't tell her. Perhaps because if anyone was likely to encourage her to do something different with her life, it was Katie – but right now Hannah wasn't sure she actually wanted to be persuaded. She let her friend ramble on about her prospective date, listened and encouraged in all the right places, and berated herself afterwards for being useless. God, she needed to pull herself together, forget this bonkers idea and get on with day-to-day life.

That was the plan, anyway. Later, she wondered whether if she'd arrived home to a house that didn't look like a bomb had gone off, and if she hadn't had to shoulder open the door (blocked by a pile of Ben's football kit, which he'd clearly dumped before heading out the back door that morning), she might not have started to think again that she was entitled to a life of her own. She'd swept her eyes across the hall. Phil had left a folder of paperwork and a load of work-related crap on the dresser, but there was no sign of him.

She went upstairs and peered cautiously into the gloom of Ben's lair. It smelled equally of Lynx and sweaty football kit – she wasn't sure which was worse. His bed was unmade, too, and his curtains completely closed. She stepped slightly warily into the bedroom and pushed open the curtains, opening the window wide at the same time. At least by the time he got home later it might smell less hideously toxic.

Downstairs there was a sticky note (only Phil, she thought – who left notes these days?) propped against the fruit bowl. Bright pink and printed with the logo of the company that seemed to take up more of Phil's time than anything else, it said in his untidy scrawl *Ben out at footy, I'll be back at about nine.*

She glanced up at the clock that sat squarely in the middle of a kitchen wall festooned with Ben's curled and faded artwork, which had been hanging there since he was in primary school. It was only four now – where on earth was Phil on a Saturday afternoon? And why on earth was he leaving a note, like someone from 1994? She pulled her phone out of her jeans pocket and tapped his name.

Beep beep beep. Hannah frowned. That noise meant out of service. She tried again. Or did it mean the phone was switched off? Either way didn't make a huge amount of sense. And not only that, but Phil had one bloody job, and that was to be on parenting duty while she was away at the funeral and driving home today. God only knew what Ben was getting up to.

'Hello,' said a voice from the hall, making her jump.

'Ben.'

'That's my name,' he said, leaning across and giving her a kiss of greeting. She smiled to herself and didn't say a word. Sometimes he was still the cuddly little boy she'd spent hours snuggled up with on the sofa watching TV – even if now he was taller than her, with a voice deeper than his father's.

'How was the match?'

Ben hitched himself up – filthy knees, muddy boots and all – onto the kitchen island and made a face. 'Not bad. Harry got an assist and kept a clean sheet and we won three-nil.'

'That's good.'

'Harry got man of the match.'

'That's good too.' Harry had been Ben's best friend all the way through primary school, until Ben had drifted off and started hanging around with the dodgy gang from the streets nearby.

She bit her tongue again. It would be so easy to ask if he'd like to have Harry round for tea, ask how his mum was doing, see if there was anything she could do to get her son back on the straight and narrow. The only saving grace was football – when he was playing, the focus he had for the game kept him from messing up – or messing about. Afterwards, particularly if the team had played as well as they clearly had today, the rush of endorphins and exhaustion would flatten him and he'd be content to stay home, showered and flopped on the sofa in a t-shirt and shorts, yelling at the Xbox. She didn't even mind that. At least he could take the Xbox with him if they moved. She pictured the golden stone of the post office and imagined herself standing in the doorway first thing in the morning, waiting for a delivery of eggs, or newspapers, or whatever else arrived before the rest of the village was awake.

Ben, grabbing two bananas and a bowl of cereal, disappeared upstairs to shower. She gathered an armful of washing that was lying on the kitchen table and sniffed it – thinking *ugh, I can't believe I'm doing that* as she did so – to establish whether it was clean or dirty. If she was going to be busy running a shop, she'd have to get this lot a bit better house-trained.

Ben reappeared half an hour later, by which time Hannah had turned the kitchen back into some semblance of order, found and hung up four of Phil's work shirts in the tiny little utility room, and made herself a coffee.

'Can you do my kit before tomorrow morning? I've got a Sunday match covering for one of the other teams.'

'Course I can, darling. Stick it there by the machine.' She paused for a moment. 'In fact, can you just empty it and put the washing out on the line?'

Ben looked at her for a moment with an expression that suggested she'd lost the plot completely.

'I don't know how.'

'Well, now's a good time to learn. The pegs are in the bag hanging on the line.'

He gave her a very old-fashioned look and said nothing, but opened the machine and hauled the damp washing out, taking it into the garden. Hannah kept her mouth shut and didn't laugh as he stood for a moment on the patio, random pairs of knickers falling out of his arms, before he settled on the wooden table as a reasonable place to put the washing (she only cringed slightly) and then proceeded to hang it up in a haphazard manner that made her want to burst into flames of frustration. He wasn't going to learn if she didn't actually let him get on with it.

'Right,' he said, fifteen minutes later, coming inside and heading straight for the fridge. 'If that's everything, I'm going on the Xbox.'

'It's not.' Hannah suppressed a giggle. Turning him into a responsible adult was quite satisfying, actually. 'You want your kit washed?'

'Oh my *God*,' Ben said, as only a teenage boy could.

*

She'd made pasta and salad and they were sitting at the table when Hannah's phone beeped.

Caught up with some stuff at work, don't wait for me to eat.

'S'that Dad?' Ben looked up, forkful of pasta mid-air.

She nodded. 'He's stuck doing work stuff.'

'He's always working,' said Ben.

Hannah glanced up at him. Things were getting serious if even Ben was noticing. This situation was going to have to change, and fast.

Just once, she thought, stacking the dishwasher, it would be nice if Phil was actually around when something happened. He wasn't ever going to be the most empathetic husband on the planet – after being with him since the age of eighteen, she'd managed to get her head around that – but just once, it'd be nice if she got home from a family thing and he was there with a glass of wine, a bath with candles – now she was pushing it – and a listening ear.

'I'm going to have a shower.' She had a sudden need to wash the weekend out of her hair and just climb into pyjamas and flop.

The shower was utterly filthy, though – as usual – so she found herself turning it on, stripping off her clothes, and climbing in with a microfibre cloth and a bottle of Mr Muscle bathroom spray. Standing bare-skinned under the water, she squirted spray over all the surfaces and scrubbed them clean. It was hardly the same as a luxury spa treatment.

Later that evening, lying on the sofa watching *Antiques*

Roadshow with a glass of Malbec, she heard the familiar clunk of Phil's car door closing and sat up, readying herself for him to come in. Maybe she'd go and grab him a glass – he'd had a long day, after all. She pottered through to the kitchen, pulled a wine glass out of the dishwasher and poured him a generous measure, taking the bottle through to top up her own.

'This is a surprising item,' the man on television intoned, seriously. *'One which we've never seen on this programme before in all the long years we've been producing . . .'*

'Oh, get on with it,' said Hannah, irritably. 'We all know this is the money shot.'

A crowd of people gathered round as the experts cooed over a hideous-looking china bowl that looked weirdly similar to one that was sitting in Hannah's garden shed, full of random DIY bits and pieces.

'This vase is unusual in that it was produced in the potteries in 1934 at a time when the factory was closing down, and so there aren't many of them left.'

The woman who owned the bowl was doing her best not to salivate, and the audience drew closer still. This was the moment when she discovered whether the ancient bit of tat she had shoved into a drawer was actually worth a fortune.

'This is a rare collector's item, and I think if you were going to insure it . . .'

'Or sell it, more like,' Hannah said under her breath.

'. . . you'd be looking in the region of thirty to forty thousand pounds . . .'

It was another five minutes before Phil finally materialized.

'Hello pet,' he said, standing in the sitting room doorway. 'You okay?'

She nodded and indicated the glass of wine. 'Got you a drink.'

'Oh, I won't,' he said, patting his stomach. 'Trying to start a bit of a get fit campaign, you know?'

She snorted. 'Well, I've heard of them, yes, but . . .'

'You have it. Nice to see you back safely. I'm just going to nip up and have a shower. Completely pooped after this afternoon.'

It wasn't until she was halfway through his glass of red that she realized he hadn't even given her a kiss hello.

Chapter Five

'I'm going to be late tonight. Got a meeting over in Leeds.'

Phil was up and out of bed at six thirty on Monday morning, moving purposefully around the bedroom, buttoning his shirt, spraying on some new aftershave he'd bought recently that Hannah privately thought smelled a bit too much like Ben's Lynx for her liking. She lay back with her nose peeking out from under the duvet, trying to will herself awake. Sunday had been swallowed up with domestic tasks and Ben's extra football match, so she still hadn't found the right moment to bring up the whole 'let's turn our entire lives upside down and move 150 miles away' issue. But the idea had been snowballing in her mind, and she now felt a steely determination that she'd never experienced before. She was going to make this happen, somehow.

'What time will you be back? I wondered if we could maybe go for a walk, or something.'

Phil turned and looked at her, an expression of bemusement on his face. 'A walk?'

'People do,' said Hannah, slightly injured. 'I mean . . . it might be nice to spend some actual time together.'

'Yeah.' Phil looked unconvinced. 'Sure. If you fancy it.'

'What time will you be back?'

She sat up, stuffing his pillow behind her back and straightening the collar of her blue-and-white-striped night-shirt. Phil fiddled with his cufflinks and didn't look up.

'Darling?'

'Hmm?'

'If we're going to go for a walk, you need to tell me when. I need to cook, and—'

'Oh, by the way, Ben's got a detention.' Phil ran a hand through his hair, sweeping it back. He was definitely thinning on top, Hannah noticed. She wasn't sure he had, though, so she didn't say anything. He had always been sensitive about ending up completely bald, like an egg, exactly like his dad.

'Another one?'

'Seems like it. Anyway, I don't know what time I'll be back – bit of a how long is a piece of string thing, really. What's with the sudden obsession with walking?'

He sat down on the dressing table stool for a moment and gave her his full attention.

'I just wanted to talk to you about something that happened at the weekend.'

Phil bit his thumbnail, frowning. 'Yeah, sorry, I feel bad. I just had so much on, and you kind of had to deal with the whole funeral thing yourself.'

'I did,' Hannah began, and somehow the words just tumbled out. 'And Beth offered me the chance to take over the shop and live there. I mean, us, not me. I mean, you can work anywhere, that's pretty much part of the deal, right? Ben needs to be somewhere without all the distractions, and . . .' She tailed off, realizing that her plan to bring the topic up carefully and in a well-thought-out, strategic manner had just fallen by the wayside in favour of a classic Hannah blurting out of news.

'You want to up sticks and move to the Cotswolds because your cousin has offered you a shop?'

'Basically, yes.'

Phil stood up and moved to the window. Hannah looked on, watching his silhouette as he stood still for a long moment, not saying anything. It struck her again in that second that not once – not since the day she'd realized she'd missed two periods and it wasn't down to end-of-term exam stress, but a pregnancy that ultimately ended up with Ben – had she asked for anything. She'd gone along with everything: leaving their friends in Manchester to move around the country, endless interminably dull nights out while Phil entertained clients. And she had never once said *what about me*? She braced herself for the inevitable disappointment.

'Fair enough.' Phil turned round, his expression slightly bemused. 'If it makes you happy, fair enough.'

'If it makes me happy?'

'Well, you must think it's a good thing, or you wouldn't be suggesting it.'

'I do.'

He looked at his phone and made a face. 'I need to go, babe.'

'Can I send you more info about it? You can't just say yes without knowing what the hell you're getting into.'

'I can,' he said, pocketing his phone. 'I think I just did.'

And then he was gone. She was left sitting there, slightly stunned, not quite able to figure out why he'd capitulated – actually, that wasn't the right word for it. He hadn't even seemed that bothered.

For the whole of that day, Hannah spent every spare moment on her laptop, sending messages about the shop to Phil by WhatsApp, rambling excitedly about all the plans she had. She couldn't stop thinking about her idea to turn the little alcove into a tiny second-hand bookshop, and found herself sketching little pictures on one of Ben's discarded A4 notebooks at the kitchen table.

Beth, of course, was delighted.

'Oh my God,' she shrieked, dropping the phone in her excitement so that she had to call back again. 'Sorry. I just can't believe it. It's *perfect* for you and selfishly I'm so bloody relieved I can actually get out of this place. Not that there's anything wrong with it, of course, just . . .'

Hannah laughed. 'I know, I know.'

Phil was messaging her between meetings:

The thing is, babe, there's just one consideration – we need to work out what to do with our place.

We could rent it out, Hannah typed. She squirmed with excitement on her chair. It was all so much simpler than she'd expected. Phil seemed to be not just enthusiastic but actually on board in a way she hadn't seen for a long, long time.

We could. In fact, I've been thinking. What if you take Ben over a bit early, and I can get things sorted and up to scratch before we put it on the market.

Good thinking, Hannah responded, privately delighted at the thought of how peaceful it would be to have the place to herself – or at least, with no men in it. Ben didn't count, in her eyes. Even if he did leave man-sized piles of washing and mess everywhere.

All we need to do is have a chat with Ben about it.

Together?

Nah. It looks like my meeting tonight is going to run late. Why don't you have a word with him, see how the land lies?

Okay, she replied, bracing herself. Growing up, Ben hadn't been a fan of their constant house moves, and he seemed more settled now they were back in Manchester. Although given the group of friends he was hanging around with, that wasn't exactly a good thing.

She took him to McDonald's in the end, working on the assumption that any news for teenagers was best heard on a stomach full of junk food. Ben, who was deeply in the 'please don't be seen within fifty metres of me in case people think we're related' stage, insisted that they get a drive-through meal and then sit in the car. It was baking hot even with the windows open, so they parked in the supermarket car park in the shade.

'Normal families have this sort of conversation over dinner,' Hannah pointed out, reasonably.

'Normal families don't have conversations.' Ben peeled a gherkin off the top of his burger and placed it on the box.

The weirdest thing, she reflected afterwards, was that if she'd had to guess how it would go, she would never have imagined that Ben would take it on the chin.

'Don't you want to yell at me about ruining your life?'

Ben shrugged, and no matter how she pushed, he wouldn't be drawn further. It wasn't an enthusiastic yes, but it wasn't a no, either. Maybe that would have to do.

Back home, Hannah stood at the back door thinking about everything she'd have to do if they moved. The grass was shaggy and strewn with daisies – Phil had promised he'd cut it at the weekend, but he'd clearly forgotten. She'd have to get organized and do it herself. The whole garden was looking a bit overgrown – neither of them were gardeners, and it was more a case of cutting things back and hoping than actually creating a flower-filled room outdoors. The scruffy lawn – scarred by one too many games of football – had a sagging, cracked goalpost at one end and a slightly tired-looking wooden table and chairs at the other. If they were going to move, all of this would need a major tidy-up.

'I've been Googling,' Ben said, from the kitchen table. Despite the fact they'd just been out and spent a small fortune on fast food, he was buttering a mountain of toast and had poured a pint of milk into a glass. He caught her looking. 'What?'

'Nothing.' Hannah smiled at him fondly. 'You're just like a bottomless pit.'

'I need all the energy I can get,' he continued. 'Particularly if I'm going to make it into the team down there.'

'There's a team? You mean at the school?'

'No, there's a football academy place. I reckon if I worked hard, I could get a place there and go next year, after GCSEs.'

'Okay, that sounds positive.'

'And David Beckham has a house near there. Maybe he'll spot me and I'll get scouted.'

'I can't imagine he's in the habit of wandering around looking for football players,' she said, and immediately regretted it. It sounded like the sort of negative thing her mother would have said when she was growing up – the sort of thing she tried to avoid. She wanted Ben to grow up and think all kinds of things were possible, not that they were out of reach.

She started again.

'That sounds really good. There's probably a decent local team until then. If we move over the summer holidays, that'll mean you can sign up when term starts.'

'If they'll have me.'

'Of course they will.'

Ben shrugged. He picked up his phone and was lost for a moment, staring at the screen.

'I'm going to go out for a bit, if that's okay?' He gave her a look. It was the look of someone who was absolutely chancing his arm. One eyebrow raised, hopefully, a half-smile at the corner of his mouth. It was this exact look that drove his teachers crazy, but despite everything, Hannah was enough of a soft touch that it made her heart melt. She could remember the same expression on his face when he was a chunky-legged little toddler, messing about in the park after reception class.

'Okay. Just don't get into trouble.'

When the doorbell went at eight thirty, she assumed it was him having forgotten his key. She opened it, and was halfway through 'You need to remember to take it with you . . . what if I'm out?' when she realized she was addressing a very stern-looking police officer. Behind her, parked on the road right outside the house (where she could already see Mrs Harris from across the road twitching her curtains furiously) was a white police van.

'Oh.'

'Are you Mrs Reynolds?'

She nodded.

'We've got your lad in the back of the van here. Caught him and a couple of other boys messing about with a load of spray paints down at the railway bridge, and I'm just delivering them home out of harm's way.'

'Oh God.' Hannah pushed her hair back from her eyes and felt a lurch of horror.

'Right you, out you get.'

There was a clonk as the back door of the van opened and a moment later a sheepish-looking Ben slunk out. Hannah was relieved to note that he looked more than a little scared.

The police officer stood back, arms folded, watching as Ben made his way up the little front path and stood beside a tattered-looking rose bush that had never really taken to life in a pot. He picked off a leaf and fiddled with it, not looking Hannah in the eye. His expensive trainers were apparently the most fascinating thing he'd ever seen.

The police officer looked from him to Hannah and raised an eyebrow.

'I'm certain by the look on her face that your mother will have more to say. Now if I were you, I'd get inside, and I'd think hard about what you want the rest of your life to look like, because if you're not careful, you'll be back in my van and I'll not be delivering you home to your mam.'

'Sorry,' mumbled Ben.

'I should think so too,' said the police officer. 'Get inside with you and don't let me see your face again.'

'I'm so sorry,' Hannah began.

'No need.' The officer cocked her head to one side thoughtfully. 'I was in enough trouble like that for wagging off school when I was his age. If someone hadn't given me a short sharp shock, goodness knows where I'd have ended up.'

'Was he with anyone?'

'Bunch of older lads. Couple of them got a warning, couple of them are in the back there, being delivered home with a clip round the ear – metaphorical, mind – and a warning.'

'I only let him out because he acted like he was—'

'Don't beat yourself up, love. Just keep him on a tight leash.'

Phil eventually returned home at nine thirty, by which time Ben was upstairs in a bath (which seemed the safest place for him) and Hannah was halfway down a bottle of corner-shop red wine that was so acidic it made her feel slightly sick. She swallowed the last mouthful from her glass as he walked into the kitchen, where she was sorting washing at the table.

'Everything all right?'

'Apart from our son being delivered home in a police van and you being incommunicado all bloody afternoon and evening, yes.' Hannah folded a tea towel as crossly as she could (not as easy as it might sound) and put it down, looking at her husband and crossing her arms.

'Oh God, don't give me a hard time. I've been in a bloody meeting all day and then a sales thing that went on for ages.'

'And I've been explaining why we're moving to the Cotswolds and dealing with soft lad upstairs getting into all sorts of trouble.' Her accent always got stronger when she was angry – not that she tended to get riled often, but Phil's matter-of-fact attitude was really pissing her off after what had been a very long day.

'I thought he was grounded?'

'Oh God.' She rolled her eyes. 'He was. Yes, I know. Then he was really good about the whole move idea, so I gave him a stay of execution.'

'Well, it sounds like that went well.' Phil reached over and poured some wine into her glass, before heading to the kitchen cupboard to find one for himself.

'Not my best idea,' Hannah conceded, sitting down at the table. Phil sat down at the other end, and they surveyed each other across a landscape of folded clothes and bedding.

'So I've been thinking about this move thing all day.'

'You don't think I'm insane?'

He shook his head and smiled. 'We need to get Ben out of this place. He can't get in trouble if he's living in the back end of beyond and there's nothing to do.'

'He could.' Hannah made a rueful face. 'I mean, if anyone's going to, it's him.'

'True enough.' Phil picked up some of Ben's football socks from the washing pile, and started pairing them. 'But it's got to be safer than living in the suburbs of Manchester, right?'

'You'd think.'

'Okay.' He seemed surprisingly settled with the idea, considering she'd only mentioned it this morning. 'So I'm thinking what we need to do is get you and Ben down there ASAP before September term starts, and I'll hang back, get this place sorted, and then we can rent it out for – six months? A year? What d'you reckon?'

'Beth said a year to start with. It feels like a decent amount of time to see if we like it.'

'Okay. A year. And then if it's working out, we can sell it and maybe buy something down there.'

Hannah didn't like to point out that the difference between the cost of houses in the leafy, expensive-looking Cotswolds and their little street was astronomical. She just nodded agreement and decided to focus on celebrating the fact that she'd somehow managed to get her own way over a suggestion she'd expected would cause major ructions. She got up from the table, a wave of exhaustion washing over her.

'I think I'm going to go up to bed.'

'Hmm?' Phil was distracted already, looking at his phone. He placed it face down on the table beside the pile of washing.

'Bed.'

'Okay, love. I've got a bit to do – I'll see you later.' He swiped his hand in her general direction, landing a vague pat on her thigh as she passed his chair.

Climbing the stairs, Hannah wondered what it would be like to be their friends Rowan and Jack, who – ten years older, in their mid-forties – had been together for twenty years but still fancied the pants off each other and couldn't help showing it. They didn't say goodnight with a pat on the leg, she suspected.

Chapter Six

Jake knew as soon as he turned his car off the A41 and onto the expensively tarmacked surface of the drive at Ridgeway Grammar (est. 1896, old boys including cabinet ministers and the great and the so-called good of society) that he had made a massive error.

There was a split second when he wondered about just swinging round in the huge turning circle outside the big house, crunching up a spray of gravel and heading back home. But that split-second moment of weakness was his downfall . . .

'Ahh, Jake,' cooed Melissa Harrington, the glamorous and charming head teacher. Somehow she had her head in the window of his Range Rover before he'd even pulled it to a halt, and was beaming at him from close quarters, the car filling with the heavy, heady, seductive scent she wore. Her grey silk blouse had one button too many undone, so as she leaned in the passenger window he had to avert his gaze to avoid looking straight at the swell of her breast rising out of a lace bra the colour of red wine. He swallowed. This was going to be a tricky sort of day.

'Let me just hop out,' he said, switching off the ignition and climbing out. He dusted his hands down the front of his trousers and held out his hand for her to shake. She was round his side of the car, taking his hand and swooping in for a kiss on the cheek, murmuring 'Let's not be too formal,' into his ear at close range.

The interior of Ridgeway Grammar wasn't anywhere near as posh as he'd expected. Wooden floorboards sagged and creaked, the walls were chipped, and classroom doors had scuff marks all around their bases – just like the school he'd gone to when he was young. He'd expected the place to be as luxurious as a five-star hotel. It bloody well should be, he thought, following Melissa towards her lair. The fees were £30,000 a year and he knew whole families of footballing friends were there, the kids wanting for nothing. Somehow he'd been roped into being the figurehead for a posh school soccer (they never called it football, he noticed) contest.

'Make yourself at home – Louis will look after you.' Melissa stood back as a tall, gangly boy with a huge mop of dark curls opened the door to what looked like an expensive sitting room. 'I've got a couple of calls to make and then I'll be with you.'

'Can I get you anything? Tea? Coffee?' Louis pushed a hand through his hair and lifted his chin to gaze at Jake directly – he had the confidence and self-assurance that came with money. Jake tried to imagine his sixteen-year-old self faced with an adult of any kind, let alone an ex-England player. He'd tended to avoid adults, unless he was being picked up for loitering (in which case he was being slung into a police van) or getting detention for skipping lessons to play footy at the back of the field when he should have been doing his GCSE English coursework.

'Coffee would be great, thanks.'

'Milk?'

'And one sugar, please.' Posh people always had it strong and black. If he was completely honest he actually preferred instant, but that was a no-no in the circles he was moving in. Louis measured spoonfuls of ground coffee into a cafetière and set it on a tray with a little bowl of rough brown sugar cubes, a Cath Kidston jug full of cream, and a plate of tiny chocolate chip cookies.

'There you are. Miss Harrington won't be long, I don't think. If there's anything else?' Louis glanced fleetingly at the door.

'No, I'm fine, thanks, Louis. You get off.'

He poured himself a coffee and took it across to look out of the window. Huge, impeccably manicured lawns stretched out, dotted with ancient oak trees and flanked with low stone walls. In the distance a ha-ha dropped away and beyond that he could see the football and rugby pitches, huge and professional standard, and on them a team of lads clad all in white doing some warm-up work with colourful plastic cones. It was a far cry from his childhood football experiences.

On the table lay a neatly fanned out stack of prospectuses. The front cover suggested that Ridgeway was a welcoming, diverse school, open to all. He sat down on the arm of a chair and started leafing through one of them. Everything about it suggested money – the thick, expensively laid paper, the glossy photographs of even glossier children. The sixth form had recently become co-ed and as a result the back half of the prospectus was filled with glamorous and self-composed looking young women with expensively straightened teeth and hair which hung to their waists in a way that would have made his old PE teacher have a blue fit – he'd been a stickler for hair being tied back.

Melissa returned a few minutes later, and bustled him out into the corridor.

'Morning, miss,' said a huge, tawny-haired boy as he jogged towards them, dressed in the all-white football kit. He was holding a couple of bottles of water, and looked flustered and apologetic.

'Running late, Ollie?'

'Forgot my shin pads.' He did a double take as he realized that Jake was walking alongside her. 'Morning, um, sir.'

'Jake is fine.'

Ollie's eyes widened slightly. He gave a brief upwards nod of acknowledgement and then jogged off ahead of them.

'He's our star goalkeeper.'

'He's the right size and shape, isn't he? Built like a brick sh– outhouse.' He corrected himself in time. Sometimes remembering who he was and where he came from wasn't such a good thing.

He stood by the side of the pitch and watched the two teams warming up, taking note of the attitudes of the players, the way they attacked the ball, which of them communicated well with their teammates. They were proficient but not stellar by any means. The other team were of a similar ilk – all of them looked a little bit like they'd be more at home on a rugby – they'd probably call it *rugger* – field. None of them were small and wiry and fast – and the game he watched reflected that. It chugged along for ninety minutes and he took some notes on his phone as he watched. 'Twelve needs to come up front and mark his man more – eight is communicating well but he's losing the ball at crucial moments . . .'

Afterwards, they headed back to the changing rooms.

'Right everyone, we've got a special guest here today to talk about the game, and I'm hoping he's going to be spending some time every month in the new term coming along to talk about how you're doing, as we attempt to reclaim the Norris Hawes Cup from Giddingham.'

Mark Lewis, the PE teacher and football coach, wasn't posh. He jiggled from side to side as he spoke and bit his nails when he was concentrating. The boys clearly saw him as a bit of a joke, Jake noted, which was a pity because he was a nice guy with no side to him.

'Hi,' said Jake, giving them a brief nod of greeting.

'If you guys go and get changed, we'll meet you back at the sports hall and we can have a debrief.'

As one, the whole team scrambled to their feet, laughing and joking, and headed off to the changing rooms.

'They're good lads,' Mark said, watching Jake watching them.

'Not a worry between them,' Jake said, and realized that there was a note of something – was it envy? – in his voice. He had no idea what they had going on in their lives. Maybe football was their escape, too – but somehow he doubted it. They didn't have the hunger that he recognized in the lads he'd grown up with, most of whom had something they wanted to escape from. This lot had it all handed to them on a plate.

The vague sense of unease gnawed away at him as he waited in the sports hall for the team to return. When they did, dressed from head to toe in expensive designer-label sportswear and shod in the sort of trainers that cost £200 a pair, he had to swallow back a rising sensation of bitterness. He sat on the sidelines and waited for the rest of the team to come in, once again looking back on himself at the same age.

Back then, aged sixteen, he'd gone to football training in second-hand trackies and the cheapest trainers his aunty Jane could find in the local market. When he'd been scouted – quite by chance, in a league cup game where his team had found themselves in the final – he'd been wearing the kit supplied by the team manager, who he found out years later had subbed the extra money for Jake's kit because he knew his family couldn't afford it. The football kit was a great leveller, though – everyone looked the same and nobody could be judged on what they wore or where they came from. Afterwards, though, when everyone got changed and headed home – getting lifts from parents or riding home on expensive bikes – that's when it became apparent that he had nothing.

Maybe that's why all these boys, sitting in their posh kit looking smug and self-satisfied and wanting for nothing, made him feel so bloody pissed off. He shook his head. He needed to get a grip.

He put his professional head on and chatted to the boys about their game, taking in the positives and the negatives, finding something to praise for each one and remembering his motto, which was to treat everyone with humour and respect. It had worked all the way through his career. Hopefully doing so now might teach these boys a lesson they'd take into their future lives, where they'd all be leaders of industry or cabinet ministers . . . not one of them, he was certain, was secretly dreaming of an England cap.

On the way home, he stopped at the village shop in Little Maudley to pick up a paper. There was a flustered-looking girl outside – well, not a girl, because she was shooing a tall boy of about sixteen or so into a car and he called her Mum – with her hair tied back in a pony-tail, wavy tendrils falling loose around her face. She didn't look more than mid-thirties – young to be a mother of a teenager.

'We need to get going,' she was saying. 'Beth, I'll give you a shout later.'

She slammed the car door shut and was about to reverse away when Jake banged on the roof.

He shook his head, laughing, and handed her the half-dozen eggs she'd left sitting on top of the car. 'You're not going to get very far with these on the roof.'

She took the eggs with one hand, holding the steering wheel with the other. 'I was trying to get back to Manchester before the motorway was completely snarled up.'

'Well, unless you're planning on having scrambled eggs for your tea, I think I'd put those somewhere safe.'

The teenage boy sitting beside her took the eggs out of her hand and darted him a look before staring fixedly out of the passenger seat window.

'Thanks. Sorry again. I mean, I didn't mean to be rude.' She had an accent that reminded him of home – not strong, but definitely northern. And very pretty hazel eyes. He shook his head, realizing he was gazing at her in a way that probably made him look like some sort of weirdo.

'You weren't rude.'

'Well, that's good to know.' Her eyes twinkled as she gave him a wry smile. 'And now that you've saved my eggs, I better get off.'

'Any time.' He gave the roof of her car a pat and stepped back, watching as she reversed out of the little bay outside the post office and waved a farewell to Beth, the owner, who was standing in the doorway waving back frantically. He hovered, not able to get past until she'd done the final wave, as the car disappeared out of sight into the dip at the bottom of the road. Jake turned back to go inside.

'That's my cousin,' Beth said, unprompted, as he

followed her in. 'She hasn't a clue about football so she won't have *any* idea who she's just talked to. Of course I'm not one to gossip . . .'

Jake kept his lips pressed closely shut, having heard precisely the opposite from everyone he'd spoken to in the village. He'd been warned that Beth had a habit of taking everything she heard and relaying it to anyone who'd listen, usually with embellishments.

'. . . so you've nothing to worry about on my account. I heard you were down at the private school this morning, doing some training or something? What's going on there? Are you working at the school, or just doing some voluntary stuff?'

'News travels fast,' he said, wryly. He didn't expand on it any further than that, even though he could see that Beth was absolutely bursting to know more. He picked up some eggs, the same kind he'd just rescued for Beth's cousin – thinking how pretty she'd looked when she'd blushed and apologized for being rude – and a loaf of bread and some plump tomatoes. He grabbed a handful of chews for the dogs and placed them on the counter. Beth was still straightening leaflets and handed him one. He read it aloud. 'Little Maudley FC Under-16 team – trials starting soon.'

'You should get involved with the village team, if you're looking for something to do. They're trying to find a coach.'

There was a derisive snort from somewhere in the depths of the village store.

A girl with long hair tied back in a ponytail popped her head up from behind a shelf and said scathingly, 'I hardly think he's looking for something to do, mother.' She glanced at Jake sideways. She was a younger, much more glamorous version of Beth and looked like she would be a perfect candidate for Melissa Harrington's school prospectus. Her long hair swung over her shoulder like a glossy curtain.

Beth rang up the goods on the till and offered him the contactless payment gadget. 'Well, if you don't ask you don't get . . .' She gave him a direct look and raised both eyebrows. 'The whole thing about living in a village is supposed to be taking part in village life, isn't it?'

Jake took out his wallet and tapped his card on the side of the machine. Beth handed over his receipt with a slightly challenging expression. So far, besides hiring as many of the local tradesmen as he could to work on his house, he'd pretty much avoided village life, merely popping in and out of the shop and exchanging pleasantries. Under the circumstances, it had seemed better to keep a low profile.

He folded the leaflet and put it in the back pocket of his trousers.

'Does that mean you'll think about it?'

He cocked his head thoughtfully and narrowed his eyes. 'Let's say I'll consider it.'

As he was closing the door, he heard Beth give a triumphant 'YES' and a moment later, another teenage snort of derision: 'Little Maudley's team is hardly going to have Jake Lovatt as their coach, are they?'

That was the moment, he realized later, that sealed the deal. That, and the experience he'd had that day at Ridgeway Grammar School. Getting back to the house, looking at the life he'd somehow managed to build for himself, thinking about the boy he'd been and the chances he'd been given, he made up his mind.

Sarah was pottering around the kitchen when he got back. She'd had a shower, and her hair was tied back from her pale, watchful face with a purple hairband.

'You okay?'

It was still weird having her there. She was a reminder of a life he'd never known.

'Yep,' she nodded, picking up an apple.

'I'm making some dinner in a bit. You want some?'

She shook her head. 'I'm not that hungry.'

'What time's the meeting tomorrow?'

'Half ten.' She gnawed at a thumbnail. 'You still okay to take me?'

'Of course.'

When she'd turned up on the doorstep last month, he'd had to make a decision. Growing up without his mother had been hard. Where everyone at school had some sort of family unit, he'd always felt that being brought up by his aunt and uncle made him stand out. He'd daydreamed about a day when his mother would reappear and want to be part of his life – want to make up for all the years he'd missed. But it had never happened, and eventually he'd become accustomed to the family he'd been allotted. That was, until the day

Sarah turned up – completely drenched, on a late June afternoon where the sky was bruised purple and the rain was clattering against the windows in a manner more suited to November.

'Hello,' she'd said, shivering.

He'd sized up the situation in a split second. Whatever her problem was, she didn't pose a threat – she was probably eight stone soaking wet, and her hair hung in sodden tendrils around her face. She'd pulled a piece of paper out of her bag – tattered, the writing faded with age – that showed who she was.

'Come in and get dry,' he'd said, installing her on the armchair beside the Aga. He'd fetched some of his ex-girlfriend's old clothes, which were still folded neatly in the drawers, and offered her a dressing down and a towel.

'Get yourself in a shower before you get hypothermia.' He showed her the downstairs shower room and paced the corridor outside for the fifteen minutes she was in there.

'Okay.' He handed her a cup of tea. She shook her head when he offered sugar. 'So – what's the story?'

She looked at him through watchful eyes, hands clasped around the mug. Even Diana's yoga pants and sweatshirt were hanging off her.

'So,' she said, after a long pause. 'I'm guessing you didn't know you had a sister.'

And that was how they'd started off.

Chapter Seven

The first day, he'd left her pretty much alone – not so much because he thought it was the right thing to do, more that he hadn't a clue what else to do. There was a woman floating around his house – one to whom he was related, as was glaringly obvious not just from their identical high cheekbones and blue-green eyes, but her height, her build. She was genetically connected to him, but he didn't feel anything at all except a basic human instinct to make sure she was okay.

While she was sleeping, he nipped into Bletchingham and went to the only shop that sold women's clothes. Guessing her size, he picked up some pyjamas, a couple of pairs of jeans, a hoody, some t-shirts. He baulked a bit, standing in the underwear department – that felt awkward. But she'd turned up with nothing but the tattered birth certificate and a beaten-up black rucksack, so what the hell else was he supposed to do? Cringing slightly, he picked up a couple of packs of knickers and shoved them in the basket. He could feel his face flaming red – this was a far cry from trips he'd made in the past to places like Agent Provocateur in London, where he'd gone in (usually armed with a text message loaded with hints) and bought up sets of tiny, exotic matching lingerie.

These were practical, sensible – and the only underwear he'd be buying for his half-sister any time soon. He grimaced as the woman checked them over, calling out the size to confirm it as she bagged the shopping. He kept his head ducked low, hoping she wouldn't recognize him, but she appeared to be completely in the dark, which was a relief, at least.

He left the shop and jumped back into the BMW, only noticing the parking ticket as he put the key in the ignition. Oh, bloody hell – he reached out and ripped it off the windscreen, tossing it onto the passenger seat. Parking in Bletchingham was a complete nightmare. He hit reverse and made his way back past the pretty castle that was the old gaol, heading for Little Maudley.

The dogs were waiting for him in the courtyard – Pippa, his PA, must've let them out. Mabel and Meg hurtled up as he opened the door, sniffing vigorously. They were clearly wound up with excitement at the prospect of someone new in the house. He grabbed the bags and went into the kitchen.

Pippa was in the office, the door to the kitchen ajar. She looked up, hearing him return.

'Oh hello,' she said, and looked at him quizzically. 'You've left . . . someone –' she lifted an eyebrow – 'upstairs?'

'Long story.'

'And there was I thinking you'd taken a vow of chastity after you and whatshername broke up.' She smirked.

'Oh my God, no –' He shook his head in horror. 'No, it's not like that. She's family.'

'Really?'

'Well, yeah. Long-lost family, I think you'd say, but family nonetheless.'

There was a sound from upstairs which made the dogs bark in alarm. Clearly Sarah had woken up. He really needed to talk to her, and it would be a hell of a lot easier if Pippa wasn't there.

'Look,' he grimaced. 'Any chance you could . . .'

'Bugger off for a bit?' Like all good PAs, she was pretty perceptive.

'Uh, yeah.'

'Course I can. I'm just doing some admin on the property stuff – I'll take the laptop and finish it at home in front of *Escape to the Chateau*. That's my kind of working day.'

'Excellent.' He stepped back out of the office. 'I think I'll make some brunch, then.'

'Sounds like a plan.'

Ten minutes later, she was gone and he was frying bacon on the Aga. The dogs were lying at his feet on the rug that stretched along the foot of the range, panting, partly because it was still quite warm but mainly because they were desperate to help him with the bacon.

'And by *help*,' he said, dropping them both a piece, 'you mean eat it all.'

'Do you often talk to the dogs?'

He looked up. Sarah had clearly showered and was standing in one of the thick white guest dressing gowns that hung on the back of the bedroom doors.

'Quite a lot,' he said, smiling. 'They don't answer back, and they think I'm the best thing since sliced bread.'

'Sounds like the perfect relationship.'

'Well yes, exactly.' He tipped the bacon out and into a shallow Pyrex dish, popping it in the bottom oven to keep warm. 'D'you want some eggs? Scrambled or fried?'

Her stomach emitted a huge growl which made them both laugh. 'Scrambled, please.'

'Coffee? There's some in the pot, if you want, or I can make you tea?'

'Tea would be lovely. But only if you don't mind? You've been kind enough already. I feel a bit like I'm imposing.'

'Not at all. Sit down, I'll put the kettle on to boil.'

She didn't sit down to start with – she fussed the dogs, paced around the kitchen, looked out of the window that overlooked the long lawn that rolled down towards the woods. Meg and Mabel, clearly sensing she was anxious, dogged her footsteps, tails wagging gently. Eventually, as he poured boiling water onto a teabag, she curled up in one of the kitchen armchairs, Meg's head resting on her knee.

'Here you are. Breakfast won't be a sec.'

'I'm surprised you cook your own breakfast.' She looked at him from over the top of her mug.

'Who did you think was going to cook it?'

'I dunno.' She shrugged. 'I assumed people like you would have a chef, or a live-in housekeeper, or something like that.'

73

'People like me?' He took some toast and placed it on the side of her plate, adding a heap of crispy bacon and some eggs. 'Salt and pepper?'

'Yes please.'

He put both their plates on the long, scrubbed wooden table, so they were facing each other. She was clearly ravenous – she wolfed down the bacon in minutes, not stopping to talk.

'You must still be worn out after yesterday.'

'I am.' She chewed her lip. 'It was – well, I didn't really plan it.'

'Which bit? Coming here?' He buttered a slice of toast.

Sarah nodded and paused for a moment, fork in hand. She gazed out of the window.

'I can't believe this is your house.'

'Nor can I,' he said, simply. 'I don't actually think it's something you ever get used to.'

'Nah,' she said, shaking her head, 'I can't imagine you would.'

'So – um . . .' He wasn't sure how to broach the subject. 'I was in town earlier and I noticed you didn't have much – well, you didn't have a bag? Anyway, I picked you up a few bits, just in case.'

Sarah ducked her head for a moment. When she looked up again, her eyes were sparkling with tears that threatened to overspill her dark lashes and pour down her cheeks.

'You didn't need to do that.'

'Well,' he said, gruffly, 'I did. Honestly, it was nothing.'

She swallowed. 'It wasn't nothing. It was really kind. You don't know me from Adam.'

'Or Eve.' He gave her a brief smile. 'Except you're family, which means you're welcome, and – well, what kind of person would I have been if I'd left you standing on the doorstep in the pouring rain?'

'Oh, lots of people would,' Sarah said.

'Not me.'

'No.' She steepled her fingers together, looking down at them. 'I know. I kind of had a feeling you wouldn't. That's why I found you.'

He put his knife and fork together and rested his chin in his hands, looking at her steadily. 'So why did you come looking?'

'I didn't.' She pushed her palms together, making it look as if she was offering up a prayer to the heavens. 'I didn't have any choice. I mean I had to get away.'

'From what?'

'From who.' She looked down at the table again, and didn't say anything for a long moment. 'I was in a relationship with someone. After Mum died, I kind of went from pillar to post – I was too old to be taken into care, too young to know what the hell I was doing. The guy she was with when she passed – he was as dodgy as anything, involved in drugs and all sorts of stuff. I mean, they all were.'

'You mean she had a series of them?' He looked down at the ground, feeling awkward and somehow embarrassed for the mother he'd never known. He hadn't really mourned her passing and he'd always felt a bit guilty about that.

Sarah nodded. Her dark hair was drying in the heat of the kitchen, lifting into waves that hung around her heart-shaped face, making her look very young. There were purple shadows under her eyes and she flicked glances around the room the whole time, clearly without even realizing. What the hell was she afraid of?

He closed his eyes. All the time he'd been growing up with Aunty Jane, the subject of his mother had been a closed one. He'd learned, eventually, to stop asking. She was just something the family didn't talk about. He'd had no idea he had a sister, ten years younger, being dragged from the house of one unsuitable partner to another.

'Anyway,' she began, exhaling slowly. 'You know that saying about boiling a frog?'

'The thing about them not realizing they're in hot water or something?'

Sarah nodded. 'That's basically what happened. I met Joe and he seemed really nice – like he'd look after me. Told me I didn't need to worry about working, that he'd make sure I was all right.'

'And then?' Jake could already tell where this was going. He watched Sarah as she traced circles on the table with her finger.

'It was subtle at first. He wanted to make sure I was okay. Didn't want me seeing my friends. Didn't like me going out.' She paused for a moment. 'Then the first time he—'

He didn't speak, just waited. The clock on the wall ticked loudly, and the scrape of Meg's claws on the tiled floor as she shifted seemed amplified by the silence in the room. Sarah took a deep breath.

'He hit me, because he was drunk.'

Jake pressed his lips together to stop himself from speaking out. If he jumped in now, Sarah was going to think he was just another loud male shooting his mouth off.

'Well, he said it was because he was drunk. Then he apologized, was an angel for a few weeks. Then it happened again. Thing is, it sort of went on, and then he'd be lovely, then I'd end up feeling like it was my fault, somehow. But the gaps between him being lovely and him losing it were getting smaller and smaller, and I started thinking that I had to get away.'

'I'm glad you did.'

'I looked up the family, and realized that Mum's sister had moved abroad. But they never spoke, did they?'

He shook his head. 'Not as far as I knew. She brought me up. She lives in Spain now.'

'Anyway, I started to work on an escape plan. I couldn't go to any of my friends, or he'd have found me straight away. I figured if I could find you, maybe I could . . .' she tailed off. 'She used to talk about you, you know. Always knew when your games were on telly.'

Jake's heart contracted. Life hadn't been easy growing up. But there had been plenty of love and affection, and he'd never been made to feel like the poor relation just because he was a nephew and cousin rather than a son and brother.

He reached across the table and covered her hand with his. 'Well, you're here now. And I'll do whatever I can to help.'

'I can't believe I actually found you.' She smiled, fleetingly.

'It can't have been that hard?'

'It wasn't. It was just plucking up the courage to actually leave. I packed a bag a million times, it felt like.'

He frowned, thinking of the tattered black rucksack. Was that all she'd ever planned to bring?

Sarah laughed then. 'You're thinking that if I packed a bag, why was that all I had?'

'Well, yeah.'

'I didn't take my bag. I left everything – not that I had that much, but . . . I didn't intend to go when I did. But he'd gone out drinking, and he was in a foul mood because something had gone wrong at work, and I just knew what was going to happen next. So I grabbed his credit card and jumped on the train heading for Bletchingham. By the time I got there, he'd obviously realized that someone was using it so he'd put a freeze on the card. That's why I had to walk.'

'From Bletchingham?' Bloody hell, no wonder she'd been drenched and slept for hours.

'It wasn't that bad until the thunder started.' She made a self-deprecating face.

'Jesus, Sarah,' Jake said, feeling sick. 'I can't believe you did all that.'

'It was better than the alternative.'

Later that morning, she came downstairs dressed in some of the clothes he'd bought her. The t-shirt had a scoop neck, and when she caught him glancing at a set of dark bruises around her collarbone she pulled it up, defensively.

'Was that him?'

She nodded.

'You could press charges, you know.'

'It'd be his word against mine. I bet he'd convince them there was nothing going on.'

'With bruises like that?'

She shrugged. 'I'm just glad to be away from him.'

'Well, you're welcome here as long as you want to stay. It's not like it's not big enough.'

'Are you sure?'

Jake nodded. 'It's nice to have company. And we've got a whole lifetime of stuff to catch up on.' He hoped his tone didn't bely the apprehension he felt. It was a massive step, bringing someone into his life who he'd never even met until now. He felt a muscle jumping in his cheek and rubbed at his jaw. He'd just have to find a way to manage.

Chapter Eight

It seemed crazy to Hannah that it had been as straight-forward as it had. Driving down the motorway with Ben by her side, she couldn't quite believe that something was actually going her way. She kept expecting the car to break down, or a lorry to crash into the back of them. Things like this just didn't happen to her. Even Ben seemed to have been roused out of his habitual mono-syllabic state and had been quite chatty for the first leg of the journey. Now, though, he was dozing with his head against the window, headphones in ears, not even waking as they drove down the winding roads that led to Little Maudley.

Phil still seemed oddly laid-back about this whole undertaking. Another conversation they'd had last night had only served to reinforce that impression.

'You could totally make a go of the bookshop idea,' he'd said as they'd washed up the dishes after a takeaway meal. 'I don't know anyone as into books as you.'

'There are millions of people who love reading as much as I do,' she'd laughed.

'Yeah, but you did the whole school librarian thing. Not everyone would've volunteered to do that in a primary school.'

'I loved it.' She had smiled at the memory of hours spent sorting out the primary school library, helping to choose books the children would love, willingly giving up her free time to do so.

'Exactly.' Phil had ruffled her hair. 'Weirdo.'

They were coming into the village. Even on a rainy day like today, where the honey stone of the Cotswolds cottages was darkened to the colour of a golden retriever after an impromptu dip in the river, it looked beautiful. Hannah skirted a suspiciously deep-looking puddle at the foot of the hill and returned the friendly wave of a man giving way to her in his battered dark green Land Rover.

They pulled up outside The Old Post Office and Ben woke with a start. He leaned forward slightly, pushing a hand through untidy dark curls that flopped over his forehead. He looked so like his dad at the same age, Hannah thought.

He turned to look at her. 'What?'

'Just thinking how like Dad you look.'

'Oh my God.' He rolled his eyes and shook his head. 'Kill me now.'

Good luck.

Talk of the devil: it was a text from Phil, sending a flying message from the midst of a meeting. She smiled and typed back a quick reply.

Wish you were here. Feels like you're missing out.

His reply was immediate.

You can tell me all about it later.

She typed a reply, but it didn't send. He'd probably

switched his phone back off. Hopefully moving out here would mean he could unwind a bit, stop working the ridiculous hours that he had been. They'd sneaked up over the last year or so – all because of the big project his team was working on, but it was time for the whole family to focus on being together and not on work. Life was way too short for that. He gaze drifted back to her son again.

'What are you staring at?' Realizing he was being watched, Ben looked up from his phone screen.

'Just wondering how you can be almost sixteen already.'

He rolled his eyes. 'It's basic physics. Time, space, that sort of thing.' They got out of the car, and Hannah watched him expectantly. He looked up and down the quiet street. An old-fashioned plane flew overhead through the pale grey clouds, breaking the silence with a gentle thrum of its engine.

'There's genuinely nothing to do here at all, is there?' Ben propelled himself off the wall he'd immediately leaned on and shoved his phone in the back pocket of his jeans.

'There's a WI meeting next Tuesday,' Hannah said, pointing to a poster stuck behind glass on a telegraph pole.

'What's WI?'

'Not your sort of thing,' Hannah said, smiling.

'Why not?'

She shook her head again. 'Trust me on that. Unless you're into *much* older women, and given your age, that had better not be the case.'

'Ugh,' Ben grimaced. 'Mum, that's utterly gross.'

'I was only joking.'

'Well, don't. If we're going to have to live out here in the sticks, we don't want people thinking we're weirdos. Apparently everyone knows everyone in places like this.'

As if his words had summoned a village elder, an old man in a gardening apron materialized from behind a privet hedge.

'Ah – so you're the people taking over the post office?'

'I am, yes. Well, we are – my husband and I. Only he's working, and I've come up to chat to Beth about a few practicalities.'

'And brought me along for the ride,' muttered Ben disapprovingly.

'Well, I hope you'll be very happy here in Little Maudley.' He put down the secateurs he was holding and brushed his hands on the front of his apron. The strands of hair ineffectually covering his bald patch lifted slightly in a gentle breeze and he raise a hand, patting them back into place.

'I can't see how you could be anything other than happy, living here,' Hannah beamed. Ben stuck his fingers down his throat in a vomiting gesture behind the man's back.

'I couldn't agree more.' He extended a gnarled, liver-spotted hand. 'I'm Charles Brewster. Charlie to my friends. I've lived here eighty years, so there's not much I haven't seen.'

'So you're the font of all knowledge?'

'I wouldn't say that. But you get to see the patterns of life living in a village like this. People come and go, relationships flourish and fail, children grow up and move away . . .'

'That's exactly what I'm excited about. I want to be part of a community. Where we live in Manchester, there's none of that. I don't even know my neighbours and they've lived next door for five years.'

'Heh,' Charles chuckled. 'Not much chance of that here. You'll have Helen Bromsgrove on the doorstep within five minutes of getting your belongings moved in. She's a bit of a busybody, but her heart's in the right place.'

'Noted.' Aware there was a limited amount of time before Ben started getting bored and antsy, she said her goodbyes and left Charles ('Call me Charlie') standing by his front gate, watching them as they headed up the path towards the post office.

'Hello, gorgeous. You've grown!'

Ben tolerated Beth rubbing him on the top of his head with relatively good grace.

'Ben's been telling me he's looking forward to helping out in the shop,' Hannah said with a smile.

'That'll wane, mark my words,' said Beth, darkly. 'I can't get Lauren to do a thing unless there's bribery and corruption involved.'

'Oh, there's definitely bribery involved.' Hannah looked at Ben, who was waggling his eyebrows. 'He's his father's son in that regard. Doesn't do anything for nothing.'

'What are you saying about me?' Lauren appeared from the doorway leading through to the adjoining cottage.

'Ben, you haven't seen Lauren for ages.'

'All right?' Lauren, glamorous and insouciant, leaned back against the shop counter, extending endless legs clad in black workout leggings. Ben was uncharacteristically quiet – stunned into silence, Hannah suspected. Lauren was confident, pretty and slightly intimidating. His usual cockiness was gone and he stood looking ill at ease, biting his thumbnail.

'I can't believe you're voluntarily coming to live here,' Lauren said, widening her eyes in mock horror.

'*Lauren*,' chorused Hannah and Beth, giving her a look. Then they both burst out laughing.

'Genetics are bloody amazing. That's exactly the look Mum used to give me if I was in trouble,' Beth chuckled.

'And my mum.'

'Why don't I take you to look round the village so you can see what you're letting yourself in for?' Lauren nodded towards the door of the shop.

Ben gave a curt nod. 'All right.'

'She needs more than the village can offer,' Beth said, watching her daughter fondly through the window.

'And Ben needs less than Manchester has to offer. He got delivered home in a police van again the other day.'

'Bloody hell, Han.'

'I know. He's not a bad kid, he's just a bit easily led.' She'd been telling herself that for the last year, as the

85

trouble he got into increased exponentially. 'And there's nothing much to do.'

'I thought he was into football?'

'He is. It's the only thing that really keeps his interest. He's got absolutely no focus when it comes to school stuff.'

'The village team is pretty good. They came second in their league last year, but they've lost their coach – Gary's got something wrong with his heart so he can't spend all winter freezing his arse off on a football pitch. You just need to get Ben training with them.'

'I do. He's got it into his head that he's going to be spotted by David Beckham because he lives in Chipping Norton.'

Beth snorted with laughter as she flipped on the kettle in the little ante-room behind the counter. 'Coffee?'

'Tea would be lovely if you've got it.'

'There's not much chance of bumping into the Beckhams. We don't really see them in our neck of the woods.'

'Little Maudley isn't exactly overflowing with famous people, you mean?' Hannah took a sip of Beth's tea, wincing slightly. It was so strong that a teaspoon would probably stand up in it. She put the cup down on the counter.

'Well, there's that lovely author I told you about – Anna Broadway. She writes books for teenagers. Lives in a thatched cottage on the edge of the woods behind the allotment – I'll take you for a walk up there before we move. Anyway, she's got a little writing class she runs from the cafe here. And there are a couple of TV actors – they're pretty low-profile, but you might know the woman from that series set in Cornwall about the fishing family? And an ex-footballer, and someone who used to be in an indie band back in the nineties. And that's about it.'

'More than we have in Salford,' said Hannah.

'Well, that's true. But you've got the BBC on your doorstep, and all those glamorous TV people.'

'I've seen them in the morning. They don't look that glam when they're getting off the train at Media City.'

'Anyway . . .' Beth nodded hello as someone walked into the shop. 'Hello Vera, how's your leg doing?'

The elderly woman smiled briefly in acknowledgement and picked up a copy of the local newspaper. She handed over the exact change and then left, without getting involved in conversation.

'She's one of those silent types,' Beth said as she left. Hannah, who hadn't thought anything of it, looked at her cousin sideways. Beth shrugged.

'Let's leave this place for five minutes and I'll show you round the cottage properly.' She came out from behind the counter. 'Just nipping into the house, Zoe,' she called to the girl who was wiping down tables in the adjacent cafe on the other side of a connecting archway.

'I'll keep an eye out.' Zoe smiled.

The cottage was tiny, but even prettier than Hannah remembered. The kitchen window looked out over the street and down across the village green. At the opposite end of the green, Hannah could see the neatly painted telephone box library. As she watched, a woman with a little girl on a balance bike strode up, opened the door and helped herself to a couple of books. The little girl tucked a book under her arm and they headed off down the main street together.

'It's a hit, the library?'

'Definitely,' Beth nodded. 'Even more so since they closed the WHSmith in town, so now there's nowhere people can buy books locally besides the supermarket.'

'Really?'

'Yeah, we used to have a little bookshop in Bletchingham – it was really cute – but the owners moved away. The lease was taken over by the Costa Coffee next door and they expanded. Then when WHSmith went, that was it.'

Later on, once the kids had returned from their wander round the village – Ben, she was pleased to see, had returned to his normal ebullient self and was chatting quite happily to Lauren – they said their goodbyes.

'Hang on,' Beth called, 'let me just give you a couple of bits, that way you don't have to worry about dinner when you get home.'

'You don't have to give me—' Hannah began, but it was too late. Beth had pressed a packet of deliciously scented cherry vine tomatoes into her hands, along with a crusty loaf of sourdough ('Baked this morning – Finn is amazing, you'll love him. I must tell you the story of what happened with him and his wife, mind you, you'll never believe it . . .'). There was also a huge chunk of cheese, made locally by the nineties indie star, who had a reputation for being a bit of a character . . . at least that's what Beth said, raising her eyebrows to the heavens.

'You are an angel,' Hannah said, placing everything into the back seat. 'And I must go.'

'I'll tell you the whole saga next time.' Beth tapped the side of her nose with a finger. 'Ooh, hang on, some eggs. You can do scrambled eggs on toast with roasted cherry toms – that'll be amazing.'

Hannah, who agreed that the food looked wonderful but was privately planning an emergency stop at McDonald's on the way home, said nothing but smiled gratefully.

'Here you are.'

'I might just run to the loo, hang on.'

She left the eggs sitting on the roof of the car and popped back inside while Ben leaned against the little wall, scrolling on his phone.

Finally, when they were both settled in their seats and about to reverse out of the little parking bay, there was a bang on the roof. She stopped the car, startled, and looked out the window. A man – over six foot, handsome, with an amused-looking expression on his face – looked in at her.

'You're not going to get very far with these on the roof.' He passed her the eggs. Beth, standing in the shop doorway, was giggling and pointing, having realized her mistake.

The handsome stranger smiled at Hannah, the corners

of his eyes crinkling in a way that made her feel a bit – well, like she hadn't felt for a long time. And he was oddly familiar-looking, as if she'd seen him before. Whatever it was, he was *way* out of her league, and she needed to get a grip and remember that she was a married thirty-five-year-old mother in a beaten-up Ford Focus.

'I was trying to get back to Manchester before the motorway was completely snarled up.' It was a good thing she wasn't trying to chat him up, because as sexy lines went, that wasn't exactly up there.

'Well, unless you're planning on having scrambled eggs for your tea, I think I'd put those somewhere safe.'

She picked up a hint of a northern accent – flattened, perhaps, by years of living down here in the Home Counties.

And then she realized that Ben was peering cautiously at the man, whilst trying very hard to look as if he was still looking at his phone. He took the eggs out of her hand, put them at his feet, and then looked very hard out of the window as if the post box had suddenly become completely and utterly fascinating.

'Thanks. Sorry. I mean, I didn't mean to be rude.' She made an apologetic gesture with her hands raised, palm up, and shook her head.

'You weren't rude.' His eyes met hers for a second. They were an unusual blue-green, fringed with thick, very dark lashes.

'Well, that's good to know . . . and now that you've saved my eggs, I better get off.' Who on earth was this person speaking words in her voice through her mouth, but actually sounding – was she actually being *flirty*?

'Any time.' He tapped lightly on the roof of her car and then stepped back, still looking at her with the same slightly amused expression.

It wasn't until they'd driven down to the bottom of the village and out past the sign thanking people for driving carefully in Little Maudley that Ben exploded.

'Oh my *God* Mum, I can't believe you.'

'What?'

'Eggs. He handed you eggs.'

She turned to him, one hand on the wheel. 'And?'

'You don't know who that was?'

'He looked familiar. Does he read the news or something?'

Ben dropped his head into his hands and groaned in disbelief.

'It's Jake Lovatt. You know, the England player who broke his leg in the Championship?'

A vague recollection of news articles, horrible clickbait videos on Facebook and front-page photos spun through her mind. She wasn't a football fan by any means, but living with Ben meant that it was ever-present on TV, on the radio, being talked about with his friends. Phil had never taken an interest, claiming he wasn't a football person – so it had always been Hannah who'd spent Saturday mornings standing in the pouring rain watching Ben play, learning the offside rule (well, mostly – she was still a bit hazy on it) and cheering him on. It felt like the least she could do, given his father's lack of interest. And now here she was presented with one of the biggest players in the country and all she could do was – oh God, she'd flirted with him. He probably got that *all* the time. She cringed.

'I remember now.' God, she was actually blushing at the thought of it.

'And you acted like that.'

'Like what?'

Ben groaned. 'You acted like a *mum*.'

Hannah rolled her eyes.

She drove home, not even minding the hideous traffic on the motorway, thinking about how excited she was to be moving to Little Maudley and daydreaming about the possibility of her very own tiny little bookshop. And she definitely didn't think at all about the green-eyed, egg-rescuing ex-footballer. She smiled secretly to herself as she pulled into Beulah Avenue and saw Phil's car parked outside. A tiny little flirt once in a while was probably good for the soul. It wasn't as if it was going to go anywhere.

Chapter Nine

It was a grey and slightly damp Saturday morning – August seemed to have forgotten it was summer and the weather had changed, bringing leaden skies and an abrupt end to summer – when Jake walked the dogs down to the park. Meg and Mabel, both yellow labradors, were delighted to have an extra-long walk and trotted along by his side, tongues lolling.

Despite it only being half nine in the morning, the park between Little Maudley and Much Maudley, its neighbouring (and even more upmarket) village, was already busy. The newly built tennis courts were full, as they always were for a couple of months after Wimbledon time when everyone fancied themselves as the new Serena Williams or Andy Murray.

Over on the far side of the park, shaded by horse chestnut trees, he could see a group of lads messing about with a ball and a man in a tracksuit laying out some colourful flat plastic cones. There was a moment, as he picked up the ball and threw it for the dogs, when he found himself hesitating, and then he headed towards them.

He was standing on the sidelines, feeling awkward, half waiting to be noticed and half wondering what he was supposed to do. Despite everything, it felt like a massive ego trip to actually just turn up and say – what?

And then the problem was solved.

'Oh my God,' said one of the boys, nudging another. They both shot him a sneaky glance.

He was used to it – the first time it happened when he'd signed for Southampton at the age of seventeen, he'd gone to the shop with Aunty Jane and been surprised when the man behind the counter had pulled off a piece of receipt paper and asked for his autograph. He'd never even thought about what his signature should look like, so he'd just scribbled a vague doodle on the paper and given a shy smile before leaving, face scarlet with embarrassment. But as the years had passed and he'd adjusted to it, he'd learned to make himself invisible – despite what the papers would have you think, it wasn't that difficult. A baseball cap, travelling early in the morning or late at night – just keeping your head down was the secret.

'All right?' The man in the tracksuit came over. 'Heard you've been doing some training with the lads over at Ridgeway. How's it going?'

'Good, thanks,' Jake said, picking up the ball that had been dropped at his feet and throwing it as far as he could. They both watched as the two dogs hurtled off in hot pursuit. He hadn't actually done anything more with them – having pretty much decided straight off that they didn't need him – but he couldn't face an inquisition, so he just let it drop.

'Have you come to check us out? We're all a bit knackered – end of summer, everyone's boiling hot, and half of them haven't done any exercise all holidays.'

'I dunno, you've got a few decent players. That lad at the back communicates well. That's always a good start.'

The man beamed. 'I'm Gary, by the way.'

'I guessed.' Jake shook his hand. 'Beth in the village shop mentioned you guys were looking for some help with coaching?'

Gary took a step back and started to laugh, which turned into a fit of coughing. 'And you're offering your services?' He chuckled to himself.

Jake nodded. 'If you're still looking for someone.'

'You're offering to train this lot?' The boys, who had gathered and were hovering close by, weren't saying anything. 'This is the quietest I've seen them in – well, forever,' Gary added.

'I don't need them quiet,' Jake said, turning to catch their eyes. 'If I do take this on, I'll need as much communication as I can get, and I'll need you all focused on what the rest of the team is doing at all times.'

Not one of them said a word. They looked shell-shocked, and more than a little bit like rabbits in headlights.

'Well, this is a first,' said Gary. 'Nobody got anything to say?'

They shook their heads, still mute.

Jake looked at him. 'I understand you've had some trouble with your heart?'

'Yeah, I just can't spend as much time on my feet as I could. And you can't coach while you're sitting on the sidelines.'

'True.' Jake tapped the ball, which had rolled to his feet, back towards one of the taller boys in the team. 'Come on then, let's see what you lot are made of. Shall we do some tackling drills?'

The boys played surprisingly well. Gary was a good coach – encouraging those who were quieter, nipping the occasional bit of teenage attitude in the bud and redirecting the mouthy ones. Jake was surprised by how much he enjoyed being back at grassroots level, where there was nothing to focus on but the love of the game.

'You certain you want to give up your Saturday mornings to do this?' Gary sat on a folding travel chair, clearly worn out from his exertions. The boys were dismantling the net, stacking up the cones and messing about with the ball. In the distance, several cars lined up by the road, waiting for them to finish.

'Yes, I am.' Jake nodded. 'It's not like I have anything else to do, to be honest.'

'I'd have thought you'd be busy doing lots of . . .' He tailed off. 'I dunno. What *do* retired footballers do on a weekend?'

'Not a lot.' Jake shrugged, smiling. 'I'm single, no kids, nothing like that.'

'Sounds bloody peaceful to me,' Gary laughed.

They shook hands, swapped mobile numbers and

agreed to meet up to discuss the practicalities later in the week. It was the most normal thing Jake had done in a long time, and he liked it. If he could keep it out of the papers and they didn't come sniffing around, he could actually have a stab at a normal life. But it depended on people not mouthing off to the press.

The last thing he needed was anyone getting wind of what was going on at home. The newspapers would have a field day – he could just imagine the headlines. Despite everything, he felt a fierce sense of loyalty towards the mother he'd never known – and to Sarah, who seemed so fragile and broken by everything. She'd been at rock bottom when she'd turned up on his doorstep and he felt, somehow, that helping her to find her way out of what had brought her to him was the least he could do. If she could develop some self-confidence, she'd be far less likely to end up in another relationship where she was treated the way that Joe had treated her.

He'd picked up enough intel over the last twelve months to know that Beth at the village shop was a complete gossip hound. Anything she heard was shared with the next person who came into the shop – so he'd just have to try his best to avoid her. If there was one thing his time in the Premiership had taught him, it was that it was possible to be discreet if he had to.

With that in mind, he walked home with the dogs and then drove quickly into Bletchingham instead of doing his shopping in the village. It mightn't fit in with the much-repeated call to support local business, but he decided that he'd go easy on himself for once. He picked up some nice bits and pieces for dinner.

Back at the house, he unloaded the dogs from the back of the car and whistled for them to follow him inside. The sky had cleared and it looked like being a nice afternoon. Sarah, however, was nowhere to be seen. The only evidence she'd been up was that the dishwasher had been emptied and the wellies he'd bought her were missing from the porch. Perhaps she'd actually ventured out for a walk? He unpacked the shopping and made himself a coffee. If she wasn't about, he might as well sit down and see what was happening with today's Premier League games.

What felt like moments later, he woke with a start as the door banged. The coffee he'd made stood undrunk on the table beside him, and the game had almost finished. All this doing nothing was turning him into the sort of person who dozed off on a Saturday afternoon. Thank God he was going to be working with the kids in the village.

'Hello,' said Sarah, walking into the room and perching on the arm of the sofa. Her dark eyes were watchful, as always. She pushed a strand of hair back from her face, tucking it behind her hear.

'Hi. Fell asleep watching TV,' he said, shaking his head and laughing. 'Where have you been? Out for a walk?'

'Went to the shop,' she said.

'In the village?'

'Yeah. Thought maybe I should venture out a bit.'

'That's good.' He hoped Beth hadn't winkled out the story of his secret past before Sarah had even realized what was going on.

'I – I just want to say thanks, again,' Sarah said, hesitantly. 'You didn't need to put me up.'

'Course I did,' he said, gruffly. 'You're family. It's the least I could do.'

'I know, but – I mean, I could have been anyone.'

'But you're not. Have you told – I mean, does anyone—'

'Know I'm here?' She shook her head. 'Nobody to tell, really. That's the thing about growing up the way I did. You sort of lose people along the way. Then when Mum died, I lost myself.'

'How did you know where to find me?' It had been nagging at him for ages. He'd tried to stay below the radar, and he thought he'd done a decent job of it.

She looked at him for a moment, then laughed. 'It's not exactly hard – you're famous.'

'Hardly.' He still struggled with the idea that people knew who he was – or thought they did, at any rate. In his head he was still the same lad from back home. That's why he found the whole idea of fame so uncomfortable. Other friends of his had lapped up the whole footballer lifestyle – but to him it was everything he hated. He loved the game, loved the camaraderie that came with being part of a team – but he hated the whole high-fashion, image-conscious bit.

'Well, anyway. All I had to do was Google a bit, use my initiative . . . it wasn't that hard. I don't know what made me find you.' She looked down at the floor and scuffed her toe along the edge of the rug. 'But I'm glad I did.'

'Me too.'

Chapter Ten

'I can't believe you're just upping sticks and disappearing to the sticks.'

A surprise farewell-to-Manchester party was Hannah's idea of hell, which was probably why Katie had left her planner open on her kitchen dresser a week before the event with HANNAH'S SURPRISE PARTY written in bold and highlighted in such a way that it was hard to miss. It meant that Hannah – who would otherwise have been in the uniform of filthy, dust-covered leggings and t-shirt that she'd been wearing as she blitzed the house and packed up their belongings – was showered and dressed in something respectable, and had even managed to get a cancellation at the salon so her hair was falling in sleek waves instead of its usual tangled, curly muddle.

Katie had gathered all their friends – she had a knack for it, in a way that Hannah could only admire – and they were all hovering around Katie's kitchen island, scoffing the delicious and expensive M&S canapés that had been delivered by UberEats earlier.

'There'll be no getting food delivered in the middle of nowhere,' Georgie said darkly. She tucked a long strand of blonde hair behind her ear and popped a piece of sushi into her perfectly painted scarlet mouth. Georgie worked for an investment bank and was – like Katie – one of those friends who made everyone else feel like a scruffy underachiever. She had no children, but was embroiled in a complicated sort of relationship with Naheem, who was unhappily married but seemed to show no signs of leaving his wife. As Hannah watched, she picked up her phone and started typing into it furiously.

'In the immortal words of Nora Ephron,' began Katie, looking at Hannah and laughing as they chorused in unison: 'He's never going to leave her.'

'I know.' Georgie put her phone face down on the work surface and scoffed another two pieces of sushi. 'Anyway, enough about me. What's the deal with Phil staying here while you disappear off to live in bucolic splendour?'

Hannah took a large mouthful of wine and looked across the room at two of her other friends, who were laughing at something on a phone screen. 'It's fine,' she said quickly. 'I'm only going ASAP to make sure I get Ben away from this dodgy gang he's been hanging around with – and of course Beth is keen to get moving as soon as she can.'

She watched as a fleeting glance passed between Georgie and Katie. She knew what they thought – they'd made it clear often enough. Both of them felt like Phil didn't pull his weight. They were probably right, but – well, sometimes it was easier not to rock the boat for the sake of a quiet life.

'Maybe you'll fall head over heels for some handsome farmer before he turns up.'

'Not likely.' Hannah laughed a little too brightly. She'd found herself thinking about the gorgeous footballer quite a lot over the last couple of weeks as she'd gone back and forth between Manchester and Little Maudley, learning the ropes and being taught the basics about shopkeeping and how the post office was run. Not once, though, had she seen him. Not that she'd been looking, of course. But daydreaming about him on the drive to and from Little Maudley seemed perfectly respectable. It wasn't as if she and Phil had much of a sex life . . . in fact, if she was honest with herself, it had been quite some time since they'd done anything more than sleep together. Having Ben in the room next door was a bit offputting, but it wasn't just that – they'd been together so long that in lots of ways they were more like friends than anything else. And (she made a face into her wine glass, thinking about it) you couldn't just grab your mate and start snogging them, randomly. Katie caught her eye and raised an eyebrow.

'What are you lost in thought about?'

Hannah giggled. 'Nothing.' She was hardly about to admit that she was contemplating whether or not snogging her best friend would be more or less surprising than leaping on an unsuspecting Phil when he walked in the door that evening.

Later on, having been delivered back home slightly the worse for several glasses of wine and some celebration champagne, Hannah decided that maybe tonight was the night to actually break the drought. It had been . . . how long had it been? She couldn't actually remember.

Phil was lying on the sofa watching *8 out of 10 Cats* when she lurched into the sitting room. She was aiming for more of a lazily seductive prowl, but someone had moved the pile of washing that sat permanently behind the door, so instead of shoving it open and it giving way slowly, it swung with force and hit the wall with a clatter and she fell through the gap, giggling.

Smooth, she thought to herself. She straightened up, catching a glimpse of herself in the big mirror above the fireplace. Her hair looked good for once. Eyes still smoky, and the lipstick reapplied in the Uber home was a dark red. All in all, she decided, ruffling her hair and shaking it before turning to face him, she didn't look too bad for the mother of a teenager. She readjusted her boobs in her bra.

'You all right?' Phil looked up from his prone position, a slightly quizzical expression on his face.

'Yes.' She sat down on the coffee table so she was looking down at him. Perfect position to launch herself into – well, she could launch herself on *top*, but that might freak him out a bit. It really had been bloody ages. She'd basically turned back into a virgin. Maybe she'd have forgotten how to do it altogether.

'Are you okay?' Phil repeated. 'How much have you had to drink?' He sat up, which completely scuppered her plans to lean over and tenderly kiss him on the mouth.

'Just some wine. And some champagne.' She eyed the bottle of brandy that was sitting on the bookshelf. 'Maybe we should have a nightcap?'

'I think you've probably had enough.' He stood up. Well, this was going brilliantly. Hannah pushed herself up from the table so she was standing face to face with him. Phil looked slightly alarmed. His arms were rigid by his sides. She took one of his hands, which was balled in a fist. He looked at her again. 'Han, are you okay?'

And then she decided to just go for it. Propelling herself forward, still holding his balled-up fist in one hand, she landed an open-mouthed kiss on his closed, rather stubbly and definitely resistant mouth. There was a split second when she wondered if he was going to part his lips – she held herself there, waiting, frozen in between one moment and the next, and then recoiled backwards.

Phil laughed. 'What on earth was that?'

She plopped back on the sofa with a gentle thud. 'It was affection, Phil.' Her voice was crisp.

'Well, obviously, but what inspired this sudden burst of passion?'

And as if someone had pulled out a plug, all her feelings came rushing out. 'We haven't had sex in forever. We never kiss. There's no physical affection between us. You don't—'

'I've been flat out at work and you're wrapped up in sorting out the shop and making plans for a village bookshop. What d'you expect?'

'It's been longer than that.' She exhaled, and sagged back onto the cushions. He was looking at her as if she was a little bit simple, and talking to her as if she was a very young child.

'It really hasn't. Look, you're drunk, I'm tired, and I've got some work to check before I come up. Why don't you go and warm the bed up, and I'll be there before you know it. I'll cuddle you to sleep and we can talk about this more in the morning.'

She bit her lip. The sitting room wall was lined with cardboard boxes full of books she'd already packed. She'd promised to travel light, but going without her familiar friends had felt too hard. Right now she wanted to pick up a copy of John Donne's poetry and comfort herself, but he was locked away somewhere in the depths of the pile.

Phil was still standing there, looking at her as if she were a dementia patient or something. He held a hand out to help her up. 'Go on, blossom, up you go.'

She allowed herself to be pulled up to standing and headed for the door, feeling slightly more the worse for wear than before. Maybe red wine, white wine *and* champagne had been a bit much. 'I'll see you in a second,' Phil said, patting her affectionately on the bottom as she left the room.

She was asleep seconds after washing her face and brushing her teeth.

The next morning, she woke – dry-mouthed and fuzzy-headed – to find the bed empty. Creeping downstairs – it was still early and she loved the peace of having the place to herself – she found Phil snoring on the sofa, sleeping laptop open on the coffee table beside him. He hadn't made it to bed last night. A tiny, creeping sensation of unease passed over her, but she brushed it to one side. Once they got to the village, everything was going to be okay.

Chapter Eleven

The amazing thing, Hannah thought, was just how quickly everything seemed to slot into place. Never before had she experienced anything like it – normally life had so many bumps and twists and turns in the road that she'd become used to things taking twice as long as planned. Instead, the whole experience seemed blessed in some way. Beth and Lauren were so desperate to get away from the village that it was only going to be another week before the big move took place.

She had one more trip to make, to sign some paperwork and meet the woman from the farm that supplied the post office with locally reared meat ('You'll love her, she's hysterical!' Beth had said, which somehow only filled Hannah with foreboding) – and then the next time she'd be there was when she was taking over. She felt a flurry of nerves at the speed of it all if she stopped to think about it for too long. But beneath that, there was the strangest feeling of certainty that she was doing the right thing.

The next morning she headed down the M6 again. She'd done the journey so many times of late that it felt as if she was wearing tracks on the route between Salford and

Little Maudley. Pulling off the motorway and into the increasingly familiar countryside, she felt her shoulders dropping and the tension easing as the roads grew narrower. The sun was high in a pale blue sky. Pausing at a temporary traffic light, she looked out of the window and saw a group of cows gathered under an oak tree, sheltering from a burst of unexpected Indian summer heat. The temperature guide on her dashboard said it was twenty-four degrees, and it was only half past eleven. It was definitely warmer down south. Maybe they'd all get tans from lying in the back garden next summer – maybe they'd even be able to use the inflatable swimming pool they'd bought three years ago when there was a two-week heatwave in the north of England. Although – a horn beeped, and she realized the lights had turned – back then Ben had been twelve, and she'd still been the centre of his universe. God, she hoped village life wouldn't be too boring for him. But also, she really hoped it was boring enough that Ben could focus on his GCSEs or his football or *something* that didn't involve coming home in a police van.

When she reached the centre of the village and parked outside the post office, she saw that the green was abuzz with people hanging coloured bunting and setting up trestle tables.

'Well, *hello* again!' It was Helen Bromsgrove, de facto queen of the village. 'I've heard all about your plans from Beth. I'm Helen – you probably remember that, of course.' She was so self-assured. Hannah never expected anyone to remember who she was from one day to the next. 'You must come round for drinks when you get settled. When is your husband joining you?'

Beth appeared, waggling a finger. 'Now then, Helen, stop trying to get all the gossip out of my cousin before she's even settled in.'

Another woman had entered the shop – plumpish, dark hair, expensively dressed in floral patterns that looked like Joules or Boden, which seemed to be a uniform down in the Cotswolds. She gave Helen a fleeting sideways glance with eyebrows raised, which Hannah clocked. The dark-haired woman flushed slightly and turned to busy herself with folding up some paper napkins and placing them beside pretty floral cups and saucers.

'Come on,' Beth said, giving the woman's back a glare. 'Let's get you inside. I've found something you'll love.'

'What's the story with that woman with the dark hair?'

They went into the cottage kitchen and Beth poured two glasses of iced water, passing one to Hannah and taking a sip of her own. She looked at her cousin over the top of the glass, mouth pursed in thought.

'Just one of those people who likes to be at the centre of everything. And of course Helen's queen bee here in the village – chair of the PTA, on the WI committee, a parish councillor, all that sort of thing. Mina kind of tags along behind her, and she's a bit of a cow.'

Hannah stirred the ice in her drink with a finger thoughtfully. 'I guess village life sort of magnifies all that stuff?'

'It can do, yes. Little Maudley likes to present itself as a tight-knit community, but it's like any group of people – there's always loads of stuff going on behind the scenes. I end up hearing it all because I'm in the shop all day.'

After they'd had a drink, Hannah took a walk around the village to see what was going on. There was a huge hand-painted sign hanging on the side of the village hall, proclaiming that the annual fête was taking place the next day. She bumped into the dark-haired woman again and smiled at her, but the woman's answering smile was tight-lipped and she quickly scuttled off. In the car park of the village hall, an elderly woman with bright blue eyes was sitting on a bench watching proceedings. She had a shrewd, thoughtful expression, and she lifted her chin and sized up Hannah for a moment before she spoke.

'Hello,' she said.

'Hello.' Hannah smiled.

'I gather you're moving to the village.'

'I am, yes.'

'And you're going to be taking over the shop.'

Hannah's eyes widened. This woman might look like a sweet old dear, but she was clearly very switched on.

'I – yes?'

'Such a strange habit, answering a question with a question. I blame those Australian soap operas.'

Hannah, who had often pulled Ben up for his upward inflection at the end of sentences, laughed. 'Sorry. I think I've caught it from my son.'

'So what brings you to this village in particular?'

'I didn't expect any of this to happen. It's all been very sudden.'

'The best things in life often are,' said the woman, looking off into the middle distance for a moment. She was lost in thought for a while before she shook herself and extended a gnarled, liver-spotted hand in greeting. 'I'm Bunty, by the way. How d'you do?'

Hannah smiled. 'I'm good, thank you.' And in that moment, she realized that actually – she was. It was a strange feeling.

Chapter Twelve

She'd planned the first morning a million times in her head. She was going to have an early night, set the alarm for half five, get up and be ready bright and early for the newspaper deliveries. Beth had told her a million times that she didn't need to do that – they were shoved into the secure porch, covered from the rain (not that they'd had any all week) – but she wanted to feel like she was doing the whole thing right.

Of course, it didn't exactly go to plan. Ben was up in the night with an upset stomach. The streetlight outside shone a glowing orange through the curtains which kept her half-awake, and then she woke at three – and four – and four thirty, just in case she slept through the alarm. Then the birds started yelling from the clematis that grew outside the bedroom window. When the alarm finally did blare through her brain she was in the heaviest of dead-limbed slumbers and waking felt like dragging herself through a sea of thick, oozing mud.

Stopping to turn off Ben's bedroom light – he had a terrible habit of falling asleep with it on – she staggered downstairs and put on the kettle, dragging a brush through her hair. Once she'd mainlined a huge mug of coffee, though, she started to feel more human. The village street was deserted save for a lone jogger who gave her a cheerful wave as he trotted past. She recognized him as David, husband of Helen, the village linchpin.

'Morning,' he said, stopping for a moment to catch his breath. 'How's it going? I gather Beth's gone and you're on your lonesome?'

'First day nerves.' Hannah made a face. 'I'm just hoping it all goes okay.'

'It'll be fine. You've got Flo in the cafe if you get stuck, and no doubt Helen will be in later to see how it's going.'

Helen was a bit of a whirlwind, but Hannah quite liked her. And frankly, today she would be pleased to see any friendly face. It seemed like a terrifying prospect all of a sudden: Phil wasn't there for backup, she felt like the butterflies in her stomach were wearing Doc Marten boots, and the reality of being responsible for everything without Beth to guide her suddenly seemed quite terrifying. She hadn't worked full-time in – well, in years. And now, if she messed up, there was nobody to blame but herself. She swallowed hard and tried to take a deep breath. How hard could it be?

'Morning, love,' said a man pulling up with a white van. He jumped out and hefted a huge bundle of papers. 'Didn't get the personal treatment with Beth. This is nice.' He winked.

'I'm not sure you'll be getting it with me every day.' Hannah stopped a yawn with her hand. She headed inside as he pulled away, unwrapping all the newspapers and placing them carefully on their racks. Then she straightened the already straight piles of leaflets and flyers that stood by the front of the counter and looked around. Everything had been organized neatly by Freya, one of the sixth-form students who worked there after college. She'd done a brilliant job and left it looking absolutely impeccable. Hannah looked at the clock – it was only six. The shop didn't officially open until eight. Maybe she could just lie down for a quick half-hour snooze and then she'd feel more human.

'Mum?'

Hannah could hear a distant voice. She pulled the pillow over her head and tried to burrow back into sleep.

'Mum!' The voice was more urgent now.

'I'm sleeping. There's lots of cereal in the kitchen cupboard.'

'There isn't, because we've only just moved and you haven't done the shopping yet. But there's lots of cereal on the *shop shelves*,' Ben said meaningfully.

'Oh shit.' Hannah sat bolt upright.

'Language,' said Ben from her bedroom doorway, raising a sardonic eyebrow.

'Sorry. *Shit*. What time is it?' She grabbed for her phone, feeling sick with having just woken from a deep sleep and a sense of overwhelming nausea that she'd managed to screw things up before she'd even started.

'Quarter to eight. I thought you said the shop opens at eight?'

'It does.'

'Didn't you say you were going to be up super-early?'

'I did.' She pulled on a pair of cropped leggings and a long tunic vest, quickly tidied her hair and headed to the bathroom to brush her teeth and wash her face. There was no time for the shower and pretty sundress and light-but-casual make-up she'd been planning. The villagers were going to have to take her as they found her. In this case, that would mean a bit scruffy and bleary round the edges.

'Morning.' An elderly woman was tying a terrier to the post outside as she unlocked the front door. It wasn't even eight yet, but there were two people waiting. The woman and the teenage boy (who had thrown his bike carelessly against the wall) both made their way inside before she could even remark that the shop wasn't officially open yet.

'Can I just have this, please?' The boy handed over a can of some sort of energy drink.

'I'm afraid you can't, no.'

'What d'you mean?'

'You're under sixteen. I can't serve you energy drinks. It's the rules.' Beth had drilled it into her – and given her a crib list of all the teenagers in the village liable to come in and try their luck buying alcohol with fake IDs.

'Fine,' said the boy, rolling his eyes at her and giving a cheeky smile which suggested he'd only been chancing his luck with the new girl behind the desk. 'I'll swap it for a Diet Coke, then.'

'Just these, please,' said the woman, meanwhile. She

placed a copy of the *Daily Telegraph* and a pint of milk on the counter. Hannah rang it up and handed back the change. And that was it – she was in business.

There was a flurry of customers after the bread delivery – people came in and swooped down like locusts, clearing the baskets almost as soon as they were filled. She was under the counter looking for a replacement till roll when she heard someone clearing their throat.

'I guess I'm too late for the famous sourdough,' the voice said. It was faintly northern and vaguely familiar. She stood up. Standing opposite her, sunglasses pushed back in his dark hair, which stood up in slightly untidy spikes, was Jake, the handsome footballer. She felt her knees give a disobedient wobble.

'I'll save you one next time, if you ask nicely.' He was so far out of her – married, in any case – league that it actually felt quite safe to be vaguely flirtatious.

He gave her a crooked half-smile. 'Special treatment?' He lifted one of the wonkily cut, colourful flyers announcing that Little Maudley Junior FC was seeking a new coach.

'Call it a thank you for saving me from losing my eggs the other week.' She looked down at the leaflet. 'Are you considering a new career?'

'Funny you should say that. I was about to say that these are out of date now, so you can chuck them in the recycling.'

'Really?' She took them from him and absent-mindedly placed them back down on the counter.

'Yep. You're looking at the new coach.'

She recoiled slightly, snorting a giggle. Since they'd bumped into him, Ben had done nothing but go on and on about how amazing it was to discover The Actual Jake Lovatt living in the same village. 'Isn't that a bit . . . beneath you?'

He looked at her directly with his strange, green-blue eyes. 'There's no such thing.'

She flushed. 'Sorry, it's just – I mean—'

Jake laughed. 'Yeah, I know. I'm at a loose end, though – and grassroots is where I started, so it feels like a good thing to give something back.'

'My son – Ben – he's obsessed with football. He's hoping to join the team.'

'We've got a trial tomorrow. Bring him along.'

'What time tomorrow?'

'Half eleven on the playing field. We'll be there for an hour and a half. Come and say hello if you're passing.'

'Ben might die of horror. I've gone from the person he wants there cheering him on at every match to the most embarrassing mother on the planet.'

'I bet he can't wait to tell you if he scores, though, right?'

She nodded, smiling. The games she didn't watch, he always rushed in the door to give her a blow-by-blow account of what happened.

'Thought as much. All right, tell him to be there ten minutes early so I can fill in the paperwork. And remind him to bring his shin pads, or he won't be able to play.'

'I will.'

'Ah, hello!'

They both jumped as Helen Bromsgrove bustled into the shop. Catching sight of Jake, she put an automatic hand to her smooth blonde hair. Hannah felt even scruffier by comparison, remembering her lack of make-up and untidy tangle of curls.

'It's lovely that I've bumped into you, Jake – have been meaning to ask if you'd like to pop round for dinner one night.' Hannah watched as Jake's eyes flickered from left to right, like a cornered animal looking for escape. 'David and I would *love* to introduce you to some of the locals, and of course there's so much you could get involved with, village-wise. Would be very quiet, just a few chosen guests. Shall I give you my card? Or perhaps you could pop your number in my phone?' She started fishing in her handbag, and Jake took the opportunity to make his escape.

'I'm already tied up with some village stuff, actually – but I must get on. Got somewhere to be this morning.' He glanced up at the clock above Hannah's head. 'Is that the time?'

Hannah was gratified – and Helen more than a little miffed – that as he left, he popped his head round the door and said, 'Don't forget about tomorrow.'

'Well,' Helen said, with some asperity, putting her phone back in her bag, 'I was *going* to ask how you were settling in, but it seems you've caught us all on the hop.'

She fixed Hannah with an unreadable look and then

119

disappeared to the back of the shop, pausing only to collect a wicker basket. She returned a few minutes later with it stacked full – gratifyingly so, Hannah thought. She had been wondering how profitable a village shop that sold everything you could buy in the supermarket, only for quite a lot more, could actually be.

'Important to support our local shops,' Helen said cosily, helping to unload the things onto the counter. 'And important for us to support our local shopkeeper,' she added. 'Why don't you pop round this evening for a drink, and we can have a chat about your plans?'

'That sounds lovely,' said Hannah automatically, wishing at the same time that she was the sort of person who had ready-made excuses for things like that up her sleeve. It didn't take a genius to work out that she was going to be completely wrecked by the end of a day of trying to learn the ropes and keep the shop going.

The rest of the day flew past – as Beth had instructed her, there was a busy period first thing, then a lull, and another rush of people coming in around lunchtime. The early afternoon saw walkers coming by, and of course a steady stream of people made their way into and out of the cafe. But she managed to find half an hour when the village volunteer was manning the till to stand in the alcove where the bookshop was going to be and draw a sketch of what she wanted. There was room for shelves on both sides, and even a little space under the window where children's books could sit. Maybe she could even get Ben to do some painting on the whitewashed walls, or make a sign. The one subject he'd always flourished in at school besides sport was art. It would do him good – give him a bit of confidence, and hopefully make him feel part of things.

And that was how she ended up sitting at Helen's kitchen table that evening, watching as Helen, notebook in hand, sat holding court with a glass of wine in front of two other women she'd only just met.

'This is Mina. She's my right-hand woman.'

Mina, the dark-haired women from the day of the fête, was dressed almost identically to Helen. She gave Hannah a thin smile.

'And Jenny. She's new to the village, like you. Jenny, Hannah's cousin Beth was running the shop until this week.'

Jenny was very slim, with hooded eyes and a slightly beaky nose. She was dressed in a floral dress and a pair of silver sandals. She looked at Hannah and narrowed her eyes briefly. 'The one you—'

Helen widened her eyes and shook her head, imperceptibly. It wasn't the first time that Hannah had picked up on something – some sort of atmosphere – about Beth. She knew her cousin could be a bit of a gossip, but her heart was basically in the right place. It felt like the villagers weren't convinced about that, though.

'I'm sure Hannah has her own ideas about how to run the shop. New broom sweeps cleanest, and all that.'

Jenny flicked a glance at Helen. Hannah, feeling like the girl at school who everyone was picking on for no reason, shifted uncomfortably in her chair. She placed a hand over her wine glass as David, Helen's husband, appeared, brandishing a brand new bottle of Sauvignon Blanc. 'No, I'm fine, thank you. I've got to be up in the morning.'

'You'll be glad to have Sundays off, though?' David smiled. He seemed far less spiky than his wife.

'Definitely.' Shifting in her seat, she absent-mindedly twisted her wedding ring round on her finger. She was exhausted, and all the work she'd been doing over the last few weeks was catching up with her. All she wanted to do was go home, order a pizza and curl up on the sofa to watch something mindless on television.

'So tell me,' Helen said, turning to face her. 'What exactly have you got in mind for the shop?'

Hannah began cautiously at first, not wanting to tread on any toes. But as she warmed to the bookshop idea and explained what she hoped to do, she knew that her excitement was showing. To her relief, all of them seemed to be on board.

'This is just the best idea ever,' Helen beamed. 'We've found the telephone box library has been rather a victim of its own success. Poor Lucy, who said she'd be in charge of book distribution, has been completely flooded with donations.'

'I met her the other week,' Hannah said, taking an olive. 'She seems lovely.'

'Oh, she's a gem.' Helen nodded approvingly. 'And such a good teacher. An asset to the village. And it looks like you might be too,' she added, squeezing Hannah's arm. 'Coming up with ideas for fundraising for the village hall when you've only just arrived. Goodness. We'll have to get you on the WI committee. And you must come along to the Parish Council meeting, too. Oh, and while I think, you need to—'

'I—' Hannah began, alarmed.

'Cool your jets,' said Mina, laughing and shaking her head. 'Don't mind our Helen. She can't help herself.'

'I am here,' Helen said, indignantly.

'You're going to scare her back to Manchester at this rate,' Jenny said, joining in the laughter.

'So sorry,' Helen said, offering Hannah some more wine. 'I can get a little *over-enthusiastic* at times.'

You're not bloody joking she can, Hannah texted Katie later that night when she'd made it home and was tucked up in bed, eyelids drooping.

You said you wanted all that village stuff, Katie replied, with a laughing face emoji.

I did! Hannah agreed. *Just not all of it in one evening.*

Chapter Thirteen

The morning of the football trials, Jake woke early and went for a run. Sarah was up and cooking bacon when he got back.

'What are you up to today?' She pointed to the frying pan. 'You want a sandwich?'

'Football trials,' he said, nodding. It'd cancel out the run he'd just done, but never mind. He could never resist a bacon roll first thing in the morning.

'I thought I might go into town and have a wander about.'

'Bletchingham?'

Sarah nodded. It was nice to see her coming out of herself a bit more. For a long time, she'd seemed content to just sit at home like a cat that had been caught out in the rain.

In the park he set out cones for some training drills, trying to convince himself he wasn't looking out for the pretty woman from the shop. But every couple of minutes he found himself glancing across the field, looking for anyone that looked like her. He checked his watch – quarter to. The rest of the boys were milling about, some kicking a ball back and forth, others jogging on the spot and chatting.

'Hello,' said a familiar voice.

She was standing behind him. He spun round, still holding the coiled rope for the sideline.

'Jamie, can you put this out?'

One of the boys nodded and took it from his hands.

'I'm taking my life in my hands being here,' she said, laughing and nodding in the direction of her son, who'd joined the others and was passing the ball back and forth.

'Plenty of other parents here today,' he said, pointing to a group of them standing nearby. 'I think trials are a bit different.'

'Well, I'll just keep my head down and try not to do anything embarrassing.'

He watched as she headed over to join the other parents, and then the trial session started in earnest and his focus was completely taken up with the boys and how they were performing. It was a relief that Ben, her son, wasn't just averagely good – he was genuinely promising. Every time he could, he put himself between the opposing player and the goal, putting on speed and showing some incredibly nimble footwork. And best of all – in Jake's eyes – he was a generous player, happy to share the ball and not determined to hog it at all costs. That was something that was instinctive, as he explained to Hannah when they finished up.

'He's good,' he said, not wanting to be effusive. 'Really good.'

'I think he is,' she said, proudly. 'But you don't know, do you? I mean, I'm not a football person. All I know is

125

he seems to get results, and he loves it. He comes to life when he's on the pitch.'

'Sounds familiar.' Jake nodded. 'I was exactly the same. Hated school, was happiest when I was outside. Not everyone's cut out for academia.'

'You're right.' Hannah threw the hoody she was holding across to Ben, who'd ventured over and was hovering just a few metres away, clearly desperate to know how he'd got on.

'You did well,' Jake told him. 'See you next weekend for training?'

Ben's face burst into a huge beam of happiness. 'Really?'

'Really.'

'Cool.'

'I think he means "thanks Jake, that's a real honour and I promise I'll do my best",' teased Hannah.

'Yeah,' said Ben, ducking his head and looking embarrassed. 'That as well.'

'Off you go,' Jake said, laughing. 'You lads might as well have a kickabout while I talk to the parents.'

Hannah – feeling shy, because all the others seemed to know each other – hovered on the edges of the group as Jake spoke to the parents about training times and his plans for the team. It was clear that most of them were in awe of him to start with, but once he started chatting and the ice was broken, everyone relaxed. Jake seemed to relax as well, and looked markedly less stressed than he had when they'd spoken earlier.

She was touched when he came over to talk as all the

other parents drifted back to their cars or headed across the field with their dogs.

'It's a bit weird being the new person,' he said, pushing his hair out of his eyes.

'Tell me about it.'

'So you've taken over the shop from your cousin?'

She nodded. 'It was a last-minute thing.' She looked across at Ben, who was laughing and kicking the ball to one of the other boys. 'But it seems like it's working out okay. I wanted to get him away from . . . well, he was hanging around with a dodgy crowd.'

'I was the same at that age. Football's a good way of focusing the mind. There's not much time to mess about if you're taking it seriously.'

'That's what I'm hoping.'

'Well, he's got potential, so that's a start. So how's it going, taking over from your cousin? She was . . .' He paused, clearly trying to choose his words carefully. 'She seemed like a village stalwart.'

'That's one way of putting it.' She caught his eye and they both laughed. 'I adore Beth, but she's always been a gossip.'

'Well, I didn't like to say, but . . .'

'Oh, I know exactly what she's like. And so does everyone in the village, it seems.' She bit her lip thoughtfully. 'The trouble is, it sometimes feels like I've been tarred with the same brush. I got here thinking it was going to be like living in an episode of *The Archers* where everyone was super-friendly, but they've all been kind of . . .'

'Standoffish?' He finished her sentence.

'Not quite.'

'Are you feeling the North-South divide?' He grinned.

'I dunno.' She lifted her shoulders slightly. 'I think maybe I just need get used to village life. It's a big change from back home.'

He picked up the bag of kit and shouldered it, but didn't make a move to leave. When he spoke, Hannah noticed, he had a habit of focusing very intently, so you felt like you were the only person in the world. It made her knees go a bit weak.

'Yeah, it's a bit of a change, isn't it? Have you seen the village Facebook group?'

She smiled. 'I have. Are you on there?'

'Under an assumed name, ridiculously. But yes, I can't stay away because it's hysterical.'

'Did you see the post about the escaped goats?'

He laughed. 'And the one complaining about someone rifling through the contents of a skip?'

'I'm sort of weirdly addicted to looking at it.'

'Me too.'

'Are we going, or what?' Ben ran up, barely out of breath despite having been playing for a good two hours.

'Yes, come on.' She rolled her eyes, laughing. 'I better get this one home before he starves to death, plus I've left someone in charge of the shop when I've only just taken over. I don't want to get a reputation as a slacker.'

'And I've got stuff to do, too. Good game today, Ben. Look forward to seeing you next week?'

He looked at Hannah as he said it. Afterwards, making cheese on toast for lunch, she replayed it in her head. He obviously meant Ben, not her. But she couldn't help daydreaming about what it would be like to have a handsome, charming, kind man paying her that sort of attention. God, she really needed to get a grip. And phone Phil, her perfectly pleasant – if not exactly demonstrative – husband. He was probably pining away back in Manchester, missing them terribly.

Chapter Fourteen

On the day Beth had handed over the keys and full responsibility to Hannah, only the briefest flicker of guilt had crossed her face as she mentioned the village AGM that was imminent.

'It's nothing major – just a chance for the villagers to get together and iron out any problems, check we're all singing from the same song sheet, that sort of thing . . .'

'I don't even know what song we're singing!'

'Oh, you'll pick it up. It's easy enough. Helen's in charge – that won't come as a surprise – and all you have to do is turn up to the village hall for seven on the Thursday after next, say a few words and it'll be fine.' Beth had had the good grace to look a tiny bit shamefaced at that, but only briefly.

And so it had come to the day of the meeting. Hannah left Ben installed in the little sitting room on Beth's slightly lumpy sofa, Pinky the cat curled up on a striped crochet blanket by his side.

'I don't know how long I'll be, but I can't imagine it'll be much later than nine. You can ring me if you get stuck, but I'm sure you'll be okay.'

Ben looked up from his Xbox game, headset askew. He pushed one headphone off an ear and frowned.

'What?'

'I said –' Hannah began, then sighed and shook her head. 'Never mind.' She lifted the headphone back over his ear and pointed to the door. 'Going out. Back in two hours.' She lifted two fingers and waggled them in the air. Ben gave a vague grunt of acknowledgement.

The village hall stood at the side of the road, opposite a row of neat red-brick houses that reminded her a little bit of the ones back home in Salford. Where everything else in Little Maudley seemed almost too perfect and regimented, these were scruffier around the edges – the gardens weren't perfect, the cars outside a bit older and less pristine. She was just gazing at them when a small, slight woman with a mass of light brown curls and a pair of glasses perched on the end of her nose emerged through a bright yellow door.

'Hello,' she said, giving a smile so welcoming that Hannah felt for a moment she might burst into tears of gratitude. 'Are you going to the village meeting?'

'I am.'

'Me too. Let's go in together – it's always less scary when you go in with someone else.'

She smiled again and they crossed the road, Hannah following a second behind her.

'I'm Nicola.'

'Hannah.'

'Oh, of course! You're the person who's taken over the shop from Beth.'

The door opened just as Nicola was about to push it.

'Oh, this is a nice surprise – nice and early, you two.' Kirsten, one of the shop volunteers, gave an approving nod of her head. She was holding a clipboard and ticked off Nicola's name. 'You're not on here yet, Hannah, so I'll just add you to the bottom and then we can tick you off. I do like a nice list. Keeps everyone organized.'

Hannah caught Nicola's eye briefly. Nicola widened hers slightly, making Hannah giggle.

'Right, that's you two officially in attendance. Why don't you go and get a nice cup of tea and sit down? We'll be starting business at seven prompt.'

'It's very serious stuff,' Nicola said, her grey eyes dancing with amusement. They joined the tea queue behind an elderly man who was trying to juggle his tea, a plate with an iced bun, and a walking stick. 'Let me help you with that.'

'Thanks very much, my dear.' He handed Nicola the iced bun and his teacup, and she saw him to his seat.

'Lovely to see you here,' said Helen. She was standing behind the counter of the village hall kitchen, flowery Cath Kidston apron tied neatly over her crisp white blouse, wielding a huge stainless steel teapot. 'Tea?'

'Yes, please. And I think one for Nicola?'

It was surprising how many people had turned up for the meeting. There were about ten rows of chairs, all serried neatly, and almost all of them were full. The room was filled with the sort of excited chatter Hannah was used to hearing at the start of a school performance,

132

when everyone was catching up with one another and hearing all the latest playground gossip. She sat beside Nicola, who was checking her phone, and listened in surreptitiously.

'The thing is, we can't expect the Neighbourhood Watch scheme to just run itself . . .'

'I don't know what he was thinking, leaving her for that woman. Imagine doing it in the middle of harvest, as well. She's had to pay contractors to come in and do everything.'

And then (quietly, but not so quietly that she couldn't hear) someone behind whispered, *'Just remember, she's Beth's cousin, so she's probably . . .'* The rest was indistinct. Nicola clearly heard that bit and looked up from her phone, giving Hannah a reassuring look.

'Don't worry about it. People can be a bit – well, it's a small village. They don't have much to do but talk things over until they've created a whole mythology about stuff.'

Hannah felt her stomach clench uncomfortably. It wasn't the first time she'd heard mutterings about Beth, but when she'd tried to ask the women who worked alongside her in the shop, everyone had clammed up. It was awkward, and she'd felt like she used to in primary school the year when one of the popular girls had decided she was *persona non grata* because she had the wrong kind of shoes.

'Honestly, don't worry. They'll find something else to dissect soon enough.'

Helen Bromsgrove, pinny removed and no doubt hung

up neatly, made her way to the front of the village hall. A row of trestle tables had been set up as a barrier between the committee and the rest of the village, and Hannah watched as they all settled into their seats, sipping water and shuffling papers.

'Lovely to see such a good turnout for this committee meeting, everyone. I'm sure it's not just Margaret's cake that's done it . . .' She looked down the row of committee members to a woman in her late sixties and smiled. The woman gave a little smirk of recognition and shook her head so her highlighted ash blonde hair shifted slightly, before settling back into its neat bob. '. . . But it must have been a significant lure. Don't forget, you can place your orders with Margaret for cakes for all occasions – there's a mention of her new business venture on the back page of the village newsletter, which we'll be handing out at the end of play this evening.'

Hannah stifled a yawn. She had a suspicion this was going to be a very long evening and she was absolutely shattered. Two weeks in, she'd been relieved to discover that she wasn't expected to get up every morning and deal with the early shift – that was shared between the volunteers – but even so, standing on her feet all day was proving to be exhausting.

'We'll go through the agenda first – village business to start, and then we'll get on to the community shop and our latest plans.' At that, a few people glanced Hannah's way and she fiddled with the silver bracelet she always wore, twisting it round on her wrist. God, she could murder Beth for dropping this on her. She'd hated anything like this since school, and she'd never really had experience of it in a work context. It felt like the entire room was staring at her. Her hands were clammy and she could feel her face flushing.

Luckily, there was a distraction: a woman entered the hall, dark hair tied back in an untidy bun, wearing a t-shirt with a stained Iron Maiden logo on the front and a pair of cut-off jeans. She tripped on the step as she came in and fell through the door, grabbing the handle, which slammed hard against the wall. The noise reverberated through the hall.

'Mel!' hissed a laughing voice from behind her.

'Sorry.' The woman looked up and burst into fits of giggles like a teenager. 'Sorry, everyone.'

'It's always you, isn't it?' Helen, from her position at the front, was mock-reproving, but Hannah was relieved to see that she clearly had a sense of humour. Meanwhile, a dark-haired woman – Hannah recognized her as Lucy, who she'd met in the shop over the summer – followed Mel in, holding hands with a man with untidy dark hair. They were both clearly trying not to laugh as they filed into the row of seats behind Hannah. Nicola turned round, smiling, to mouth hello.

'Now that we're all here,' Helen said archly, 'let's get on.'

A half-hour-long waffle about paint markings outside the village hall, flower planting ideas for next year's Britain in Bloom, and a Memories of Little Maudley celebration went over Hannah's head as she sat there feeling increasingly queasy. Nicola shot her a sideways look at one point.

'You okay?'

'Just not very good at this sort of thing.'

'It'll be fine.'

'And now, we'll have a quick comfort break – don't forget your donations for the village improvement society – and then get on to the next part of the meeting.'

Helen gave a quick clap of her hands. There was a huge screech of chair legs on wooden floors as people who'd been forced to keep quiet for an unnatural period of time surged into life.

'Hi,' said the dark-haired girl, tapping Hannah on the shoulder. 'It's Hannah, right? Nice to see you again. We've been away on holiday, we're just back – this is Sam.'

Sam leaned forward to shake hands at an awkward angle. 'Hi.'

'And I'm Mel.' The girl with the untidy bun gave a wave. 'But we've met already.'

Hannah tried to look as if she remembered. The last fortnight had been such a whirlwind of faces and new things and people. 'You're the dog trainer, right?' God, please let her have got that right.

'Got it in one.' Mel beamed. 'You ready for your big scene?' She waved an arm towards the front of the village hall, where Helen was standing talking to someone, hands on hips, looking disapproving.

'Less so when I see Helen looking like that.'

'Her bark's worse than her bite. Anyway, I'm looking forward to hearing about this bookshop idea.'

Hannah swallowed. It had felt relatively safe and comfortable, discussing the bookshop in Helen's sitting room over a glass of wine. Explaining her plans in front of an entire roomful of people, all of whom had a stake in the business, felt more than a little alarming.

There was enough time for her to nip to the loo – checking her phone as she dried her hands – and then when she got back, Helen was beckoning her to the front of the room. Her throat felt tight as she approached, and her tongue as if it was made of sandpaper and twice its usual size.

'I'll just shove along,' said a kind-faced man with a very red nose. He shuffled his chair along the trestle table, making space for her in the middle beside Helen. What felt like the entire village looked back at her expectantly.

'So this next part of the meeting is our Community Store AGM. And as you know, with Beth having left us, we're in the rather *unusual* –' Helen paused, and the red-nosed man looked at Hannah and then squeezed her arm, taking her by surprise – 'situation of her having taken a unilateral decision to install Hannah as her replacement manager.'

The knot in Hannah's stomach coiled up more tightly, filling her with a sense of growing unease. Unilateral what?

'Anyway,' Helen said, giving Hannah a look which she decided was supposed to be comforting, 'the good news is that everyone seems to be on board with it, even if it is rather unorthodox, so the first thing we have to do is take a vote of approval. All in favour, raise your hand.'

For a horrible moment, Hannah wondered what would happen if there was mass dissent and everyone in the village rejected her as community shop manager.

'Nobody else is going to do it, are they?' said a wag from somewhere in the third row, making everyone laugh. A sea of hands went up.

'Well, hopefully that'll make you feel a little bit more at home,' Helen said, scribbling something down on her expensive-looking leather notepad. 'Accounts and things we'll leave for the secondary meeting,' she continued.

'That's because everyone falls asleep if she tries to do them here,' said the nice man under his breath, chuckling quietly. Helen shot him a look, and he abruptly stopped laughing and adopted a serious expression.

'So I think we'll start by getting Hannah to do a little introduction,' Helen concluded.

For a fleeting moment Hannah wondered what would happen if she leapt out of her chair, shot across the room and hurtled out of the door. Then she thought of Ben, sitting at home on the Xbox, having been uprooted from his life in Manchester. If he could be brave, so could she. She cleared her throat and folded her hands together, trying to look more confident than she felt.

'Um, hello.'

Silence. A sea of expectant faces looked back at her.

'So yes, I, um, I'm Beth's cousin. And I have to admit,

I didn't realize that she'd taken me on without consulting the committee—'

'Just as bloody well, or she'd still be here,' said the heckler, making everyone laugh again.

Hannah felt herself going pink again. Honestly, life would be so much easier if she didn't blush like a schoolgirl every time someone so much as breathed in her direction.

'Anyway, it's been a dream of mine to live in a village like this, and everyone's made me so welcome.'

That wasn't strictly true. In fact, a few of the sniffier villagers had been rather standoffish, and certainly not as warm and welcoming as she'd been led to believe was standard for village life. A couple of people in the audience looked slightly uncomfortable and shuffled their feet around, dropping their gaze. There was a vague murmur of approval. Hannah sighed with relief. Helen's shoulders dropped almost imperceptibly.

'And you've had rather a brilliant brainwave, haven't you?' God, Helen might be a bit bossy, but right then Hannah could have hugged her. She gave her a fleeting smile of thanks and took a deep breath.

'Well, it was just an idea.' Her voice was wobbly, but at that moment she caught Nicola's eye. Nicola gave her an encouraging smile and did a little thumbs up, which somehow gave her the boost she needed. She cleared her throat and started speaking, clearly this time.

'I found out that the village is trying to raise money for the kitchen here, and that the local bookshop had closed – and it's always been another dream of mine to run a bookshop. So when I discovered that there's a massive overspill from the telephone box library, it seemed like the perfect solution to make some space for second-hand books within the shop.'

'Excellent idea, isn't it?' Helen turned to one of the other committee members, nodding in approval.

'Are you planning to stock new books as well?' someone asked.

'I'm not sure yet. It's just in the early stages; and of course –' she was finding her feet now – 'it's a village bookshop, so I think that sort of thing is something we all need to agree on?'

'Sounds like you've got lots of ideas,' said Charles, the red nosed man she'd met when they first arrived. 'Nice to have some new blood in the village making a difference.'

'Any questions, anyone?' Helen spoke over the hum of discussion.

'Could we have a book club?' Nicola half turned to look at Lucy as she asked and Sam, Lucy's partner, leaned over and whispered something that made her giggle.

'I think that's a brilliant idea,' Helen said.

And then there was a flurry of questions about various other village-related things, and the rest of the meeting flew past in a whirlwind of suggestions and plans and ideas. Before she knew it, Hannah was standing by the door of the village hall and Helen was patting her on the shoulder.

'That wasn't as bad as you thought, was it?'

Hannah shook her head. Sam, Lucy and Mel headed off, waving goodbye. Nicola was helping to gather up teacups. A small but efficient army of middle-aged women began stacking chairs, and someone was sweeping the wooden floor with a huge, wide brush.

'I have to admit I had my heart in my mouth when you spoke up about the bookshop idea. One can never tell how things are going to land. But I think that was rather a success, don't you?' Helen squeezed her arm.

'I do.' Hannah felt suddenly overwhelmed with exhaustion.

'Well, we can get together and make plans over the coming week. I think perhaps I'll gather together a little working group, and we'll get things underway.'

It was, Hannah reflected, walking back down towards the cottage, rather a relief to have someone like Helen taking charge. Village life seemed to thrive on people like her. And with her support, despite whatever Beth had done – she pulled out her phone to text her cousin and then thought better of it, deciding she'd wait and call her in the morning – anything seemed possible.

Chapter Fifteen

The following week flew past. Hannah found that she didn't have time to miss Phil, who called to say that he'd been unexpectedly called up to Scotland to work at a conference. Ben was settling into school, taking advantage of the still-light evenings to go out and play football most days with his new friends. He came home exhausted and muddy, face pink with exertion, and collapsed on the sofa with vast bowls of cereal before hoovering up enormous helpings of dinner. They'd settled into a pattern over the three weeks, just the two of them. It wasn't that different to home, she reflected – Phil had been away so much with work of late that they'd been used to just getting on with things. Nicest of all, Hannah thought, as she sorted out the till at the end of the day, was the knowledge that Katie was on her way for a visit.

She arrived the next morning, dressed for her visit to the village – jeans and colourful Converse, a striped Joules t-shirt and her hair tied back in a ponytail with a navy blue bow. Being Katie, of course, she launched straight into a line of enquiry about the missing Phil.

'And you're fine with this?'

'Fine about what?'

'Well.' Katie waved her arm around airily. 'You're here

in bucolic splendour, and he's still up there ostensibly *sorting out the house*.' She raised an eyebrow, almost imperceptibly. The emphasis was faint, but definitely there.

'It's fine.' What did fine actually mean? Hannah turned away, busying herself with putting on shoes so they could go for a walk around the village.

'Seems a bit weird to me. Anyway, what's the latest on the bookshop idea? Is your sitting room going to be some sort of holding area for books?' Katie lifted up the lid of a box and took out a copy of *Bleak House*. 'God, that's grim. I loathe Dickens. Reminds me of being forced to read it at school.'

'Someone else must feel the same way – we've been given a complete set of his works, brand new. D'you reckon they'll sell?' Hannah asked.

'You're the bookish one. How do you feel about Dickens?'

Hannah picked up a copy of *A Christmas Carol*. 'Well, I quite like this,' she said, turning it over and looking at the cover art. 'I mean, it's very . . . All right, I'm not exactly a fan.'

'You need to think about what you want to sell in this little bookshop thing of yours. You can't have boring old classics taking up space on the shelves. You need stuff people are actually going to want to buy.'

'Oh God, don't you start. I've had a meeting over coffee this week with Helen and Nicola and a couple of others. Everyone's got an opinion on what we should be selling and how.'

'Nicola? She helps in the shop, doesn't she?'

'Yeah, she's lovely.'

Nicola had appeared in the shop the day after the AGM, keen to help with plans for the bookshop. She was married and worked part-time at a nursery school in Bletchingham, but seemed to be at a loose end.

'Is she going to be your new BFF? Do I have competition?'

'Shut up, you,' Hannah laughed.

'I'm only teasing. So what's the deal with her? Is she a local?'

'No, they've not been in the village long.'

'Ah,' Katie nodded. 'That's quite nice, then. You're newbies together.'

They headed out, leaving the shop in the capable hands of one of the volunteers. It was lovely to be able to take time off to spend with Katie – and even nicer that the village looked so gorgeous on a day like today. They walked along in silence for a while, just taking in the scenery. Two riders on sleek brown horses trotted past, nodding hello as the sound of the metal horseshoes rang out in the quiet of the village street. George was outside his cottage, pruning some roses, and waved hello. They walked up and Hannah pointed out Helen's huge, beautiful house, set back from the road with a neatly tended gravel drive.

'This is beautiful.'

'I know. You can see why I wanted to move, can't you?'

'Well yes, it's hardly suburban Manchester, is it?'

Katie cocked her head in the direction of a heavy wooden gate that stood open, revealing two extremely expensive cars. 'There's a *lot* of money here, isn't there? There must be people who could just put their hand in their pocket and pay for a brand new kitchen for the village hall.'

'Probably, yes.' Hannah had thought the same, several times. It never ceased to surprise her how much money people would spend in the village shop, nipping in and buying six bottles of wine and not even checking the cost. She and Phil hadn't ever got out of the habit of buying bog standard supermarket stuff, so watching people happily blowing fifteen pounds a bottle just for a weeknight was a revelation. Not that she was complaining – the village shop was doing wonderfully, with profits week on week already rising, which was a nice surprise.

'How far d'you want to go?' Katie was super-fit and routinely ran for miles. Hannah thought quickly, knowing that if she didn't come up with a route they'd end up walking a half marathon round the country lanes.

'Let's walk up here. You can have a look at Jake Lovatt's place from the top of the hill.'

'Ooh, d'you reckon we might bump into him?'

'I dunno.' Hannah tried to look unenthusiastic. The truth was she'd seen him in the shop yesterday afternoon and the second he'd walked in – dark hair ruffled from the wind, a thick navy jumper over a checked shirt – she'd been flustered. He'd stood chatting for ten minutes, asking about her plans for the bookshop, surprising her with his interest, until a group of schoolgirls had come in and she'd had to turn her attention to serving them.

They walked out of the village and up the hill, Katie striding along and Hannah trying not to sound puffed as they chatted.

'So what's the deal with Phil?'

'He says he'll be here next weekend. I'm flat out to be honest – I had no idea how tired I'd be. I haven't really had time to mind that he's not here.'

Katie shot her a sideways look.

'What?'

'Nothing.'

They carried on in silence for a bit, and then as the road twisted round and the hill dropped away, Hannah grabbed her friend's arm. 'There, look. That's his place.'

Nestled in a dip in the fields, Greenhowes looked like something from a period drama. There was a plume of smoke curling up from one of the chimneys, and the trees that encircled it were huge and imposing.

'My God, if I come back in another life I'm coming back as a premier league footballer.'

'I'm not,' Hannah snorted with laughter. 'Far too much effort.'

'You can be my wife, then,' said Katie, linking arms with her as they started to walk down the hill. 'Can we get any closer? I want to see what it's like inside.'

'Yeah, that's a brilliant plan. Why don't we just casually walk down his driveway and pretend we're lost.'

'You could tell him you wanted to borrow a cup of sugar. You're neighbours, after all.'

'Neighbours we might be, but I run a blooming shop. I've got all the sugar anyone might need.'

Katie raised an eyebrow. 'He might like some of your sweetness.'

'Oh my God.' Hannah shook her head, laughing. 'You are a complete disgrace.'

'Just saying.'

'Well, don't. I'm a happily married woman.'

'Are you?'

A few moments later, just as they were approaching the driveway for Greenhowes, a sleek black BMW purred to a halt at the top of the drive.

'Hello,' Katie said, peering in. Hannah could see Jake sitting at the wheel. A second later her stomach gave a slight lurch as she saw a pale, extremely slender, dark-haired woman with high cheekbones sitting in the passenger seat. Of course he had a girlfriend – he was handsome, charming, loaded . . . and she was married, so it didn't matter one bit.

'Hi,' Jake said, briefly catching Hannah's eye and lifting one eyebrow slightly. 'You looking for me?'

'Out for a walk,' she said simply. Why on earth was she feeling faintly sick and a bit stupid?

'Oh, that's a pity,' he said. 'I'll see you tomorrow for training, maybe?' He gave a brief wave and, winding up the window, pulled away.

'Okay,' Katie said, turning to face Hannah with her

hands on her hips. 'You're going to have to explain exactly what's going on. You can do it now, or over a bottle.'

'There's nothing going on.' Hannah chewed at her thumbnail. Who was the woman in the car? How hadn't she known he had a girlfriend? God, she was turning into Beth – expecting to know everything about everyone in Little Maudley. Was this what working in the village shop did to a person?

'Right, then,' said Katie, who clearly wasn't going to be deterred. 'Let's go home. It's six o'clock somewhere, in any case. We can have wine, gossip and watch trashy TV. It'll be like the old days.'

Back in the shop, Katie snaffled a bottle of red from the shelf. It wasn't one of the cheap ones, either, Hannah noticed.

'Come on, there have to be some advantages to living beside the shop,' she said, waving it merrily as she headed for the door.

'I need to pay for that,' Hannah tried to protest.

'I'll do it.' Katie shoved her through the little passageway that led to the cottage and disappeared, brandishing her bank card in the direction of the girl who was working behind the counter. 'In fact, can we make it two?'

Hannah collapsed on the sofa, removing the detritus of Ben's afternoon of gaming and sticking it on the coffee table. When Katie walked in, she picked up the tube of Pringles and shook it, hopefully.

'No chance of him leaving any food that isn't nailed down, is there?'

'Nope.' Hannah pulled off her shoes, throwing them across the room.

'You're quite enjoying this student life with no Phil around, aren't you?'

She couldn't quite imagine how it would feel to have Phil there all the time. All he'd managed so far was one night and a flying visit on his way to a client in Oxford, where he'd popped in, taken her out for lunch to the village pub and apologized for being so busy. He'd been perfectly charming, but oddly distant. Living miles away from someone who worked the hours he did was hard.

'You okay?' Katie touched her arm, nudging her out of her reverie.

'Sorry, yeah. I was just thinking it'll be weird, him being here.'

'Ben seems quite happy without him.' Katie had located a couple of glasses and unscrewed the bottle.

'He's fifteen. He lives half the time in FIFA-land and the other half on a real football field. I swear if I didn't cook him dinner and hand over his washing, he wouldn't even notice I exist.'

'You're doing yourself down.'

As if summoned, Ben appeared out of his bedroom, hair standing up on end, and Katie gave him an affectionate high five.

'How's village life?'

'Not bad.'

'Not missing your mates too much?'

'I'm on Xbox Live with them, so no.' Ben perched on the arm of the chair. He'd always had a lot of time for Katie, who'd been like an aunty to him. It helped that she was a pretty hot gamer ('for a girl', he'd tease her) and talked to him as if he was an adult rather than a child.

'Well, that's something. And I hear you're going to be taking the world of football by storm?'

His face became animated. 'Yeah, did you hear? Can you believe we've got Jake Lovatt as a coach? It's insane.'

'Totally insane.' Katie took a mouthful of wine. 'Mmm, that's nice. I'm glad I decided to stay overnight. So what's he like? Besides absolutely gorgeous, I mean . . .'

'Katie!'

'Oh come on, you can't tell me you haven't noticed.'

'He came in the shop the other day and was talking to Mum for ages,' Ben said, reaching across and lifting his own tub of crisps. 'Thought I finished these. Can I nick some more from the shop?'

'You may not.' Hannah gave him a stern look. 'There's leftover pasta in the fridge from last night.'

'Take this,' Katie said, handing him her bank card, 'and get a couple of tubes. And some of those nice cashew nuts in the posh bag.'

'You're such a soft touch,' Hannah chided her as Ben disappeared out of the room.

'He's a good lad. And I want crisps. You're telling me you don't?'

'Fair enough.' Hannah wrinkled her nose and laughed. She curled her feet up underneath herself and turned to look at Katie, who was checking her phone.

'Sorry, work stuff.'

'You're as bad as Phil.'

'Nobody's as bad as Phil.'

'That's not fair.'

'Okay, come on. If he works that hard, why aren't you two millionaires?'

Hannah chewed the inside of her cheek and thought. It was something that had nagged at her before. She'd been working her backside off in the time since she got to the shop, and already she'd changed round the shelving (triggering consternation and a mild scandal on the village Facebook group). She and Helen were drawing up plans for the little bookshop. Meanwhile, the state of her and Phil's finances remained fair to moderate, at best. They definitely weren't going to be taking an anniversary trip to the Maldives any time soon.

'We're not really anniversary trip people,' she said, thinking out loud.

'What's that got to do with anything?'

'Just musing. Anyway, when you've been together as long as we have, you can't exactly expect it to be all hearts and flowers.'

'The occasional heart or flower might be nice, though?' Katie took one of the tubes of crisps from Ben as he reappeared, handed her the bank card and disappeared back into his room. A moment later his music blared out.

Rather than yelling, Hannah picked up her phone to message him to turn it down.

'More chance of him actually paying attention that way,' she explained.

'So when's the last time Phil bought you flowers?'

'Ugh, leave it, Katie. Can we talk about your online dating adventures instead? They're far more interesting.'

'No hearts or flowers there, either,' Katie said, smirking. 'But on the other hand, who needs hearts and flowers when you're in bed with a red-hot twenty-five-year-old?'

'Twenty-five?' Hannah felt ancient all of a sudden.

'That's only eleven years younger than us.'

Hannah laughed, shaking her head as she stood up to go to the loo. When she was washing her hands, she looked at herself in the mirror. Thirty-five wasn't old – in fact, Nicola was the same age, and trying for her first baby. Maybe it was being the mother of a teenager that did it? She felt ancient and worn out and unattractive. And there was a wrinkly line in the middle of her forehead that seemed to be getting deeper by the day. She pulled her eyebrows up and tried to imagine how she'd look with Botox. Then she remembered the *love yourself* mantra and let her face drop back down again.

She still had nice eyes, and her hair was definitely a good point. But. She'd been standing in the shop, covered in dust from clearing out the bookshop space the other day when Jake had walked in. Ben, who'd been helping her, had been shaken out of his habitual cool and was genuinely excited and happy to see him, chatting away about the team's plans for the new season. Hannah had tried to wipe a cobweb off her nose and, unbeknownst to her, had smeared a dirty smudge across her face that she hadn't noticed until afterwards.

Not – of course – that she'd been looking, because she was happily married to Phil. Well, married. *Were* they happy? She pulled her phone out of her pocket and went to send him a message on WhatsApp.

Online, his status said.

Hi darling, she typed, *can't wait to see you and show you what's been happening here at the shop.*

She waited a moment. He was still online, but he hadn't seen her message. She waited, wiping the bathroom sink absent-mindedly with a cloth. Still online, still hadn't seen her message.

That's weird, she thought, shoving her phone back in the pocket of her jeans. Phil had been loath to install WhatsApp, saying it was just another way of wasting time. He'd insisted he only had it because she wanted to have a family group chat. Hannah shook herself. She was being stupid. It was probably some sort of technical error.

Have you heard from Dad? she couldn't help asking Ben by message, when she returned to the sitting room and pulled out her phone.

Nope

Oh okay.

'Everything all right?' Katie looked at her quizzically. She'd filled up their glasses and passed Hannah's over.

'Yeah, fine. Just trying to get hold of Phil and ask him

about something. It said he was online but he didn't see my message. It's probably some WhatsApp glitch.'

Katie looked at her and raised an eyebrow. 'You want me to check in on him when I get back? I can do. And I can break some kneecaps if I need to.' She looked half-serious.

'It's fine,' Hannah said, taking a large mouthful of wine. It *was* fine, wasn't it?

Later that night, though, with Katie fast asleep in the single bed in the tiny spare room and Ben staying up too late playing online, she found herself lying in bed looking at her phone. There were two blue ticks beside the message she'd sent, meaning they'd been read. And yet there was no reply. Strangest of all, it said that Phil Blake had last seen the thread at ten thirty p.m. But something stopped her from picking up the phone and ringing him. Maybe she'd get Katie to stop by the house tomorrow on her way back and see what was going on. She fell asleep with a weird, nagging sense of unease.

The next morning she didn't have time to think about it – the morning shift was her responsibility and she was up and organizing papers and deliveries before the inevitable red wine hangover had time to hit. Katie, showered and ready to go, was standing in the shop eating a slice of toast. Ben was fast asleep, and would be for hours yet.

'Katie?' Hannah waited until her friend was almost out of the door before she spoke.

'Hannah?' Katie pulled a red lipstick out of her bag, flipped open a mirror and applied it perfectly.

'Would you mind popping by the house? I know it's weird, but I feel like something's going on.'

'Course.' She blew Hannah a kiss, careful not to dislodge her lipstick. 'I'll do a reconnaissance mission on my way back. Do a detour. You want photos?' She gave a half-joking smile.

'I just want to know what's going on.'

'It's probably nothing,' Katie said, squeezing her on the arm. 'You know what Phil's like, he's probably fallen asleep with his phone in his hand or something. Maybe he's been looking at—' Her eyes widened suggestively, and she snorted with laughter.

'Perhaps,' said Hannah, forcing out a laugh. But she felt weird all morning.

Later on, once the morning rush was over and just before Ben was heading off to training, she took a walk along the road to clear her head. For a second she hesitated – should she call him?

Might as well take the bull by the horns.

'Hello?'

'Oh, you are alive.' She could hear the edge in her tone.

'What?'

'I sent you a message last night. You saw it but didn't reply?'

'Oh, my phone was playing up.'

'I thought it was probably something like that.'

'You'll be pleased to hear I've been packing some stuff up.'

'Miracles will never cease.'

'Yeah, well, I thought maybe I'd better get some of the eight billion books you own off the shelves and into boxes. It's going to take forever.'

She hung up after a brief goodbye and turned back to look at the newly cleared-out window where the bookshop would be very soon – she'd managed to transform the shop in just a few weeks' time from a space that felt very much Beth's territory into her own. Soon, with Phil at home, she could stop feeling like she was living in limbo.

'Morning,' said George, walking by with his little border terrier.

'Lovely day,' she beamed, shoving her phone back into her pocket and turning back towards the shop. If Phil was coming next week, she wanted the place looking amazing. She decided that after seeing Jake with his girlfriend yesterday, the last thing she wanted to do was bump into him again. Instead, she'd spend some more time getting the alcove all sorted. Sam, the treehouse designer who was Lucy's partner, had promised to come in and put up some shelves – he'd popped by yesterday and taken some measurements. Soon they'd have a little village bookshop, and all the books that were waiting in boxes would have new homes to go to – and the funds for the village hall kitchen would be through the roof.

That was the theory, anyway. She felt a bit sick with nerves when she thought about it – what if nobody bought anything?

Chapter Sixteen

She'd reached the point where organizing the volunteer shop workers into their shifts was going to send her insane – Beth had definitely undersold that part, with her casual comment in passing that Hannah 'just' had to swap one Excel spreadsheet for another. In fact, when she went to set it up, she found a tranche of emails from people who *couldn't make this month because . . .* and who *would be more than happy to do a double shift the following month if they could just . . .*

Shutting the laptop rather harder than she meant to and making Lily, an elderly woman who was dusting the bookshelves, jump in surprise, she stood up and straightened her back with an alarming crack.

'Right. I'm going to get some fresh air, because I think I'm going to go mad if I have to stare at a screen for much longer.'

'Very good idea, my love.' Lily paused, feather duster in mid-air. 'You'll give yourself a headache, spending all that time looking at a computer.'

'One of the afternoon girls will be here in about quarter of an hour.' Hannah scrunched up her face, then gave a huge yawn. 'Will you manage?'

'I should think so,' Lily said. 'I used to run the department store in Bletchingham back in the day.'

'You did?'

'Oh, yes. Years back, before everyone hopped on the bus to Oxford or Milton Keynes to do their shopping. I was the manageress. We closed down in the early nineties, when the big shopping centres were at their peak. It's a shame, really – Bletchingham could do with somewhere like that where you could pick up bits and bobs without having to go to town. I miss Woolies, too. But anyway . . .' She tailed off, shaking her head. 'No point living in the past. So don't you worry about me, I'll be just fine.'

'Thanks, Lily.' Hannah grabbed her phone and bag and headed out of the door.

Outside, the sky was a pale, uncertain grey. It was still just warm enough to go out for a walk in just a cardigan and a top, and Hannah looped her bag across her body to keep it from sliding over her shoulder. Perhaps she'd take a wander up to the community gardens and sit for a moment in the sensory garden.

Little Maudley was just as pretty in early autumn as it had been at the height of summer. The Cotswold stone glowed against the grey sky, and the well-tended gardens were still overflowing with the last of the summer blooms. A row of sunflowers stood against the whitewashed wall of Bunty's thatched cottage opposite the telephone box library, their petals beginning to curl and brown. As she walked further up Church Lane, Hannah paused to admire a swathe of bright dahlias growing outside one of the little stone houses by the old school.

'Morning,' said Jim, the owner of the cottage, emerging

from the front door with a pair of secateurs in hand. 'Admiring my dahlias?'

'They're gorgeous.'

'They've done well this year. Now, how's it going up at the shop? You settling in?'

'I am, yes, thank you.'

'And your boy?'

She thought of Ben, who had disappeared out the door to catch the school bus that morning, grabbing a piece of toast as he shouldered his rucksack.

'Really well.'

'Glad to hear it.'

'I must get on,' she said, hoping it wasn't rude to disappear in the midst of a conversation. Or was it passing the time of day? She still hadn't quite figured out the mysterious rules of village interaction – all she knew was it was a far cry from the vague nod hello she'd have given her neighbours back in Salford.

The pretty circular community garden had been planted to commemorate the centenary of the First World War, and at the centre of it stood a huge iron sculpture of a soldier, a dog at his feet, with a verse by a local writer to remember the villagers who'd been lost in battle. Around it, in widening concentric beds, were an all-year-round selection of plants and shrubs and some wooden benches where people came to sit and enjoy the peace. One quarter of the circle was given over to the sensory garden, which was planted with a deliciously scented jumble of herbs and flowers as well as plants like stachys with soft, appealing leaves that felt nice. The residents from the care home at the top of the hill were often wheeled down here by their care workers, but today it was empty save for Bunty, the woman who lived in the white thatched cottage. She was sitting there with a thermos travel mug by her side, eyes closed, her expression peaceful. Hannah didn't want to interrupt so she tried to sidle past quietly, but her bag rattled against the huge seed heads of some exotic plant, making enough noise that Bunty's watchful pale blue eyes snapped open.

'Oh hello,' she said, sounding as crisp as ever. Hannah was a tiny bit afraid of Bunty. Every time she came into the shop she half-expected to get a telling off for not having done something or other, but of course she never did. Bunty had never been anything but perfectly charming, in her very old-fashioned manner.

'Afternoon. It's lovely out, isn't it?'

'Well, it'll do,' Bunty said, looking up at the sky. 'One has to take advantage of the decent weather at this age. You never know when you might pop off.'

'I—' Hannah opened and shut her mouth. She wasn't quite sure what she was supposed to say in response to that.

Bunty gave a hearty chuckle and shifted over on the bench, moving her thermos mug. 'I'm not going anywhere any time soon,' she said, her eyes sparkling with amusement at her own joke. 'How's village life treating you?'

'Good,' Hannah said, sitting down at the opposite end of the bench. The wood felt smooth to the touch, worn down over the years by countless bottoms sitting down on it. She ran a hand along it, feeling the grain, briefly imagining who might have made it and where they might be now.

'I remember when I moved from London to the village during the war, it felt like a huge change. Everyone wanted to know everything, and one felt rather like one had no secrets.'

'Exactly,' Hannah nodded. 'People come into the shop and ask me all about how I ended up here, and where my husband is, and what my son's been up to.'

'And how does that make you feel?' Bunty looked at her with a shrewd expression, and for some reason Hannah found herself opening up.

'It's weird. I think everyone expects moving to a village to be easy, but a lot of people here are working in London, or just not around. And when you work in the shop you're sort of part of the fixtures and fittings – I mean, people say hello and pass the time of day, but it's not . . .' she tailed off. 'Sorry, I sound pathetic.'

'Not at all,' Bunty said. 'I remember when I moved here the strangest thing was how quiet it was at night. I couldn't sleep because there wasn't a sound – especially during the blackout, of course, but even afterwards I used to lie in bed listening to owls hooting and the sound of the wind in the trees and think how funny it was that there weren't any cars going by, or sirens from the factories.'

'It is quiet, isn't it? I'm surprised by how easy Ben's

found it to adjust. I thought he'd struggle, but he seems to have settled into life here perfectly.'

'He's got his friends from school, though, hasn't he? And a ready-made social life with football. It's easier when they're tots and you can pop along to mother and baby groups and that sort of stuff. When they're teenagers, it can be quite lonely.'

Hannah sighed. 'It can, a bit. I've been thinking about what to do – I wondered about setting up a book group or something like that, so I might meet some people outside of work.'

'That sounds like a lovely idea.'

'Would you come?' Hannah looked at Bunty, who recoiled, chuckling.

'I would not.' She shook her head. 'I have never been one for organized fun – and I have a daughter-in-law who is completely obsessed by the idea of getting me out and about, doing the most awful things. She thinks she's being helpful.' Bunty made a face like a child, which made Hannah giggle.

'I won't save you a spot, then.'

'Please not,' Bunty said, easing herself up from the wooden bench. 'But I look forward to hearing how it's going. Perhaps you can pop round for a cup of tea one afternoon while the shop's in capable hands. I gather my young friend Freya is working there?'

'She is.' Freya, who was Sam's daughter, was one of the teenagers who was actually paid to work there a few hours a week – part of the village's decision to try and do something positive for its younger residents. She was a friendly, funny girl – Hannah loved the afternoons when she was in – and a definite candidate for the book group, as a voracious reader.

'I think you might be onto something rather fun,' said Bunty, as Hannah stood up and offered her arm. 'Now, shall we walk back to the village together?'

'I'd like that,' Hannah said.

Chapter Seventeen

She rose even earlier than usual on the day Phil was expected.

'Mum,' Ben groaned, as she pulled open his curtains. 'What the hell are you doing? It's half six.'

'I want this place looking nice for when Dad gets here.' She looked around his bedroom, which looked like a bomb had hit it. The contents of his school rucksack were spilling out all over the floor; his filthy football kit was tangled up with a muddy football and a pile of plastic training cones he'd taken back from the park the other day. The desk was covered in revision papers – that was something, at least – he did seem to be more involved with schoolwork now he was at Bletchingham School. Lucy, who taught history there, had even mentioned when she'd popped in the other day that he seemed to be settling well.

'It does look nice.'

'It looks like we've been living like students for a month. Now, if you clean the bathroom for me, I'll get the sitting room and the kitchen tidy.'

'I don't know why you're stressing.'

Hannah didn't either. But she dusted and tidied and polished the little cottage sitting room, straightening up the odd collection of ornaments Beth had left behind. Once Phil was really here to stay, the place might stop feeling like a temporary fixture and start feeling like home. And of course he was bringing more boxes full of things from home that she'd packed up and left behind, thinking they could wait. But – she headed into the kitchen, wiping the surfaces and shoving a pile of washing into a basket – it was the little things that made a place feel like home.

It was strange, moving to a village. In the middle of a city, you could be anonymous and it was to be expected. But here in Little Maudley, there was a lot of talk about the amazing community spirit of the village, but so far – if she was completely honest with herself – she'd felt a little bit disappointed. She picked up her phone and checked Beth's cheery last message.

Hope you're settling in well – Lauren is having an absolute ball here, and has got herself an apprenticeship working in one of the top Oxford salons. I'm up to my eyes in paint samples, redecorating Mum's place. How are things in sleepy Little M?

Great, Hannah had replied. *Settling in well, village people are so sweet.*

The truth was that she'd been there almost a month, and apart from work, she'd hardly done a thing besides go to the AGM. There was, at least, an invitation to dinner at Helen's tonight to look forward to, so she and Phil could have a giggle about that; they'd never really been dinner party people. She'd mentioned it to him earlier in a message, although come to think of it – she checked her phone – he still hadn't seen that. Considering it was his job to stay on the ball and keep in contact with people, he was the most uncommunicative person . . .

The one saving grace was Nicola. She'd offered to help get the bookshop ready, and turned up with a pot of white paint and two brushes later that morning. Hannah managed to juggle serving customers with painting, and when they stopped for a break Nicola pulled a series of sketches out of her bag.

'I've been thinking about the ideas you had, and I . . .' She hesitated. 'I did some sketches so we could get an idea of how we might arrange things. What d'you think?'

Hannah bent her head over the papers to look. They were beautiful – Nicola clearly had a real talent for art.

'We could sell these, you know.'

'Do you think?' Nicola looked embarrassed. 'They're just some pencil drawings.'

'Yes, and they're gorgeous. I love how you've made it look – it's exactly how I imagined.'

'I was thinking you could get Ben to do some artwork for the walls. You said he was good at graphics?'

'Graffiti, not graphics,' Hannah said, deadpan, making Nicola giggle. 'Well, both, really. He'd love that. Might make him feel like he's part of this, too.'

'That's what I was thinking. And if you look, I thought we could have a little shelf with picture books, because they're more accessible for the little kiddies when they come in.' Nicola's voice was wistful. 'I'd love to do a little storytime or something – do you think we could?'

'I think it'd be a brilliant idea. Someone was saying that the community centre in Bletchingham has closed down, so the toddler group that took place there has nowhere to meet.'

Nicola's face brightened. She pulled her hair loose from its ponytail and shook out her curls, then tied it up again.

'You don't mind me hovering about?'

'Not at all. It's lovely to have the company. And it's supposed to be a community bookshop, after all.'

'It's just I'm at a bit of a loose end these days. When I stopped working full time, the idea was supposed to be that I'd get pregnant, get the house sorted, and by Christmas we'd be cosied up here with a new baby.' She bit her lip and looked down, twisting her wedding ring, which hung loose on her finger. 'Only now it's October in a couple of days, and . . .'

'I'm sorry.' Hannah reached across and put a hand on her arm. Nicola was the same age as her – thirty-five. But while she had Ben lying upstairs on the sofa, resolutely ignoring her exhortations to get out and enjoy the autumn sunshine, Nicola was at the other end of the spectrum, desperately hoping she might become a parent.

'It's not the same at all, but I do remember when I . . .'

Nicola looked up. 'Go on?'

Hannah shook her head. 'No, it's insensitive, I'm sorry.' She swallowed.

'Please.' Nicola looked at her directly. 'Nobody talks about it at all. It's so bloody awkward. My family just keep making little digs, thinking they're being funny.

Chris has gone all weird about it and I feel like a sex pest. My friends are getting pregnant left, right and centre and it's awful and I feel like a bad person for being jealous and –' She gave a rueful laugh. 'I don't know why I'm telling you this.'

'I got pregnant when I was eighteen,' Hannah began. 'And I honestly didn't know what to do. Everyone assumed I'd – well, you know.' She pulled a face. 'But I had a feeling that it wasn't the right thing to do for me. So along came Ben. And all my plans went out the window.'

'You don't regret it?'

She shook her head vigorously. 'Not at all. But I've – well, all my life for the last sixteen years has been focused on Phil's career, my being a parent . . . there hasn't been much space for me. What I was going to say was that I did try and have another. It's not the same, I know. But it just never happened.'

'Oh, I'm sorry.' Nicola's voice was gentle.

'It's fine.' Funny how two little words could sum up those two years when she'd been so focused on having a little brother or sister for Ben, the monthly disappointments, building herself up and hoping against hope, only to have to deal with the reality that it was never going to happen. *Unexplained secondary infertility*, the consultant called it. Whatever it was, eventually she had just stopped hoping and accepted that for whatever reason, Ben was going to be an only child. 'The funny thing,' she said, after a long pause, 'was that Phil wasn't that worried.'

'Mmm.' Nicola sighed. 'Sometimes I feel like Chris just wants me to forget about it. I don't know, maybe I'm being unfair.'

'Hello, you two,' said Helen, clattering into the shop. 'Oh my goodness, what a wonderful job you've done of the painting. It's looking awfully good, isn't it?'

Nicola and Hannah exchanged a fleeting look and both turned, putting on their best game faces.

'It does, doesn't it? I'm looking forward to showing Phil what we've done.'

'Gosh, he's going to get a shock. He won't have seen the shelves all filled up – it was in the midst of being built when he was here last, wasn't it?'

Hannah nodded.

'Well, it's lovely that you're going to have some backup, Hannah. And we're looking forward to seeing both of you this evening.'

The day passed in a whirl. Nicola was back in the bookshop again, stocking the second-hand shelves with some expensive-looking hardbacks that had been delivered by a woman in a spotty midi dress who'd pulled up, leaving her engine running, and dashed inside.

'Can't stop, got to get to the divorce lawyer before lunch. But these cost a fortune and I'm bloody well donating them. If he's going to sleep with his secretary, I'm going to give away all his possessions. Might as well make some money for the village fund, don't you think?' And with a brittle laugh, she'd dumped a huge plastic box on the floor of the shop and stalked out.

'Who was that?'

'Alicia Rowlands. She lives in a massive house on the outskirts of the village. Four children, huge garden, loads of money, and – well, I always thought her husband seemed too good to be true. He was a charmer. Helped with the school PTA, on the village council, all that sort of thing.'

Hannah puffed out a breath of relief. 'Thank God I don't have that problem. I always thought I was doing quite well if I managed to get Phil to come to parents' evening.'

And then, half an hour later, Phil appeared. Nicola was on her way out the door as he walked in. She smiled a greeting, but he didn't acknowledge it.

'You have to say hello to people here, it's part of the whole village thing.' Why on earth had she started with a criticism? Hannah shook her head, dusted down her hands and came out from behind the shop counter. 'Hello, darling.'

'Hi.' Did he sound weird? Maybe he was just tired.

She reached up to put an arm around his neck, pulling him in for a kiss hello, but he didn't bend to meet her, and his face when she stood on tiptoe to kiss him was rigid. Stepping back, she could see a nerve jumping in his cheek.

'Are you okay?'

'Fine.' He took a step back, knocking against a display of cereal boxes that wobbled precariously for a moment, then settled. 'Where's Ben?'

She perked up a bit. She might be struggling, but the lads from football had picked Ben up and really taken him in as one of their own. He'd headed back out again after training earlier, ball under his arm, a huge bottle of orange squash in his rucksack, eating an apple. 'I'm off to the park. See you later.'

'He's out with the boys from his new team, down at the park. We could take a walk down in a bit?' She checked the clock. 'I'm expecting Fiona to come and do the last couple of hours, she'd be fine on her own.'

Phil shook his head. 'It's okay. Why don't we go up and make a coffee? We need to have a chat, anyway.'

'We do?'

She followed him through the archway and into the cottage. 'What about the boxes? D'you want to bring them in now?'

'They can wait,' he said, collapsing on the sofa. He ran a hand through his hair, leaving it sticking up untidily.

'I'll make the coffee, then,' she said, walking past the back of the sofa. She noticed that the slight thinning at the back of his head was turning into a definite bald patch. God, they were getting old. It was weird to think of Phil turning forty.

'Here you are.'

He took the coffee, set it down on the low table and sat up, hands on his knees, looking at her directly for a moment. Hannah wrapped her hands around her own mug, suddenly conscious of the late September chill.

'We need to talk, Han,' Phil began.

Almost before the words were out, she felt something inside her stomach dropping like a huge, leaden weight.

'Talk about what?'

'You must've worked out something was up. You've been here a month, and I've – well, the thing is . . .'

Her heart was thumping so hard in her chest that she looked down, half expecting to see it crashing around underneath her striped t-shirt and the embroidered shop apron she was still wearing. 'The thing is what?'

'You've been managing really well, haven't you? I mean, the shop and Ben and everything?'

Hannah was still holding onto the coffee mug, her arms rigid and her back straight. She lifted her chin slightly, as if bracing for an attack.

'I've been managing because that's what I do. But I've been holding on, waiting for you to come.'

'That's the thing,' Phil said, and he dropped his gaze and looked down at the carpet for a long moment. 'I don't want to come.'

'What?'

'I like living in Salford. I like being in the city. I like being able to go out for dinner and go to the theatre or to the cinema. I don't want to live in the middle of nowhere.'

'This isn't the middle of nowhere. Oxford isn't far, and there's a supermarket and shops in Bletchingham, and there's Milton Keynes and there's a lovely pub here – we had dinner the other week, you liked it. You said it was nice.'

'It was nice.' He looked up at her. 'But I don't want to live here.'

'You can't do this,' Hannah said, her voice raising an octave. 'You're moving in this weekend. Ben is expecting you. We've been invited for dinner tonight. You said this was what you wanted – you can't just change your mind and pull the rug out from under me now.'

'Hannah,' he said, and ran his hand through his hair again. 'I'm not coming.'

'You can't say that.'

'I am.'

'You're just going to – what? You're not going to rent the house out? You're going to carry on living there?'

'No, I'm going to rent it out as we planned, but I'm getting a flat.'

'A flat?'

She felt like an echo machine. Everything he said, she repeated back to him, her voice getting higher and higher. If she wasn't careful she was going to reach a point where only dogs could hear her. She giggled wildly at the thought.

'Are you okay?'

'Me? Oh yes, I'm fine. You've just turned up out of the blue and gaily informed me that you're not moving in, you're moving out. And I'm living in a cottage surrounded by –' she picked up a piece of Beth's hideous discarded porcelain – 'by *this*. And Ben has had so much change to cope with already, and what the *hell*, Phil?'

'Sorry.'

'That's it? That's what you've got to say?'

And then there was a buzz. He picked up his phone and looked at it for a split second, before pocketing it and looking at her. That, as she told Katie later, was when she realized.

'You don't pick up the phone when *I* message you.'

'I do.'

'You do not.' And the sinking stone feeling increased, so Hannah felt as if she was pinned to the sofa by some heavy weight and she couldn't have moved if her life had depended on it.

'Look, Han,' Phil said, raising his tone slightly in the way he did when he was trying to close a sales deal on the phone. 'I'm going to be straight with you. I think it's for the best.'

'No.' She stood up, which took a tremendous effort, and crashed the coffee down on the table with shaking hands. It slopped out and made a little lake, which turned into a river and started moving at speed towards the edge of the table. 'Hang on.'

'You don't need to get a bloody cloth,' he said, banging his hand on the arm of the chair in frustration.

'Yes I do. This isn't even my house.'

'It's Beth's, and she's said you can stay as long as you want.'

'She said *we* could.' Hannah disappeared into the kitchen, grabbed a J-cloth and returned, mopping up the spillage.

'Sit down.'

He looked at her then, and for a moment she was reminded of the person he'd been back when they first met.

'I don't want to.'

'I know. But we need to have this conversation.'

'Do we?'

'Yes. I don't want to lie to you.'

Bile rose in her throat and she covered her mouth with her hand. 'I think I'm going to throw up.'

'You always think that, and you never do.' He gave her another look. 'Right. The thing is, I've met someone. And I've been trying to work out how to tell you, so I've been avoiding the situation. But it's like ripping off a plaster.'

'It's nothing like ripping off a bloody plaster!' Hannah exploded.

'Shh, your village gossips will be having a field day with all this.'

'They will not,' Hannah said, defensively. 'In fact, it turns out that the only village gossip was my cousin Beth, and that's half the reason why I'm finding it so bloody hard to settle here, because everyone assumes I'm the same as her and as soon as they see me, they zip their mouths shut.'

'Really?'

She nodded. 'I'm not talking about this with you now, Phil. You've just told me you're having an affair. We're not having a friendly chat. In fact –' she raised her voice, completely forgetting about the people in the shop – 'you can go – *now.*'

'We need to talk practicalities.'

'Go. *Go!*'

He hovered for a moment, as if he wasn't quite sure she was serious. Then the phone buzzed once again in his pocket, and she gave him a look which made it more than clear that she wasn't joking. He said, 'I'll give you a shout,' quietly, and walked out of the tiny sitting room, leaving her sitting there in a stunned silence.

Being Phil, of course, he still unloaded the boxes from the back of the car and left them stacked neatly in the walkway between the shop and the cottage. When Hannah – having washed her face, swallowed very hard, and decided that she was going to do what she did best and be practical – came through, she found the shop tidied up, the door locked, and the cashing up done by one of the village volunteers. There was nothing obvious to suggest that someone had just dropped a very precise bomb on all of her hopes and plans.

Chapter Eighteen

'Oh gosh, Hannah, it's lovely to see you. Where's hubby? Just parking?'

Helen opened the door to her huge house with an equally huge beaming smile of welcome. Inside, it was every bit as beautiful as Hannah had imagined. An enormous bouquet of flowers spilled voluptuously from a glass vase on a dresser in the hall. The stairs – the banister a gleaming dark wood that only served to highlight the spotlessness of the white walls – curved upwards, lit from above by a huge skylight that filled the whole hall with buttery yellow late evening sunshine.

'He's not, no, he couldn't make it.'

Helen gave her a very brief look which Hannah ignored. 'Well, I'm glad you've come along, because it turns out we're one down in any case, so the numbers are balanced. I'll just have to shuffle the place settings around a little.' She gave Hannah a slightly mischievous smile. 'In fact, I might just give you something – or someone – rather nice to sit beside. You look like you could do with cheering up.'

And that was all it took. Hannah's chin started to wobble, and she put a hand to her face to try and cover up the fact that her lower lip was trembling, too.

'Sorry,' she whispered. 'Sorry. I'm so sorry.'

'Nothing to be sorry for, my sweet,' said Helen, putting an arm around her shoulder. 'Come on, come with me.'

Hannah followed her obediently up the stairs and into a beautiful blue-and-white bedroom. Helen put a hand on each of her shoulders and pressed her firmly but gently onto the end of a massive king-sized bed, where she sat on top of a blue-and-white-checked throw.

'Now then, sweetheart, you don't have to say a word. Let me get you a tissue.'

Tears were rolling silently down Hannah's cheeks. She tried to bat them away without smudging the make-up she'd applied to try and hide how dreadful she looked. 'I'm sorry,' she said again.

'I don't think it's you that has to apologize, is it?'

Hannah shook her head.

'The thing is, I didn't expect – I mean, I know it's not perfect, no marriage is, is it?'

Helen's face softened and she dabbed at Hannah's tears with a neatly folded handkerchief. 'No, that's absolutely spot on. What has he done to you?'

Hannah took a shuddering breath, and it all came out.

'I feel like it's my fault.'

'What on earth makes you think that, my love?'

'Well . . . I pushed for this move, and I didn't once think about what Phil might like.' She took a fresh handkerchief from Helen and blew her nose noisily. 'I mean, the thing is, I've always done stuff he wanted, and now I've done something for me, it's all gone wrong.'

Helen sat down beside her on the bed and put an arm around her shoulder. 'It's not a bad thing to want to do something for yourself, Hannah. I bet you've spent the whole of your marriage doing the right thing for other people.'

Hannah looked up at Helen, who gave her shoulder a little squeeze. 'I've tried to.'

'Exactly. You're a lovely girl, and it's glaringly obvious to everyone just how much you want to make this work. And you must've been missing him while he's been away. I'm sorry.'

Hannah gave a sort of half-laugh, half-sob. 'That's the thing, though.' She twisted the corner of the hanky, looking down at the floor. 'I haven't been missing him. Is that awful?'

'Not at all. I have to confess, you haven't really struck me as someone who's been pining away.'

Hannah looked up and pulled a face. 'I love him,' she said, realizing as she said it that maybe somehow along the way, the love she'd felt had shifted from romantic – she cringed inwardly, thinking of her fruitless attempt to seduce him – to something more, well, brotherly. 'I mean, he's Ben's dad, and we've been together since we were teenagers, and . . .' She tailed off.

'That doesn't mean you have to stay married for the rest of your life, though, does it?'

Hannah chewed her lip. 'I suppose not?'

Helen tucked a strand of hair behind Hannah's ear, maternally. 'It most certainly does not. And you've got

179

your whole life in front of you – you're only thirty-five? Thirty-six?'

'Thirty-five.'

'A baby!' Helen laughed. 'Most people aren't even married at that age. Not that I'm suggesting you start signing up for online dating or anything like that, just yet. I'm just – well, I don't want to see you thinking your life is over when it's all in front of you.'

Hannah leaned forward, peering into the mirror. 'God, I look absolutely awful.'

'Nothing a bit of make-up won't fix. And you look lovely, as always.'

'I'm not going to be able to fix my marriage though, am I? It's not that easy.'

'Probably not, my love.' Helen put an arm around her waist. 'I'm afraid not. But you're amongst friends here, and we'll look out for you.'

'You will?' Hannah raised still damp eyes to look at her.

Helen nodded. She didn't even seem to mind that Hannah had somehow smudged mascara on the arm of her pristine white and pink blouse. 'Yes, we will.'

'I've felt a bit like – well, like everyone here in the village has been judging me on Beth's behaviour. And I know she's my cousin, but I've managed to gather that she wasn't always exactly the best behaved.'

'Oh, Beth could be a minx. She likes gossip, and she can't resist stirring it. Too clever by half, if you ask me, and Lauren was just the same. If you get chatting to Mel and Sam – I saw you getting on at the committee meeting – they'll tell you that Lauren caused both of their girls no end of trouble when they were at school together.'

'I thought Sam was with Lucy?'

'Yes, they got married last year. But he and Mel have been friends since school, and their daughters grew up together. They're at sixth form college now – you know Freya, of course – and they'll be off to university soon. Funny how time flies.'

Hannah, thinking of Ben and having to tell him, gave another gulp. He'd never been particularly close to his dad, mainly because Phil had always spent so much time away – but that didn't mean he was ready to hear that he was now part of a broken family. She cringed again at the thought of those words – they sounded so dramatic and old-fashioned. What on earth was she thinking? Loads of people managed as single parents. She needed to pull herself together and stop sounding like a marriage guidance leaflet from the dark ages.

'You're a lovely mum,' Helen said, pre-empting her. 'Now before you go downstairs, let's fix your make-up and get you a hefty gin and tonic. Where's your boy tonight?'

'Staying over with one of his new friends for a gaming party.'

'Excellent. Well, I'll make a couple of calls, sort out the shop arrangements for the morning, and we can get you well and truly sozzled on gin.'

'I can't—' she began.

'You jolly well will.' Helen was firm. 'Now there's every kind of make-up under the sun in the en suite, and some nice Clarins cleansing balm and some cotton-wool balls. I suggest you get in there *tout suite* and get yourself tidied up, and I'm going to make you an enormous drink.'

Helen hadn't been joking about the make-up – which was a surprise, given that her handsome, square-jawed, slightly horsey face was only ever adorned with a slick of tinted moisturizer and a pale pink lipstick. Hannah wiped away the smeared, tear-stained mess and looked at herself in the mirror. Her eyes were red-rimmed and shadowed from crying. She took a glass of water and drank it down, then splashed her face after letting the tap run for ages until the water was icy. It made her gasp, and brought some colour back into her cheeks.

'Well that's better,' Helen said kindly, reappearing with a glass of gin that clinked promisingly. 'Now I'm going to insist that you drink this, and then we're going downstairs and we'll have no mention of errant husbands or anything else.'

Hannah nodded obediently. The gin was definitely helping something – even if it was only psychological.

Downstairs, in a spacious and beautifully furnished room, Hannah was surprised to find not just David, Helen's husband, but a handful of faces she recognized from the shop and – her stomach gave a lurch – Jake. On seeing her, he stood up from his chair and headed over to say hello.

'Nice to see you,' he said, adding under his breath, 'It's a relief, actually. We Northerners have to stick together.' He was dressed in dark blue chinos and a soft, pale blue shirt, and gave her a conspiratorial smile. 'It's a long way from Manchester, isn't it?'

She nodded. 'But you'll be used to this sort of thing.' She looked around. The room was expensively decorated – of course – but tastefully neutral, with duck-egg blue cushions propped up on pale cream sofas. He inclined his head towards one.

'Shall we sit down?'

'Okay.' She managed a smile. 'So posh kitchen suppers aren't your thing either?'

He shook his head, waiting until she'd sat down at one end of the sofa before sitting at the other end, crossing one long leg over the other. 'No, this isn't really me. Football is more about nightclubs and fancy restaurants – or it was, anyway. Dinner parties with the country set hasn't really been my scene.'

She remembered photos she'd seen online – Jake seemed to have kept himself out of the limelight as much as possible, but there were still a fair number of photographs of him with a glamorous model or actress on his arm, making his way into or out of cabs in all the right places in London.

'I didn't really do dinners like this back home, either.'

David materialized by their side and handed them both a glass of champagne. 'Down the hatch,' he said, cheerfully. 'Plenty more where that came from.'

'I've had a whopping gin already,' Hannah said to Jake, taking a sip.

He smiled. 'If there's one thing I've learned about this lot – and not from experience, just from talking to Pippa, my PA – it's that there's not much else to do in the village in the evening, so they all drink like fish.'

'And you're a model of abstinence?'

'I used to be, when I was playing.' He took a drink. 'Not so much now. I mean, I don't want to be rolling up to train the boys with a massive hangover, but I don't have to be as disciplined as I was back then.'

'From what the papers say about footballers, you're all knocking back magnums of champagne in the changing room after a game. That's what Ben's hoping for, anyway.'

Jake looked at her for a moment, meeting her eyes with his blue-green ones. They were fringed with incredibly dark lashes. She swallowed, feeling suddenly awkward at his gaze on her.

'I know I've said it before, but he's got a good chance of making it.'

'Really?'

'Yes. He's good.'

'I think he is,' she agreed. 'But I can't really tell. He just – looks like he knows what he's doing. Does that sound weird?'

He shook his head as everyone stood up to follow David into the dining room. Without thinking, Hannah sat down on the chair next to Jake, then flushed, realizing that Helen had probably spent ages deciding who went where. Helen caught her eye for a brief moment and gave her the ghost of a wink.

'I was about to suggest that you two sit together. You'll have lots to talk about, with your son being in the football team?'

Hannah smiled at her, feeling relieved. She couldn't face making conversation with any of the others who were there – they all seemed nice enough, but she was tired and felt as if she'd been hollowed out. At least she knew Jake well enough to chat to him between courses, and it didn't help that he wasn't exactly unappealing to look at.

She sneaked a glance at him as Helen was putting down the starter. He was tanned – probably from some exotic trip abroad – and a sprinkling of dark hairs covered wrists that weren't adorned with an expensive watch or any of the bling she might have expected of a footballer. He had a five-day beard, which shadowed his cheeks and showed off a strong jawline, and that tangle of dark, unruly hair that flopped down over his forehead. She thought of Phil's emerging bald patch and wondered if she was being bitchy, then took another drink and decided that if ever there was a time when she could be, it was the day that he'd announced he was leaving her for – for who?

'You okay?' Jake turned to look at her. He was thoughtful, too. He turned her water glass the right way round and poured some for her, and then for himself. Meanwhile, conversation was flowing around the table.

'Very excited about this possible bookshop idea,' said one of the men, who clearly hadn't been into the shop in some time.

'It's more than a possibility now,' his wife said, rolling her eyes at Hannah. 'Jason doesn't get out much, do you, darling?'

'I do,' he protested, laughing. 'Just not in Little Maudley. I'm in the city most of the week.'

'We're lucky you've graced us with your presence,' teased Helen. 'Tuck in, everyone, there's plenty more if anyone wants seconds. I always make far too much gravadlax.'

The starter was delicious – salmon served with a lemony fresh sauce and scattered with feathery fronds of dill. Hannah ate it all, realizing she hadn't had a thing to eat all day.

'More, Hannah?' Helen was being particularly solicitous to her. She dropped a hand on her shoulder as she passed behind her chair.

'I'll save myself,' she said, turning to smile a thank you.

Helen's labrador appeared between her chair and Jake's, and he dropped pieces of salmon into its mouth when nobody was looking.

'Shh, don't get me into trouble,' he said, whispering. 'But I can't resist a starving lab.'

'Did you have dogs when you were growing up?'

He shook his head. 'Not much room for a dog in our house. You?'

'Nope.'

'I can't imagine your place looked much like this, either, did it?' He chuckled. 'Or is that being a bit prejudiced against people from the north?'

Hannah shook her head, giggling. 'No, I grew up in a red-brick terrace with a tiny back yard. No walled garden, no orangery, and our front lounge was probably half the size of Helen's bedroom.'

'Have you been exploring?' Jake looked intrigued.

'No, I popped up –' she paused for a moment as wine was passed round – 'when I got here, just to fix my make-up.' It wasn't strictly untrue.

As the evening went on and the wine flowed, she was surprised to find herself prodding cautiously at the wound that Phil had inflicted and finding it was – well, there wasn't so much a raw pain as a sort of dull ache. Maybe spending a month apart had made it easier. Sitting next to Jake definitely made it easier.

She excused herself from the table and made her way to the loo in the hallway. The light was incredibly flattering – she wiped a smudge of eyeliner away from under her lower lashes and reapplied some lipstick, looking at herself in the mirror with new eyes. So this was what it looked like to be a single parent? She wrinkled her nose and raised an eyebrow at her reflection. She ran a hand through her hair, fluffing it up, then headed back to the dining room.

By the time she returned, everyone was gathering drinks and heading back towards the sitting room.

'I brought your wine,' Jake said, standing up as she returned. He passed the glass to her, his fingers brushing hers for a split second. It made the hairs on the back of her arms stand up.

'Shall we?' He inclined his head towards the door, where everyone was making their way out.

'Come on, you two,' chided Helen. 'Far more comfortable sofas next door.'

A half smile tugged at the corners of Jake's mouth. 'Coming,' he said, giving Hannah a look.

By the time they made it into the sitting room, there was only one sofa left empty – a smallish one facing the window which looked out over the side garden of the house. Hannah hovered for a moment.

'Don't worry,' Jake said, laughing, 'I won't bite.'

She sat down, pressing her knees together and trying not to take up too much space.

'Ah, hello,' said a voice from behind them. She turned around. One of the men who'd been down at the bottom end of the table, holding court, was bearing down on them. She smiled politely, but he was clearly not remotely interested in talking to her. The next half hour was taken up with his opinions on football and the state of the Premier League. Hannah, trapped by his manspreading with his legs akimbo on the edge of the sofa, sat nursing her almost-empty glass for what felt like ages.

Eventually, though, he left.

'Do you get that a lot?' She widened her eyes in mock horror as Jake shook his head, laughing quietly.

'All the bloody time. As if I have any say over which matches are shown on the television, or who signs whom.'

'You never fancied going on TV?'

'Absolutely not. Just because I played the game doesn't mean I want to become some sort of pundit.'

'You could be on there every Saturday, with Gary Lineker and all that lot.'

Jake shook his head. 'No chance.'

'So what else do you do besides the football coaching?' Helen appeared, bringing a bottle and topping up their glasses. She gave Hannah a knowing look and disappeared.

'At the moment, not much. I've got some – well – I've got some stuff going on. Family stuff.' He rubbed his jaw and frowned. 'But I've been thinking about what I'm going to do next.'

'It must be hard, changing careers and not knowing what's ahead for the rest of your life.'

He shook his head. 'Not really. Hard is working two jobs like my aunt did when she was bringing me up.'

She ducked her head, smiling. 'All right, fair enough.'

'Oh,' he looked concerned. 'I didn't mean that the way it came out – I don't mean to sound so bloody self-righteous. Just . . . there's so much crap around footballing and footballers and sometimes I think we're all treated like special snowflakes when the truth is, it's just a game, and we're lucky enough to get to do it as a job. D'you know what I mean?'

'I do.' He really wasn't anything like she'd expected. The more she got talking to him, the more she realized she liked him and his straightforward approach to life.

And he'd be an incredible influence on Ben, especially if he was going to try and make a career out of playing.

'Anyway, how about you? Moving down from Manchester to the village must be a shock to the system?'

You have no idea, thought Hannah. 'It is a bit,' she agreed.

'Ben seems to be settling in pretty well, though, doesn't he?'

'He's loving it.' She was relieved to get onto a safer subject. She sat back against the soft cushions of the sofa and stretched out her legs, feeling more at home now she was chatting about parental stuff.

'You must've been pretty young when you had Ben? You're loads younger than most of the other parents in the team.' Jake looked at her thoughtfully. He was resting his wine glass on his knee. She tried not to look at the length of his thighs.

'I was nineteen.' She always hated this conversation, because there always felt like there was a side helping of judgement that came along with it.

'Wow. And you did it all by yourself?'

'Um,' she said, feeling a small army of butterflies crashing around in her stomach. 'No, I'm – I was, I mean – I – well . . .'

'You're divorced?' He finished the sentence for her, lifting his glass and spinning it around by the stem. He looked at her steadily. She felt her stomach contract.

'Something like that. We've recently split up.'

'Ben seems to have coped pretty well. He comes across as a level-headed sort of kid.'

'God.' She shook her head, laughing. 'He wasn't so much when we were back in Manchester. He was in trouble with the police, got suspended from school, the whole lot.'

'Weird how sometimes a move can change everything, isn't it?'

'Really weird.' She gazed out of the window. In the darkness, she could spot the lights of the next village up on the hill beyond Little Maudley. This area was such a contrast to the noise and bustle she'd lived with in Manchester. 'We moved around quite a lot when he was younger, but he never seemed to settle anywhere until we got here.'

'Strange how things turn out. I never thought I'd be living in a posh village like this when I was growing up. Did you?'

'God, no way.' She shook her head. 'I still find it a bit . . .' She searched for the right word.

'Stuck up?' He raised an eyebrow and looked over towards Helen and the others, who were gathered round the coffee table looking at something on an iPad and chortling loudly.

'I dunno.' She wrinkled her nose in thought. 'They're all very nice, aren't they?'

'Oh God, yeah. Just – well, you can't imagine them living back home, can you?'

She liked the way he referred to Manchester as *home* for both of them.

*

Later on, once everyone had been offered coffee and most had turned it down in favour of one last drink, they gathered in the big open hall to say farewell.

'Had a good time?' Helen asked quietly, as Hannah was putting on her coat.

'Really lovely, thank you.'

'Excellent.' Helen squeezed her arm. 'That's what I like to hear.' She nodded in Jake's direction. He was standing to one side in the hall, tapping out a message on his phone. 'Of course, as distractions go, he's a pretty good one, you must admit.'

'Helen!' Hannah giggled. She'd definitely had more than enough wine. God, she was going to regret it in the morning.

'Just saying,' said Helen, with a catlike smile. 'I mean, it's hard to feel too despondent with someone as handsome as that giving you his undivided attention.'

'Hardly.' Hannah felt herself blushing.

'Oh my dear,' Helen said, dropping to a whisper. 'He most certainly was. I think you've got a fan.'

Hannah shook her head. 'I think you might need to get your eyes tested.'

'Mark my words,' Helen said, tapping the side of her nose. 'I have a good eye for that sort of thing.'

'Would you like a lift?' David had been sticking to soft drinks all night, and was jangling the keys for his Land Rover.

'No, it's fine, I can walk. It's not exactly far. The fresh air will do me good.'

'Bit chilly out there, though.'

'Oh, David, you're a sweetie.' Helen linked her hand through her husband's arm and looked at him fondly. 'Honestly, Hannah, it's no trouble at all. Unless perhaps Jake wants to offer you a lift? Oh gosh, no, he's been drinking as well.' Helen was looking mischievous.

Jake looked up. 'What was that?'

'Are you needing a lift home?' David jangled the keys again.

Jake shook his head. 'Don't worry, I've got someone picking me up.'

'He's probably got a chauffeur,' Helen said under her breath to Hannah.

'I can't imagine that.' Hannah shook her head. Jake seemed the last person to be ostentatious about his wealth.

She kissed Helen goodbye and waved to the other guests. She felt oddly shy about saying goodbye to Jake, despite having spent the whole evening chatting to him and sitting by his side.

'I must get off,' she said, awkwardly. 'I'll say hello to Ben for you.'

Why on earth had she said that? God, she had a knack of making herself look like a complete idiot. She pressed her lips together carefully in case any more inane comments fell out.

'Take care,' he said, looking up. 'See you soon?' He shoved his phone in the back pocket of his jeans.

'I will,' she nodded. 'And yes. Let me know if you need a hand with lifts for the boys for that away game next week.'

'Will do. That would be really helpful.'

She made her way out into Helen's garden. The sky was velvety dark and sprinkled with stars, and her heart felt a bit lighter for an evening spent in Jake's company.

And then she heard the crunch of tyres on fine gravel. The lights dazzled her for a moment, but then she realized she was looking at the expensive black car Jake had been driving the other day – and at the wheel was the dark-haired woman who'd been beside him.

Hannah sighed. Of course he was getting picked up by whoever she was – it was ridiculous of her to think he'd be single. She gave the woman a brief smile out of good manners and trudged back to the cottage.

Chapter Nineteen

Hannah woke with a clobbering headache (thanks to the combination of red wine, white wine, gin and champagne) and a strange sense that something awful had happened, but she couldn't quite remember what . . .

She sat bolt upright, letting out a very long, slow, careful exhalation of breath, and picked up her phone. He'd sent a message.

Just checking you're okay? Can we talk later?

Instinctively, she hit the call button, then a split second later cancelled it. He could wait. She needed to gather her thoughts.

Another text message popped up as she had the phone in her hand.

I've been invited to hang out here for the day and stay for tea – have said OK.

That's fine, she tapped out a reply to Ben. She had a stay of execution after all.

Once she'd tidied the kitchen and done the usual routine tasks, she collapsed on the sofa and called Katie. Pinky the cat hopped onto her knee, trod round in circles a few times, and then curled up, purring. She stroked him absent-mindedly. He was the loveliest thing about moving to the cottage. She'd always wanted a cat, and

Phil had always said no. Lose a husband, gain a cat, she thought to herself.

'Hello, gorgeous. What's up?'

'Phil's not coming.'

'I thought he was coming yesterday?'

There was a rush of noise and a clatter down the line, and Hannah heard Katie place an order for coffee. For a moment she felt a pang of longing to be back in Manchester where her old friends were, sitting having a cake and putting the world to rights over coffee while Katie blocked out her diary and pretended to be in an important meeting.

'No, he's not coming as in *he's not coming to Little Maudley*. At all. As in, we are over. It's done.'

'Hang on. What? Bloody hell. Are you okay? Do you want me to come down?'

She rubbed her nose thoughtfully. 'Of course I'd love you to come down – that goes without saying. But – I think I am?'

'Okay?'

'Yeah.' She closed her eyes and examined her feelings. 'Unless I'm in some sort of denial.'

'Maybe the fact that he's effing useless and you've basically been operating as a solo unit for years has something to do with it?'

There was a pause. Hannah waited, pretty sure Katie had more to say. She picked absent-mindedly at some fluff on the cushion, gathering it into a little ball and tossing it onto the carpet.

'Oh God,' Katie said eventually, and Hannah could

picture her face perfectly. 'I'm sorry. That was uncalled for and I'm a bitch and it's not exactly helpful, is it? Is there anything I can do?'

Typical Katie – straight in with an action plan.

'Nope. It's not uncalled for. That's the weird thing. I woke up this morning and felt really strange – I mean, that was partly the raging hangover, but I'll tell you about that later. Mainly, though, I realized that I didn't actually feel anything.'

'Shock, probably.'

'I don't know if it is. I think that I've been making excuses for him and trying to do the right thing and stay together for ages, and now I feel like someone's given me a leave pass.'

'Well that's – surprising. Radical. Good. Bit weird?'

'Probably all of the above.'

'What are you going to do today?'

'I'm going to see if Nicola wants to come and have a look at the community bookshop in Moreton-in-Marsh. I thought we might pick up some hints.'

'Er, right.'

'What is it?'

'Um,' Katie paused for a moment. 'Nothing.'

'Look,' Hannah said, guessing what she was thinking, 'Of course I'm not expecting to come out of this unscathed, but I think maybe on some level I was expecting it to happen eventually.'

'Yeah. I sort of hoped you'd be the one to leave him,' said Katie, darkly.

'It's not a competition!'

'Yeah, yeah.'

'Oh my God. If it helps, I'll divorce him instead of him divorcing me. Does that make you feel better?'

'Much.'

'Right, I better go and get dressed. I'm working on the assumption that Nicola probably isn't doing anything. She's had a rough time herself lately, and maybe if we go out today it'll take both our minds off things.'

'Okay. Keep me posted.'

'I will. Love you – speak to you later.' Hannah went to hang up, but realized that her friend was still talking.

'What did you say?'

'I said – just look after yourself. I know you think you've just bounced back from this, but you might find you do feel a bit shitty later on. And I'll be here if you do.'

Smiling to herself, Hannah hung up.

She got dressed and headed across the village green and up the high street. The weather was definitely turning now – the trees of Little Maudley were displaying beautiful shades of orange and red, and the gardens had all been neatly tidied up for the winter. Green foliage replaced the flowers in the pots that stood outside so many of the front doors. It was as if someone had gone along and waved a magic wand, transforming the village from summer mode to autumn. She turned left and walked along the narrow lane flanked with russet-coloured beech hedges that led to Nicola's house. Before she could raise her hand to ring the bell, Nicola's black cockapoo had leapt from her vantage point on the sitting room windowsill and reappeared at the front door window, yapping furiously.

'Hang on,' called a voice, 'Belle, will you please *be quiet*.'

'Just wondered if you were doing anything,' Hannah said as Nicola appeared, hair tied back from her face and a red-and-white-spotted Cath Kidston apron tied around her waist.

'Well, I was going to clean the kitchen for the eighteenth time this week,' Nicola said, untying her apron as she spoke. 'But if you've got a better offer, I'm absolutely up for it.'

'D'you want to come to Moreton-in-Marsh for the day with me?'

'Yes. Yes please. Definitely.'

'Excellent.'

They drove in Nicola's little MG, zooming down the country lanes and listening to Radio 1.

'It feels like playing truant,' Hannah said, laughing.

'So what should you be doing?'

'Nothing much,' Hannah said, thinking of the boxes Phil had dropped off that still had to be unpacked. In them were all her books – or all her favourites, at least. She felt a bit sick then, realizing that at some point they were going to have to divide up everything they owned. Things like that made it all feel very real. She decided to block it out and just forget about it for the day – it couldn't be that hard to do, surely?

Moreton-in-Marsh was a gorgeous little village crammed with the sort of shops you could spend hours in. They wandered around, looking at expensive kitchen equipment and gorgeous hand-painted fabrics and watching a busload of tourists unloading, cameras around their necks.

'Let's go for lunch before they all descend, shall we?'

They'd stopped outside a quaint little restaurant with gingham checked tablecloths and pretty, mismatched old-fashioned tables and chairs. Nicola pointed to the menu.

'This place looks gorgeous.'

'Go on, then. We can do the bookshop afterwards when we're stuffed full of cake.'

'Exactly.'

They sat waiting at the table. The cafe was already busy. A group of fifteen tourists had followed them in and were now busily trying to rearrange the tables and chairs so they could all sit together.

'Can I get you a menu?' The woman running things looked more than a little harassed. She passed them a menu and said she'd be right back to take their order.

'So what made you want to come and look at the community bookshop?' Nicola traced a finger down the menu. 'Ooh, Welsh rarebit and salad.'

'I'm going to have the brie and red onion panini.' Hannah was desperate for a glass of water or some orange juice. 'And probably about a gallon of fluids.' She took the menu from Nicola, who was checking her phone and scrolling through emails.

'Oh God,' Nicola said, looking up and nodding slowly in realization. 'Are you feeling delicate after last night?'

'Just a little.' Hannah cringed. 'I pretty much had a glass of everything on offer. Or more than one.'

'And what did your husband think of Helen and the other guests?'

'Um.' She looked down at the gingham tablecloth. 'Well, he didn't come, actually.'

'Oh no,' said Nicola, her sweet, open face a picture of concern. 'Is he okay? Nothing happened, did it?'

'He's fine,' Hannah began. The woman came back with a notepad and pen and took their orders. 'He's fine. We just . . . well, we sort of split up last night. Not so much of the sort of. I mean, we did.'

'Oh my God,' said Nicola, putting a hand over Hannah's. 'Are you okay?'

Hannah nodded. 'I think so.'

Nicola squeezed her hand tighter and Hannah realized that *her* eyes were brimming with tears.

'Oh God, are *you* okay?'

'I'm fine.' Nicola shook her head, dabbing her eyes with a paper napkin and laughing at herself. 'I'm just – I dunno, I swear it's all these different herbal remedies I'm taking to try and get pregnant. I think they've turned me into someone with permanent PMT. I can't stop weeping at those adverts on TV for homeless dogs and lions who just need five pounds a month.'

Hannah giggled. 'Sorry, I shouldn't laugh.'

'I know, but it is bonkers. Enough about me, though.

How are you feeling? Do you want to talk about it, or would you rather we changed the subject?' Nicola shifted in her chair to allow a tattooed, studenty-looking boy to set down their drinks and cutlery.

'Food won't be long,' said the youth as he turned away. He flicked a tea towel over his shoulder as he took orders from the table next to theirs. It was surprisingly crowded despite the time of year – but through working in the shop, Hannah was learning that the Cotswolds had a steady flow of tourists all year round.

'Those ear things are so weird,' Nicola said under her voice. 'Can you imagine what happens when he takes them out?'

'I didn't notice,' Hannah said, taking a sip of deliciously cool local cider.

'He's got those ring things, so his earlobes are all stretched in huge circles. They always make me imagine taking them out at night and having big dangly spaces.' She shuddered.

Hannah shook her head. 'I have a rule that I don't get stressed out about stuff like that because as soon as I do, it's more than likely Ben's going to end up with it. Or a tattoo of a spider on his face, or something.'

'Ben?' Nicola shook her head. 'He wouldn't do that.'

'He might,' Hannah said, crossing her fingers without thinking. 'I hope not, though. The good thing about him getting so serious about football is, right now it's taking up all the space in his brain that was previously being used for mischief. He isn't even getting into trouble at school.' She paused. 'Anyway – weirdly, I think I'm okay. I know it might sound strange, but I think I realized as soon as I woke up that maybe it's been coming for a while. You know when one of you needs to say something, but nobody does?'

Nicola nodded. 'Yes, I know exactly what you mean.'

'Well, that's where I think we were for a long time. I mean, you can quote me on that when I've drunk a bottle of red this evening and watched *The Notebook* and I'm weeping at the thought of being alone forever, obviously.'

'I will.' Nicola laughed again. 'Right, so let's talk about something else. Something practical. You need something to take your mind off everything, and so do I. I swear if I spend another day obsessing over where I am in my cycle, I'm going to go bananas.'

'Okay. So let's think about the bookshop. I've got a notebook in my bag . . .' Hannah reached down and pulled it out, along with a pen. 'Let's make some plans.'

'And we can size up the opposition after we've eaten.'

'Exactly.'

They ended up sitting chatting for an hour and a half – long after the huge tourist group had left and the owner had returned all the tables to their rightful places. Stuffed full of cake and delicious flat white coffees, they left a tip and headed down the main street to the bookshop.

They paused outside to admire the window display. Like theirs, it was a community shop, with the focus on second-hand books.

'But they've got gorgeous stationery and paintings and things as well, look.'

'We could sell stationery.'

'If we sell stationery, I'll end up bankrupting myself buying it all,' said Hannah, laughing. 'It's my only vice. Well, that and wine. And chocolate.'

'Crisps?'

'Mmm.' Hannah pushed open the door. 'Them too. Living beside the shop is a blessing and a curse.'

Inside, the little shop had been designed so that every single inch of space was used well. On the wall behind the counter was a sign announcing the monthly book group, and a children's story time every Thursday.

'Oh, I would love to do that,' sighed Nicola.

'You could. As we've said, I bet Flo would love it if you did it in the cafe. She doesn't open until eleven three days a week, so you could just do it in there and clear up afterwards. And I spoke to Bunty the other day about having a book group in the village. I think it would be amazing.'

'I do too.'

Hannah ran a hand along the spines of the classics shelf. They'd clearly decided that the villagers of Moreton-in-Marsh were likely to enjoy Dickens and Wilkie Collins – she still wasn't sure if Little Maudley's residents would. This bookshop had quite a bit more room, though, while the Village Green Bookshop (as she'd taken to calling it, in her head) would be a much more bijou affair, with shelf space at a premium.

'I used to be in a book group in Suffolk, where we

lived before. Well, I say book group, it was more like a wine group,' admitted Nicola.

'Yeah, I was in one when we lived in Scotland. It was much the same. It got to the point where nobody would read the book and we'd all just get together and gossip. But I'd really like the chance to sit down and talk about books.'

'Me too.'

Hannah looked up at the wall to scrutinize the neatly calligraphed sign informing shoppers about the Moreton Monthly Book Club.

'Share your love of books with like-minded readers,' Hannah read.

'Interested in joining us?' A man emerged from behind a shelf. He looked as much like a bookshop manager as you could possibly imagine: white hair, a battered tweed coat with leather patches at the arms and a woollen pullover atop a checked brown-and-white shirt.

'We meet once a month. It's lots of fun.'

'Actually, we're from Little Maudley,' Nicola said confidently. 'We're just getting some ideas for our bookshop – it hasn't been running long.'

'A book group is the perfect answer,' he said earnestly. 'Everyone has a book to read, and it gives them something to aim for. Then we sit down and have a good chat about what we liked or didn't, and discuss the literary content. It's very intellectually stimulating.'

Nicola sneaked a sideways glance at Hannah. He was charming and incredibly intense, but very sweet.

'It sounds very – challenging.'

'It is. Rigorous.'

Moments later, having left the shop, they turned to each other, laughing.

'Rigorous,' Hannah said, raising an eyebrow.

'Stimulating.'

'I'm not sure I'm looking for either of those,' confessed Hannah. 'I just thought it might be nice to have a chat about books with some people who aren't my teenage son, because right now all I seem to do is work or try and elicit more than monosyllables from him.'

They started walking back along the high street and paused beside an old-fashioned cart selling coffees, cakes, and ice creams.

'Shall we?' Hannah looked at the rainbow of flavours on offer.

'Yes. Definitely.'

They ordered, then headed back towards the car park, ice creams in hand.

'I read a lovely book once, called *The Guernsey Literary and Potato Peel Pie Society*. Have you read it?' Nicola chased a trickle of melting strawberry ice cream down the cone with her tongue. 'These are gorgeous, aren't they? Even if it's not exactly ice-cream weather.'

Hannah shook her head. 'I haven't, no. My friend Katie loved it. There's a film of it, isn't there?'

'Yes – haven't seen it but I don't think it's supposed to be as good as the book. Things never are. Anyway, they have a book group in it of sorts, but they don't read a specific text; they just gather once a month to talk about what they've been reading and why they love it. Or something like that. It's ages since I read it.'

'That sounds like a lovely idea,' Hannah mused. If they did that, there wouldn't be such pressure for everyone to get on board with reading the same book, which had always been the problem in the past when she'd been to these kind of evenings. 'Maybe we should do something like that.'

'I think maybe we should,' Hannah agreed. Hanging out with a collection of book lovers was her idea of heaven. It definitely gave her something more positive to think about than the prospect of telling Ben about the split, which was nagging away at the back of her mind. Somehow, she suspected he wouldn't actually be that surprised, but – well, she'd have to deal with it when she got back.

Chapter Twenty

Jake was happy to see that Sarah was finding her feet a bit more in recent weeks. She'd taken up his offer of a drive through to Oxford and had spent a whole day pottering around the shops, drinking coffee and – after feeling reticent at first – spending the money he'd given her. She'd arrived with nothing and he'd opened a bank account in her name, depositing a large amount of money and telling her it was the least he could do. She'd replaced the ill-fitting outfits he'd bought her from the shop in Bletchingham with some clothes of her own choice – still simple, plain and clearly designed to make her blend in rather than stand out. But she'd begun to flourish, and it was making him happy.

He'd offered her the chance to come and help out at football training, but something about that had seemed too exposing to her. Instead she seemed quite content walking the dogs in the fields and round the woods, relaxing and watching Netflix, and cooking vast three-course meals for them both to eat. He patted his stomach absently – it was definitely slightly less concave than it had been. Maybe that wasn't a bad thing, though. Sarah had filled out and looked much less haunted and hollow-cheeked.

He checked his watch. He was giving the lads an extra midweek training session because they had a big game coming up with Melissa Harrington's Ridgeway Grammar team. If he didn't get a move on, they'd all be down on the all-weather pitch before he got there.

'I'll see you later, okay?' he called to Sarah, who was making vegetable soup in the kitchen.

'See you,' she said, then carried on singing along to the radio.

He threw his water bottle onto the passenger seat and climbed into the car. Because they'd stopped training on the grass pitch – the full week of rain they'd recently had was the final straw – and were instead using the all-weather pitch at the school in Bletchingham, he was doing a run round the village to collect the boys who weren't able to make their own way into town.

His first stop was The Old Post Office. He hadn't seen Hannah since the night of Helen's dinner, but hadn't stopped wondering how she was getting on. She'd clearly had something on her mind that night.

He parked outside and decided to go into the shop, knowing perfectly well that if he'd waited, Ben would have been outside in moments. But he told himself that he needed to pick up some drinks for half time, and crossed his fingers hoping that when he walked in Hannah would be there.

His luck was in – she was standing just inside the doorway, hands on her hips, her face flushed and wreathed in smiles. She looked fresh-faced and very pretty.

'Oh, hello!' She smiled a welcome. 'Perfect timing. Look at our finished handiwork.'

She waved a hand in the direction of the little bookshop alcove. Above the archway, the words 'The Village Green Bookshop' had been spray-painted, surrounded by stacks of stylized books, a bright-red image of the telephone box library, the date, and a graffiti tag.

'Ben did it. What d'you think?'

'It's very cool.'

Ben, who was standing by the bookshelves, looked quietly pleased with himself.

'You ready?' Jake asked him.

'Yeah.'

'Go and wait in the car, then.' He tossed the keys over. 'I'll just be a sec. Got to get you lot some drinks.'

Ben looked at the keys to the Range Rover reverently.

'They're for opening it, not nicking it and going boy racing round the village lanes, I should add.'

Hannah snorted with amusement. 'He wouldn't dare. He's been in trouble at school this week already, so he's on a warning, aren't you, my angel?'

Ben rolled his eyes as he left. 'It wasn't my fault.'

'What's going on?' Jake asked her as he gathered bottles of sports drink and put them on the counter.

'Oh, God.' Hannah shook her head. 'I don't know. I honestly thought moving down here was going to be the end of all the nonsense, but he bunked off for the second part of the afternoon with a couple of boys from his class.

I don't know if I can deal with it all right now, along with everything else that's going on.'

He looked at her, head to one side slightly. 'Everything else?'

'Oh, just –' She paused for a moment, hand on the till. 'You know. Life stuff. Getting this place sorted. Sometimes doing it all on your own is exhausting.'

'I can imagine it's hard.' His heart went out to her. He'd love to invite her round for dinner, have a chance to chat to her with nobody else there – watch her just relax and unwind from all the stress.

'Anyway,' she said, brightening, 'We've got the shop sorted, and I'm sure it's just a blip.'

'Hopefully.' He put the groceries in a bag. 'D'you want me to have a word?'

'Would you?'

'Course.'

'He listens to you. The thing is, I can do so much, but sometimes being the only parent who's actually around . . . Well, I feel like it goes in one ear and out the other.'

'Yep, I get it.' Ben wasn't a bad lad, but he needed someone to give him a kick up the backside and remind him to stop messing about.

'I'd really appreciate it.' She looked directly at him for a moment, her hazel eyes meeting his.

He felt an irrational urge to reach across and cup her face in his hands, smooth the frown from her forehead and tell her she'd be okay. He shook his head slightly and stepped back.

'Leave it with me. I'll just point out to him that if he wants to get anywhere in football, he needs to keep his nose clean.'

'Thanks, Jake.'

'No problem.' He picked up the bag and turned to leave – then caught a glimpse of the poster on the wall by the door. 'What's this?'

'Oh.' Hannah looked uncomfortable. 'It's my brain-wave. Or maybe brain fart, I don't know. I suspect nobody'll turn up.'

'A book group? Of course they will.' He paused for a moment. 'Can I come along?' He waited for the inevitable expression of surprise.

'To a book group?'

'Believe it or not, I can read.'

She went slightly pink. 'Of course you can.'

'But you weren't expecting me to be a reader, right?'

'Umm,' she teased. 'Well, it's not really – well, there aren't that many footballers who are judging the Booker Prize in their spare time, are there?'

'I might be the first.'

'You might.'

'So is that a yes, then? Am I allowed to come along, or will I lower the tone?'

Hannah laughed. 'Of course. At least there'll be two of us there.'

'That might be quite nice,' he said, almost without

thinking. She caught his eye again and for a brief moment there was a strange, electric silence. He felt his heart banging in his chest. 'Anyway,' he said, 'I'd better get these lads off to training.'

'I will.'

He pulled the shop door closed behind him and closed his eyes for a moment before heading back to the car. He liked her, there was no getting away from it. He liked her a lot.

Chapter Twenty-one

Flo had left the cafe chairs down, with Hannah assuring her that everyone would tidy up afterwards so she wouldn't have to do anything the next morning. Hannah decided as a one-off to supply a few bottles of wine, in the hope that it might get the conversation flowing.

'But this isn't an actual book group, is it?'

Ben had pinched a handful of the crisps she'd shaken out into a bowl. She slapped his hand jokily and threw him an unopened bag. 'Not this time, no. This is a discussion about having a book group.'

'Adults are weird.' Ben popped open the bag. 'Oh look, there's Jake.'

He opened the glazed wooden door to the cafe and stood for a moment. It was still amusing to Hannah that the only time she saw Ben looking apprehensive was when he was around Jake, and yet Jake was the most laid-back, unpretentious person.

'Hey,' he said, giving Ben a high five.

'All right?' Ben stepped back, letting him into the little cafe.

'This looks very cosy.'

'It's Mum's book group.'

Jake looked around at the wine glasses and lifted an

eyebrow, the corner of his lips turning up in a teasing smile. 'Book, or wine?'

'Book *and* wine,' Hannah said, thinking once again how ridiculously gorgeous he was. And so totally unaffected with it. It must be nice to be so tall and lean casually against the side of a cafe table, long legs crossed, totally unaware of the effect you were having on people. She shook herself inwardly. For God's sake. It was like being fifteen again and having a crush on the hottest boy in school – the one who wouldn't even notice you if you landed on his head in a freak accident.

'Which book are you reading?'

'We're not.' She felt a bit awkward. Despite his initial interest, she hadn't wanted to pursue him and see if he wanted to join in, assuming he was far too busy doing glamorous footballer things to be interested. And now she felt like perhaps she should have, and that she'd been rude. God, being an adult was complicated sometimes.

'Uh, right. Okay. You're not even pretending to read and just going straight for the wine?' He fiddled with the button on his shirt cuff, rolling it up absent-mindedly. He left the other one down, which Hannah thought very endearing.

'We're discussing the concept of the book group and what it's going to be.'

'I've just been reading a brilliant book – it's a sort of thriller, but it's also sort of social commentary – set in Manchester. I grew up escaping into books when I was living with my aunty. She always had loads of them because she managed a charity shop in Wythenshawe and she used to take the ones she fancied home.'

'I didn't expect you to say that.'

'Not many people do. There's this preconceived idea that we footballers are uncultured louts, isn't there, Ben?'

'Uh?' Ben, who'd been looking at his phone, looked up and grunted a response. She'd broken the news of the split to Ben, who'd taken it surprisingly well. She was still half-expecting an aftershock of some sort, though, and being a solo parent meant feeling the strain of being the one who'd have to pick up the pieces . . .

Jake fixed Hannah with his blue-green eyes and gave her the tiniest ghost of a wink. 'I can't think where people get that idea, can you?'

'Not a clue.'

'Anyway, what time are you expecting everyone?'

'About eight.' Hannah looked up at the clock. 'Assuming they all turn up.'

'I'm sure they will.' He leaned forward and picked a long hair from the shoulder of her shirt. 'You probably don't need that, though.'

Hannah, who'd caught the faintest hint of his lemony, wood-scented aftershave, exhaled slowly. She must try not to act like a teenager with a massive crush. The reality, though, was it had been so bloody long since she'd had a crush that her only point of reference *was* being a teenager with a crush. It just happened that this one was on possibly the most unattainable man in the entire village, if not the county.

'I just need to get the chairs in a circle and move these tables and—' She stepped backwards, thinking to herself that if she could try and be at least a tiny bit cool it might help, and caught her shoe on the hem of her long floaty dress. It made her stumble slightly and knock against the table.

'Oh shit,' said Jake, reaching with lightning-fast reflexes to catch an already opened bottle of red as it spun on the edge of the base in the slowest slow motion, then fell. He didn't have enough free hands for the rest, though, and three bottles of dark, jammy red crashed onto the flagstone floor in a mess of broken green glass and liquid.

'Oh shit,' Hannah echoed.

'Language, mother,' Ben said mildly, then laughed.

'Grab a pack of kitchen roll from the shop,' Jake instructed him, 'and we'll get this sorted.'

'So much for having half an hour to brush my hair and put some make-up on and all that stuff,' Hannah groaned. She bent down to pick up some of the bigger pieces of glass. Jake, who'd done the same thing, gazed directly at her.

'It's fine. We can get this sorted in no time. You go and get ready, I'll clear it up.'

'I can't ask you to do that,' she said, still squatting in an ungainly manner, holding chunks of glass in both hands.

'You're not asking,' he said, taking them from her. 'I'm offering.'

'Seriously?'

'Yes.' He put the broken pieces of wine bottle on one of the cafe tables and stood up, holding out a hand to pull her up. 'And you might need to find something else to wear. That dress has wine all over the hem.'

Upstairs, heart hammering (she told herself it was the stress), she washed her face and hands, hastily applied some make-up and ran a brush through her hair. There wasn't anything clean to hand that she could put on besides a pair of jeans and a striped t-shirt. She looped a necklace Ben had bought her years ago over her neck, and headed back downstairs.

In the cafe, there was no sign of the devastation that she'd left. The floor was gleaming wet but clean, the tables pushed to one side, the chairs sitting neatly spaced in a circle. She counted them up and realized there were eleven.

Jake followed her gaze and gave her a mock-rueful look. 'I was hoping you might not notice.'

'For you?' She tried to keep the surprise out of her tone.

'Mmm.' He nodded. 'We've managed to avoid disaster, and there's nothing like saving the day that gets me in the mood for talking about books . . . or something like that.'

Ben, who had reappeared with six replacement bottles of wine, looked at Jake as if he were talking a foreign language.

'You don't fancy joining us, then?' Hannah asked him with a smile.

'Uh, no. If you don't mind I'm going upstairs to play FIFA.' A moment later, there was a thud as the connecting door to the cottage banged shut.

Jake took one of the bottles and unscrewed the lid. 'Well, it looks like it's just us two,' he said, pouring them both a glass of red. 'I reckon we're entitled to an early drink, seeing as we've just sorted this lot out.'

Hannah swallowed. The evening was getting stranger by the moment. 'It was more you than me. I didn't exactly do anything, did I?'

'You organized the whole book group. And you're doing a good job of running this place, from what I can see.'

'Thank you.' She took a sip of wine. For one fleeting moment, she allowed herself to imagine what it would be like if this was her life, and then a bang at the door announced the first of the book group members.

'Oh!' said Freya and her stepmum, Lucy, in unison as they walked in the door. Jake caught Hannah's eye for a moment and pulled a face only she could see. It must be so difficult to live in a world where everyone makes you feel conspicuous every time you walk into a room, she realized. Maybe he secretly craved normality and the sort of life people take for granted. She shook herself. Now was time for being hostess, not daydreaming about some fantasy existence.

'Right then,' she said, putting down her glass. 'Let's get this show on the road.'

Chapter Twenty-two

The room filled up quickly, with everyone milling around drinking free wine and catching up on village gossip. Jake was relieved that after the initial – and hastily corrected – looks of surprise on people's faces, everyone had clearly decided he was just another person who wanted to get out of the house and talk about books on a drizzly October evening.

'Did you hear the dog walker from Much Maudley lost all the dogs from her van and they all went rampaging through George's garden?'

'Oh my God. Of all the people in the world . . .'

'I know. It'll be all over the Facebook group tomorrow, no doubt.'

Jake suppressed a smile. The group remained a constant source of amusement to him. Living in Little Maudley had become more interesting since Hannah had moved into the shop, mind you. He'd found himself looking for excuses to pop in and pick up a daily newspaper, a loaf of sourdough, a box of eggs. Pippa, his PA, had pointed out acidly that if he carried on buying eggs at the rate he was, he would have to start selling meringues on the roadside. He'd told her to sod off and sent her for a weekend away with her girlfriend, with two dozen and a couple of the countless packs of expensive bacon he'd bought.

It was funny, though, that Hannah never seemed to pick up on his interest. He'd offered Ben lifts to football and chatted to him about how he felt about his parents splitting up ('Not exactly a massive surprise, to be honest – Dad was never there, and they never really seemed to like spending time together.')

'So what are you reading at the moment?' Freya, who was eighteen, perched on a cafe table and looked directly at him from under her neatly trimmed black fringe of hair. She looked a little bit like a pony, with her huge black-ringed eyes.

'I've just finished a thriller set in Manchester. The guy who wrote it used to work in a bookshop, and it was set in a part of the city I know, so it was like coming home. How about you?'

'I've been reading a YA novel called *Ink* by Alice Broadway. It's amazing. You should read it. It's all about this girl who . . .' and she was off. As he listened, he couldn't help but be aware of Hannah from the corner of his eye as she made her way round the room, quiet but friendly, looking out for everyone and making sure nobody was left out. She had a habit of tucking one long, wavy strand of hair behind her ear and then twirling it absent-mindedly around her finger. He wanted to reach out and catch her hand as she did it, and kiss the side of her—

'Do you want to read it?'

He shook himself mentally. Hannah was the mother of one of his team, and clearly not even slightly interested in him. She was funny and clever and interesting, and he was – well, basically a jock who'd left school at sixteen. Not just that, but who would want to deal with all the crap that followed him? Press intrusion, people taking photos of them when they were out . . . it was a lot for anyone to deal with.

Eventually they all sat down in their circle of chairs, and Hannah – clearly nervous, but with her friend Nicola giving her a smile of encouragement – made a little speech about the book club idea.

'We thought a lot about whether we wanted to make it one of those groups where you all have to buy a book, read it, and then sit down and talk about it with questions every month, but the truth is they can be a bit prescriptive.'

'Hear, hear,' said one of the women who was sitting with a notebook and pen in one hand and a very generous glass of white wine in the other.

'So we thought – why not do a themed book group?'

'Interesting,' said a woman with vibrant dark burgundy hair called Veronika. 'This is a good idea.'

'Thanks,' smiled Hannah. 'We thought we could do a theme every month – like loss, happiness, joy, that sort of thing?'

'Holidays,' said Veronika.

'Oh, that's a good one,' said Hannah. Nicola scribbled it down on her notepad.

'Loneliness.'

'Death,' said Freya.

'All right, Mrs Gothic Misery,' teased Lucy, elbowing her in the ribs.

'That way we can bring along a book we've chosen – or one we've read previously – and talk about how it made us feel in relation to the theme. Hopefully we'll all be opened up to stories we might not otherwise have read.'

'I love that,' said Nicola, dreamily. 'It's such a lovely idea.'

'It was your idea,' said Hannah, laughing.

'I know, but you know what I mean.'

'Now I thought maybe we could split into two groups of five –' Hannah caught Jake's eye and he gave her the ghost of a wink, teasing her – 'or six, and maybe introduce yourselves and explain why you're here. And next time we can swap round?'

There were a few self-conscious murmurs: nobody, it seemed, liked talking about themselves. As they gathered the chairs around, Jake decided he'd take the bull by the horns and be the one who went first.

'Okay, I'm going to get it over with. I'm Jake, I've been living in the village for eighteen months, and I wasn't going to come tonight but it just sort of happened. And I grew up reading pretty much anything, so I'm looking forward to the chance to experience some new authors. Oh, and I love reading because it's a chance to escape from my own life and into the world of someone else altogether.'

And then he stopped talking and there was a silence which seemed to last forever. He swallowed hard, and wished the ground would swallow him.

'I'm Lucy,' said Freya's stepmother. 'I'm a history teacher, and I have to read a lot for work, but I find that I'm not getting the opportunity to read for pleasure and I thought that perhaps if I came along I might actually read something other than research books and academic history journals. Oh, and I love most books, but I do like a nice romantic comedy.'

'I'm Freya. Lucy is married to my dad. I'm going to uni to study English Lit next year, hopefully, and I'm at college just now. I love reading – YA mostly, but I like a good thriller as well –' she gave Jake a warm look – 'and I just wanted the chance to get out of the house, because there's only so much YouTube you can watch and the village pub is full of try-hards.'

Jake snorted with laughter.

The others introduced themselves, but he'd stopped focusing again because he was watching Hannah, who had got up from her chair and was tidying up glasses and wiping spills from the side of wine bottles. Quietly, he got up from his chair and slipped out of the circle of conversation.

'You okay?'

She turned to look at him, still holding a blue-and-white-striped tea towel in her hand. 'Yes.' She looked at the others, all chatting animatedly. 'I think it's been a hit, don't you?'

'Definitely. You've done brilliantly.'

'It wasn't much, really. Just had to gather people and let them talk.' Her accent made him melt. And there she was, again, lifting a hand and tucking that curl behind her ear. He wanted to catch her wrist and turn it inside out and kiss it, then kiss her, then—

'Are you two hogging that wine?' Freya's shrill little voice broke into his thoughts and he turned away, rubbing at his chin and shaking his head. What the hell was wrong with him?

'Here, I'll bring everyone some,' he said, picking up a bottle of red and one of white and heading off to circulate.

'Thanks,' Hannah mouthed, as he turned back to look at her. His heart glowed. God, he had it bad.

He hovered after everyone had left, on the grounds that he wanted to talk to her about Ben and football. The truth was, he just didn't want to leave. He wanted her to invite him through to hers for a coffee, and to sit on the sofa and talk for hours and – well, if he was completely honest with himself, he wanted to do quite a lot more than sit on the sofa with her. He gritted his teeth as he stacked the tables and chairs back up in the cafe. Hannah was ringing up the bottles of wine she'd paid for on the shop till, in near-darkness. He headed through to the counter to find her.

'Thanks,' he said.

'No, thank you.' She played with the little seahorse necklace that hung low on her chest, just above the collar of her t-shirt. He looked away, realizing he probably looked as if he was gazing at her breasts, which – well, if he was honest about that, too, he would have been more than happy to do.

'I had a brilliant evening.'

'It was right good,' she said, in a jokey strong Manchester accent.

'The good thing is we get to do it again next month.'

'It's a date.' She looked up at him through long dark lashes, and he knew in that second that he was completely, totally and utterly screwed. He'd fallen for her, and he had absolutely no idea what to do about it.

Chapter Twenty-three

Jake woke in a good mood after the first book club meeting. Spending time with Hannah had been lovely, and he'd been surprised by how much he'd enjoyed getting out of the house and doing something. The truth was that he'd been spending way too much time alone since he gave up the game, and last night had just underlined it. Maybe he should actually get off his backside and ring back some of the friends who'd left messages over the last few months. They'd all been keen to keep up with him, and he'd let them fall by the wayside, feeling like he had nothing to offer.

He wolfed down a couple of slices of toast and peanut butter washed down with black coffee, then grabbed his keys. The boys were playing Ridgeway Grammar this morning and he felt an overwhelming need for them to hammer them, just to prove a point. Unfortunately they'd played like dogs in training on Wednesday.

It turned out to be one of those days. He got to the field and realized he'd forgotten their bibs, which meant he had to get one of the other parents to nip back to the house and collect them from the porch where he'd left them sitting in a bag. Then the goalkeeper called in sick with a twisted ankle, and he had to put their second – by a long way – choice in net. And there was no sign of Ben, or Hannah.

The lads started warming up, and he pushed them in the hope of making up for the other night's training debacle. Watching them side-skipping from one side of the pitch to the other, he checked his watch and glanced back over his shoulder. Where the hell was Ben? He was the linchpin of the team. Without him they'd have little to no chance – especially without the keeper – of beating the grammar school.

Five minutes before kickoff, he saw Ben jogging across the field.

'Come on,' he yelled.

'Sorry.' Ben lifted a hand in apology and pulled off his hoody, throwing it with his bottle of water by the side of the pitch.

'Where the hell were you?'

'Just didn't notice the time.' He gave a half shrug. This wasn't like Ben – he was normally on time, happy to help out before and after the game, keen to soak up as much of the atmosphere as he could. He looked dazed as well, as if he'd just rolled out of bed.

Jake fixed him with a glare. There wasn't time to deal with this before the match, but he'd be bollocking him for it afterwards.

'Right, lads—' he began, but was interrupted by a tap on the shoulder.

'What?'

'Hello, stranger.' Melissa Harrington, dressed in

expensive country casuals with her hair curling from underneath a tweed cap, was standing beside him, looking all set for a cosy chat. He gritted his teeth and tried to look less irritable than he felt.

'Hi.' He gave her a fleeting smile and then said, 'Do excuse me, I need to have a last-minute word with the team.'

'No problem,' she said, not taking the hint and continuing to stand there. Jake longed for Hannah to appear, with her calm nature and easy-going way of making everything seem all right, but there was no sign of her.

He beckoned the boys into a huddle and gave them some last-minute instructions. 'You can do this,' he finished. 'There's absolutely no reason why we can't smash it.'

'Except their defence look like rugby players,' said one of the lads, disconsolately.

'That is precisely the attitude we do not need. Now get out there and show them what you're all made of.'

By half time, they were two goals down. Jake glanced across the field in the hope he might see Hannah as he was giving them a pep talk, trying to lift their spirits up, but it was like pushing a rock up a hill and there was no sign of her. It was pretty clear their heads were down and trying to get them back on course was going to be tough work. Melissa was delighted that she'd *popped by* to see her boys completely crushing the opposition and at the final whistle, despite a late goal, the score was 3–1 to Ridgeway. Jake took a deep breath, straightened his shoulders and went to shake hands with the other team manager.

'Such a good little team you've got here,' Melissa said, smiling at him as if at a charity case.

'Thanks.' He wasn't going to rise to it. The Ridgeway boys were joking about, slapping each other on the back, clearly feeling that they'd proved their superiority. 'Your lads played brilliantly. You must be pleased with them.'

'Delighted.' Melissa put a hand on his arm and lowered her voice. 'Of course, if you wanted to, the offer still stands. I'm sure the village team could find another coach.'

'That's kind,' he said, hoping his face didn't betray him. 'But no, I'm more than happy coaching the lads. We've got some really good players – a couple of them have a good chance of being scouted.'

'Mmm,' Melissa said, nodding. 'We were just discussing that. That tall boy with the dark hair – number twelve. He'd be an asset to our team. I wonder if his parents would be interested in chatting about a scholarship.'

'I don't think so,' Jake said, more sharply than he intended to.

'Are you sure? I think most parents would be delighted with the prospect. We could take him all the way through to university – we've got an excellent sixth form, as you probably know.'

'Mmm,' he said, politely. He had no idea what their sixth form was like, nor did he have any intention of finding out. And the idea of Melissa smarming into the shop and trying to charm Ben away made him feel quite irrationally angry. It was typical of someone who'd grown up with that sort of privilege and it riled him. Ben could go far, and he realized in that moment that *he* wanted to be the one who guided him.

He stopped by the shop on the way back, telling himself it was because he needed something to cook later. Hannah was on her hands and knees, unpacking a box of books.

'Hi,' he said, making her jump.

'Oh!' She turned, falling over in the process, and without thinking he put out a hand to pull her up. She stood facing him for a moment, her hand still in his, and he felt an overwhelming urge to pull her into his arms and hold her close. This was getting ridiculous, and he was behaving like an idiot.

'You must be a good luck charm,' he said, picking up a copy of *Pride and Prejudice* from the shelf and turning it over to read the back.

'I am,' she said, teasing. 'I hear it didn't go so well?'

'That's an understatement.'

'Yeah, sorry about Ben being late – I don't imagine that helped him, somehow.'

He shook his head. 'It's fine. Not your fault.'

'I could have got him out of bed, but I got caught up down here. Helen brought a load of books – these are all brand new, can you believe it?'

'The bookshop's going to be making a fortune in no time.'

'That's the plan. I think they might be on course to rebuild the village hall kitchen sometime in 2022 at this rate.'

They both laughed.

'D'you think I should read this?' He waved the book in the air. 'I've got to find something to discuss at the book group next time.' They'd decided on a theme of sisterhood for the next meeting.

'Well, I'm biased,' Hannah said, leaning back against the bookcase and unconsciously reaching for a lock of hair to twirl round her finger. 'I love Jane Austen. She's really funny, which is something they don't mention at school when they're trying to get you to read stuff like that.'

'Yeah, I avoided more English classes than I went to when I was at school.'

'Sounds like someone I know.' Hannah looked over her shoulder at Ben, who had just appeared in the shop, showered, his dark hair still wet. He gave a nod of greeting.

'All right?'

'I gather you were up late last night?' He fixed him with a mock-disapproving look.

'Mum,' Ben said, shaking his head.

'Just saying,' Hannah laughed. 'If you want to be a professional player, you're going to have to start taking this stuff seriously.'

'She's right.' He wanted to find the right balance between keeping Ben grounded and trying to let him know that he really had the potential to go far. This was the point where things were going to start happening, and if he wanted it he was going to need to learn to focus. When Jake had been a professional player, the game had pretty much been his life.

'I had a missed call from Dad earlier,' Ben said. 'Asking if he could come down next week. I'd have to miss the game though.'

Hannah raised an eyebrow. 'And you want to do that?'

Ben shook his head. 'Not really. Just feel like I ought to be around if he's coming down.'

'After the way we played today, Ben, we need all the bodies on the pitch we can get. He needs to fit around your game,' said Jake, speaking without thinking. 'It's only two hours.'

What the hell was he doing? He shouldn't have said that – it wasn't his place. It wasn't as if he was Ben's parent, or had any right to an opinion.

But Hannah, although she looked a little surprised, nodded. 'Jake's right, you know.'

Ben shrugged slightly. 'Yeah, you're probably right. I'll tell him no.'

'You don't need to do that,' Hannah said. 'Just tell him he needs to come after football.'

'Okay,' Ben said, and disappeared out the front door into the rain, which had started pouring down outside.

'You've forgotten your coat,' she called, but he was gone.

'Sorry,' he said. 'I shouldn't have butted in.'

'No, you're right. Phil can't just disappear from Ben's life and then randomly decide to call all the shots because he's at a loose end one weekend.'

Jake grimaced, feeling awkward. 'Yeah – I just don't want to see Ben throwing away his chances.'

'I know.' Hannah smiled at him. Then a woman and

her two children came in and started asking questions about the bookshop. Jake gave her a brief wave of the hand as he left.

It wasn't until he got back to the house that he realized he'd gone in and not bought anything. Sodden and pissed off, he got out of the car and slammed the door harder than he'd meant to, setting off both dogs uncharacteristically barking from within the kitchen. By the time he got inside, they were utterly convinced that he was a burglar and not their master. They'd clearly been freaked out by a stranger coming to collect the bibs before the game earlier, because normally they'd be more likely to lick him to death than bark at him. He stood in the middle of the kitchen, leaning on the huge island, letting them circle and sniff him until they'd satisfied themselves that he wasn't an impostor.

'At least I know you two are decent guard dogs,' he said, patting both of them on the head and peeling off his soaked coat. He slung it over a hook above the Aga – it would be dry in no time – and headed for the shower.

It was amazing how bloody cold it got in late autumn standing by the pitch for a couple of hours. He washed his hair and watched the soapy water run down his leg; the scar from the operation to repair his shattered bone went a livid red in the cold. He grabbed a towel, dried himself off and headed for the bedroom to throw on a t-shirt and some grey tracksuit bottoms.

He flicked through the channels on TV, got up, made

himself a coffee, came back to the sitting room and collapsed on the sofa, one foot up on the coffee table. Sarah was nowhere to be seen – probably in the bath, or lying in bed watching Netflix. Sometimes this place just felt ridiculously huge – a testament to the ostentation of high-level football. What the hell did he want with eight bedrooms and a snooker room? He got up and paced across the floor, looking out at the sweep of gravel and the perfectly maintained lawn. It was bloody ridiculous. He looked at his phone again – maybe he could just give her a ring? Or send a quick message, just to say sorry for being a bit off? He typed her name in and saw her face looking back from a tiny image on the screen.

Hi

Meg lolloped in and knocked his hand so that he hit the send button by accident. Oh, shit. Well, that was that decision made. Now he'd better send something else or he would look weirdly creepy.

Hello. Have you dried off? You looked soaked earlier.

Hannah's reply was instant, which threw him.

Yes, and defrosted. Had a bath when I got back.

God, lucky you – I'd love to jump in a bath right now.

Do *not* think about Hannah in the bath, he told himself, fruitlessly. He imagined her surrounded by bubbles, hair tied up, those little twirly bits that always seemed to come loose hanging around her neck. He banged his forehead with his open palm and groaned. For God's sake, man.

I just wanted to check you were . . . He paused, wondering what to type. He deleted it and started again.

Is Ben okay? I feel bad for sticking my oar in.

Yeah, his dad's ducked out of next weekend anyway – I think he's feeling pretty low on the priority list.

I'm sorry. That's shit. Is he okay?

He wanted to type *And are you?* – because really, that was what was nagging at him. Whatever the hell that ex had done to her, he wanted to get in his car and drive down to wherever he was and tell him in no uncertain terms what he thought of him and the way he was treating her – and Ben, for that matter. He was a nice lad, and he deserved better than a deadbeat who couldn't even summon up the enthusiasm to hang around and watch the game.

I'm sure he will be after an afternoon playing on the Xbox with his mates.

Jake chuckled.

That sounds about right.

He couldn't think what to say next. What he ached to say was *why don't you come up here this afternoon, I'll make you dinner and we can sit in front of the fire and drink red wine and talk?* Instead he just stared at the screen for a few more moments, then sent a brief:

Glad to hear he's okay.

He put his phone down on the coffee table, stretched his legs out and ran his hands through his still-damp hair. God, why was it so bloody difficult? He'd always found it easy enough to go out on casual dates with women, and relationships had been – well, he'd never really felt like he'd found *the one*, but he hadn't found it hard to form them. And yet somehow, now, he seemed shy and self-conscious.

Chapter Twenty-four

Hannah was relieved that after Jake's pep talk, Ben seemed to have settled back to his new state of behaving relatively well at school. Parents' evening passed uneventfully – his teachers seemed to feel he was doing fine, on the whole, and working hard towards his exams. She raised an eyebrow at that, knowing perfectly well that he was spending more time playing FIFA or actual football than working on revision, but she'd resigned herself to hoping that if he could just pass the five GCSEs he needed to get into sixth form college, he'd be all right. They'd gone along to the local sixth form, which offered a BTEC in sports science, and with that in mind he seemed reasonably focused. Chatting to the other parents on the side of the pitch at the weekends, it seemed they were all in the same boat: as Jake had once observed to her, not everyone was cut out for academia.

She still hankered after it, though, and with Oxford so close at hand it felt like a reminder of a life she could have had but which had been whisked away. One weekend they went down to visit Beth and Lauren, happily settled now in Aunt Jess's old house in the middle of the city. Ben and Lauren went off together and spent a small fortune in JD Sports while Hannah and

Beth put the world to rights over coffee and cake, then dinner and wine.

'If you ever want me to come back and do shop duty,' Beth had said, pouring them another glass of red, 'just shout.'

'Are you missing it?'

'Weirdly, a bit, yes.'

'I thought you were desperate to escape Little Maudley.'

'I was. But I miss the village gossip. What's going on? Any interesting news to report?'

Hannah shook her head. 'I don't tend to hear that much.'

'You're not asking the right questions.' Beth chuckled. 'I was an expert at wheedling info out of people. It's a talent, y'know.'

Hannah sipped her wine and didn't reply. She could hardly tell Beth how much the villagers clearly appreciated not having to fend off exactly that sort of wheedling. Often they forgot that she and Beth were related, and when they mentioned how nice it was with Hannah at the helm, she felt a little bit awkward that her cousin had apparently ruffled so many feathers.

'How's the online dating going?' Hannah changed the subject.

'Oh my God,' Beth said, shaking her head in amusement. 'You wouldn't believe how many utter idiots there are out there.'

'So you haven't fallen madly in love with any of them?'

'Lust, perhaps.' Beth looked misty-eyed for a moment. 'I had a one-night stand with a guy who was only twenty-five. Looked like Kit Harrington from *Game of Thrones*. Let me show you his photo . . .' She scrolled through her phone and passed it over.

'Ooh.' Hannah had to admit he was cute. 'What happened?'

'Well.' Beth gave a dirty laugh. 'I'll leave that to the imagination. But it made me realize that I wasn't in a rush to get into a relationship. I've no desire to wash someone's underwear when I could be out having fun.'

'Good for you.' Hannah reached forward and helped herself to some crisps.

'I take it that you've not had any excitement in that department since you've moved to the village?'

'Hardly.' Hannah suppressed a thought about Jake, and how much she'd enjoyed spending the night chatting with him at Helen's dinner party and again at the book group. Not to mention how much she was looking forward to the following weekend, when she'd offered to come along by minibus to Milton Keynes for an away match. 'No, I'm quite happy as I am.'

'Not missing Phil?'

She shook her head. 'Not at all. Is that weird?'

'To be honest, Han, it would be weird if you were. I always wondered why you two stayed together all that time.'

Hannah shrugged. 'I dunno. I think I just sort of thought that I should do the right thing.'

'The right thing being staying with a bloke who made zero effort and who you clearly didn't even fancy?'

'Oh shush.' Hannah laughed, feeling embarrassed. 'I didn't want to mess up things with Ben.'

'Because he was clearly getting *so much* out of his relationship with his father, right? How many times has he been down to visit since you split up?'

'Um, once.' It was already November, and since they'd split he'd managed one midweek visit. Hannah had bitten her tongue and not pointed out that he was combining it with a trip to Oxford for a sales conference, and had even given him the spare room. And then Ben, whom he'd come to see, had sloped off to a friend's house after half an hour claiming he had to do a project for Geography. She'd sighed in despair and left Phil at the cottage, heading into Bletchingham to pick up fish and chips for their dinner.

'And how did that go?'

'Weird. Awkward. We ate fish and chips on our knees and watched *Air Ambulance Rescue*, he told me about stuff that was going on at work, and then I went off to have a bath and when I got back out he'd gone to bed in the spare room.'

'Sounds pretty much like a standard night when you two were together.'

Hannah looked at her straight-talking cousin and laughed. 'That's exactly what I thought.'

The next morning, Phil had been up and on his way before Ben had even made it out of bed. Hannah had unpacked a delivery from the wholesaler and thought to herself all morning just how bloody thankful she was that they weren't together any more.

'You need to get back on the horse, Han.'

'I haven't been on the horse in sixteen years. I don't know if I even remember what to do.'

'It's not exactly rocket science.'

'I know, I know. I mean the whole dating thing. It's not really me, to be honest.'

'I'm loving it.' Beth picked up her phone, which was pinging with another notification. 'Look, I've got another match. I wonder if this one's pretending he's not married as well . . .'

Chapter Twenty-five

'I think I'm going to do it.'

Sarah looked up as Jake walked into the pool room. She'd been swimming lengths, and her hair was clamped to her head in damp tendrils. She looked rosy-cheeked, healthy and like a completely different person to the terrified, sodden shell who'd turned up on his doorstep all those weeks ago.

'Do what?' He racked his brain. His half-sister had a weird habit of coming back to conversations they'd had ages before, and he couldn't always keep up. Plus, if he was honest with himself, he'd been so wrapped up in plans for Bonfire Night that he'd not really been paying attention.

'Go to that course I showed you.'

'Ohhh.' He nodded, remembering. 'The one about mindfulness and stuff?'

'Yes.' She climbed out of the water and wrapped a towel around her middle, sitting down on one of the pool chairs. 'I was thinking about it when I was swimming.'

'I think that's a brilliant idea.'

'I'll show you the stuff.' She paused, biting her lower lip and looking at him, suddenly awkward. 'As long as you don't mind paying?'

'Of course I don't.'

'You are an angel.'

'I'm not,' he said. 'It's the least I can do. I've got years of big brother stuff to catch up on.'

She beamed, her smile lighting up her face. 'Cool.'

So it was sorted. Sarah was off to Cirencester for a week-long residential course in mindfulness training, where she'd be locked away from the outside world, relaxing and enjoying the beautiful grounds of the country-house hotel where it was taking place. He was quietly relieved, because it made his plans for Bonfire Night with the boys from the team so much easier.

He'd managed to keep Sarah's existence below the radar so far. Pippa was the only one who knew about her – and that was just how he liked it.

'D'you want me to order fireworks and stuff?'

Pippa was sitting in the office at her desk, which faced onto his. Where his was neat, with just a desktop computer and a small succulent plant in a red enamel pot, hers was as chaotic as she was organized. Papers were strewn all over the place.

'That would be amazing. Any other stuff I need to sort?'

'Nope.' She pointed to the screen of her computer. 'I've sorted out the tax stuff for the property portfolio, and I've set up the account for Sarah. She's lucky to have you, you know.'

'Not that lucky.' He felt automatically defensive. 'She's spent twenty-four years crashing from pillar to post and ended up escaping an abusive relationship. God knows what would have happened if she hadn't turned up here.'

'That's what I mean, silly,' Pippa shook her head. 'I wasn't suggesting she was taking the mick, more that she's fallen on her feet. In a good way,' she added, as he opened his mouth to defend her further.

'I just want her to be happy, and feel safe. And I want to make sure she never ends up going back to that dickhead again.'

'That's not likely to happen, is it?'

'I'd like to think not. But she can't stay tucked away here forever, can she? I guess this course is the start of her getting ready to live a new life.'

'You don't want people getting wind of her, do you?'

'I don't want the press turning up and making up a load of crap, no.' He shuddered, thinking about it. He'd always had an instinctive loathing of the press and their desperate desire to overturn everything in a person's past just to make up a story that would sell papers – or more likely, sell online advertising space. He'd stayed as low-profile as possible because of that, and yet they'd still made up a load of crap when he'd been injured, claiming he'd lost his nerve and that was why he'd never returned to the game. It made him furious that they could behave that way.

A week and a half later, he was pacing the kitchen waiting for everyone to arrive. Pippa had organized the fireworks and with the help of Dave, the gardener, he'd set up a huge bonfire at the back of the long stretch of lawn. They'd been careful to leave spaces just in case any late-hibernating hedgehogs had decided it looked like a good place to curl up for the winter, and he'd taken a last look before the light dropped that evening, poking about with a long branch in the hope of scaring anything that might have crept in back out again. Fortunately there was no sign of anything.

'Evening,' said Jamie, who appeared at the door followed by his twin, Tommy, and their friend Jude. They were carrying a huge effigy of Guy Fawkes, stuffed with straw and with a terrifying-looking Anonymous mask in place of a face. 'We thought we'd burn him on the bonfire.'

'Good idea. D'you want to take him round the back and stick him on, or wait for the others?'

They looked at each other thoughtfully. 'Leave him. We can bring him down when the lads get here.'

'Come on then,' Jake said, beckoning them in. 'Where's your mum, Jude? Is she coming?'

'She's got to work.' Jude, who towered over the other boys at six foot five, motioned to the driveway where his mum lifted a hand to wave hello and goodbye. 'She says thanks for the offer, but she's got something she needs to hand in by Monday.'

'That's all right.' Jake waved to Jude's mother. She was a writer and always seemed to be running to catch up with herself, muttering about deadlines and edits. Her wheels crunched on the gravel as she drove off, music blaring from her car.

'This place is so cool.' Tommy spun round on his heel,

looking at the huge open hallway. 'When I'm a famous player, though, I'm going to have one of those smart houses where everything's done automatically. This place is a bit—'

'Haunted-looking?' His twin finished his sentence. It made Jake laugh. The two of them were just as instinctive on the pitch, seeming to know where the other one was without looking. It was their team's secret weapon – and the fact they were identical helped even more. The opposition teams seemed to be thrown by it every time, not quite able to figure out how the player they'd just tackled was somehow in front of the ball and bearing down on them all over again.

'There's drinks in the kitchen,' he said, showing them through to the room where the dogs were waiting, eager to be petted. 'And snacks and stuff.'

'No beers?' Jude looked hopeful.

'No beers,' he said, firmly. 'Because you're under age, and the last thing I need is a load of crap for giving alcohol to sixteen-year-olds.'

'You said your body was a temple anyway,' Tommy teased Jude, who was always at the gym working out.

'It is.'

'So you won't be wanting any of these?' Jamie picked up a tube of Pringles and waggled it under his friend's nose.

'Nope.' Jude looked resolute for about two seconds. 'Oh go on then. Give us some.'

Jake, laughing, left them to it. A few moments later, it

seemed, the room was packed with all the lads from the team, winding each other up and messing about with the dogs. Gary, the old coach, had come along with his wife Anna, and the usual parents – the ones who made it every weekend and stood freezing their backsides off on the sidelines – were here too, more dressed up than he'd seen them before. They'd all brought warm coats and hats for the firework display that was planned for later, and he showed them to the downstairs cloakroom to hang them up before heading into the kitchen for drinks.

He'd set up a couple of games in the big sitting room. The boys had naturally gravitated towards the Xbox and PlayStation and were sitting around on the sofas, drinks in hand, teasing each other and having a laugh. This had been a good idea, he decided. They needed some downtime where they could hang out and bond away from the pitch, and it felt good to have a houseful. Greenhowes hadn't been built to be a home for just him and the dogs. He looked out of the window. There was only one thing missing. Well, two, to be exact.

'Anyone heard from Ben?' He tried to sound casual as he stuck his head round the sitting room door. Tommy looked up.

'Yeah, he's coming, I think.'

'Right.' Jake gave a brief nod and headed back towards the kitchen.

'This place is gorgeous,' Gary's wife Anna said, running a hand along the rail of the Aga. 'I've always wanted one of these.'

'D'you know,' he began, distracted by the sight of lights in the driveway, 'everyone says that, but it's like the world's biggest and most expensive radiator.'

'You don't recommend it?'

'Oh it's lovely, don't get me wrong – and the dogs love it. But as a cooker it's rubbish. You try and do a Sunday roast on it and by the time you've made the Yorkshires it's lost half the heat and the potatoes take about two hours.'

'You hear that, Gary,' she said, tapping her husband on the arm. 'Jake's not just a pretty face, you know. He makes his own Yorkshires, as well.'

'Don't go giving away all your secrets, Jake,' Gary chuckled, putting an arm around his wife's waist. 'I don't want to be expected to make Sunday lunch after all these years.'

'Shush, you,' said Anna, laughing.

'Hi,' said Hannah as Jake pulled open the door. 'Sorry, we got caught up with the shop alarm. It wouldn't stop beeping and I thought we were going to have to call the security people.'

'Did you get it sorted? Do you need a hand?'

'Yes, it's sorted.' Hannah looked at Ben with one eyebrow raised, laughing. 'Someone was typing the code in wrong.'

'*Someone* told me the wrong code.' Ben nudged her.

'Someone needs to get me a drink.' Hannah pushed Ben gently in the small of his back, propelling him through the doorway.

'I'll do that,' Jake said, turning to look at her. He reached out a hand. 'Can I take your coat?'

'Of course.' She passed it to him, taking off a red woollen hat and unwinding the scarf from round her neck. She put a hand to her hair. 'Oh God, I bet I look like a fuzzy thing now.'

'You look lovely.' He spoke without thinking. She cast her eyes down for a moment.

'Anyway,' she said, looking up again, her eyes sparkling. 'You said something about drinks?'

'I did.' He went across the hall, taking her things. They smelled of her perfume. 'Right, let's get you something. You need it after the whole fire alarm stress.'

The level of noise in the kitchen had risen as the first drinks had gone down. Everyone was chatting animatedly. He poured Hannah a glass of white wine and passed it to her.

'This should be mulled wine, really.'

'Or mulled cider.'

'Mulled anything, really. But I've got some hot chocolate and stuff down at the summer house for the boys – and us.'

She took a drink and looked around.

'This place is gorgeous.'

'Thanks.'

'So what's the history? What made you buy it?'

'I just always wanted to live in an old house. The boys came in tonight and announced that it looks like it's haunted.'

'Is it?'

'I hope not. I'm here on my own and I don't think the labradors would do much to protect me, besides barking their heads off.'

'They're not the best burglar deterrents, are they?'

'Definitely not.'

'I'd love to have a look around one day.'

'You can have a look now.' He checked everyone was okay for drinks. Nobody seemed particularly desperate to get outside into the cold, and the boys were all happily playing FIFA on the games consoles. 'If you'd like?'

'I'd love it.'

He let her go upstairs ahead of him, partly because he had good manners and partly because – if he was completely honest with himself – he wanted to watch her bottom as she climbed the stairs. The nicest thing about Hannah, he decided as he watched her standing at the top of the galleried staircase and looking down, was that she had absolutely no idea of the effect she had on him, or anyone else for that case. She was completely unaware of how pretty she was.

'Beth said this place was completely run down when you moved in?'

'Oh God, trashed. It was used during the war as a convalescent hospital, and after that the owners couldn't afford to do the work that was needed, and eventually they just gave up. It had been empty for years when I bought it.'

Hannah ran a hand along the silky wood of the banister. 'I can't believe you live in a place like this. Is that weird?'

He shook his head. 'Not at all. That's exactly how I feel. It's so far removed from what we – what I grew up in.'

'We,' she agreed, her voice low. 'No, me too. I get it.'

He looked at her for a moment then, and as if propelled by some outside force, took a step towards her. She held his gaze.

'It's just –' he began, and then – with impeccable timing – there was a crash as a ball thudded across the tiles of the hall beneath them, followed by two of the lads, who whooped with delight and picked it up before it could do any damage. Hannah shook her head, smiling.

'Think it might be time to get this lot outside, before there's some kind of incident.'

'I think you might be right.'

Chapter Twenty-six

Oh my God, Hannah thought, putting a hand to her chest to calm herself. For a second there, she'd genuinely imagined that Jake was about to kiss her. Then the boys had come crashing through and reality had brought her back to earth with a bump. The chances that he was about to declare his undying love for her when she was – well, herself – were non-existent. She shook her head, laughing inwardly.

Out in the garden, they trekked down a gravel path that curved along the side of the long stretch of lawn leading down towards the wood. The wooden summer-house – which was a misnomer, because she'd imagined a little shed type of affair and this was a huge, gorgeous alpine-looking thing with a central barbecue pit and chairs that went all the way round – was lit up with a thousand sparkling fairy lights, and a huge vat of hot chocolate stood warming on the side. On a side table there were containers of squirty cream, marshmallows and chocolate sprinkles, and next to them a huge refrig-erated tray holding biscuits, fluffy marshmallows and chocolate chunks for making s'mores. The boys got stuck in straight away.

'This is pretty amazing, isn't it?' Anna stood by

Hannah's side and spoke quietly. 'I feel like I'm in an American movie.'

'Me too.' Hannah nodded. 'Except of course they don't have fireworks night, and they think burning an effigy of Guy Fawkes is utterly bonkers.'

They both laughed.

'Speak of the devil.' Anna pointed to the boys, who were making their way across the grass with the huge stuffed body held high in the air, laughing and making lots of noise.

'We'd better go out,' Hannah said, pulling her scarf more tightly around her neck against the crispness of the air. 'I think they're about to light the bonfire.'

'Three – two – one – GO!' the whole football team chanted in delight, as Jake took a long torch and thrust it into the fire. It shot into flames immediately, and everyone cheered.

'Fireworks now, I think,' Jake said, once the blaze was satisfyingly under way and they'd all watched it for a while. He moved further down the lawn to a space that had been carefully marked off with rope and metal posts.

'Can we light them?' Ben called out hopefully.

'No chance,' Jake said, laughing.

Hannah realized she'd left a glove in the summer house and went back to get it, bumping into a returning Jake as she did so.

'This is amazing. You've given them a brilliant night.'

'Least I could do,' he said simply.

Above their heads, a succession of rockets and sparkling,

crackling colourful lights shot through the air. She turned to look at him, his face lit up by the bonfire, and realized that the fizzing heat she felt was far more potent than any of the fireworks that were illuminating the velvet of the night sky. The truth is, Hannah acknowledged to herself, gloved hand over her mouth in surprise, you are falling for this person. And you can't have him.

Chapter Twenty-seven

November flew past – the shop was decorated prettily for Christmas, and the second book group meeting was a huge hit. Little Maudley was starting to feel like home, and Hannah couldn't wait for Katie to come and visit for the weekend. It had been weeks since she'd last come down, and she was really looking forward to a girly weekend of wine and watching Christmas movies and picking up a takeaway from the Chinese restaurant in Bletchingham.

Katie arrived, arms full of bags of presents, hair misted with rain. The crisp weather of November had been replaced with a damp, sodden December, but Hannah was undeterred. She was determined to make this Christmas a good one – not just for Ben, but for her. It felt good to be making plans without having to factor in Phil's lack of interest in the season, and she was going all out.

'My God, this place looks amazing.' Katie stood outside the shop for a moment, taking it in. She peered through the window of the little bookshop. 'And this is just gorgeous. You're living the dream, aren't you?'

Hannah smiled. 'I am a bit. I honestly didn't know how much I'd love it here.'

'There's a village tree, and they've decorated the telephone box library with fairy lights.'

'And there's a carol service tomorrow. It's like living in a Richard Curtis movie.'

'All you need is a hot footballer to sweep you off your feet.' Katie followed her into the shop. 'Oh, wait. You've got that, too.'

'Don't start. He's a friend, that's all.'

'A friend who happens to turn up and help when the lights go out in the shop?' Katie's tone was arch.

'Like you wouldn't have done the same thing?'

'Yeah, right. Okay, you've got a point.'

The night before last, just as Jake was dropping Ben off from a midweek training session, the power to the shop had gone with a slightly alarming bang not long after Hannah had strung up a final set of Christmas lights along the top of the bookshelves. Jake had come in, helped work out what the problem was and then stayed for coffee and to talk about the book he'd been reading, which he thought she'd love. The next morning, he'd popped into the shop with a copy for her.

'Anyway,' Katie said, collapsing on the sofa, 'I think it's nice that you've got someone in your life – even if they're *just a friend*, before you say anything.' She gave Hannah a meaningful look. 'Who is decent and treats you nicely.'

'He does, you're right.'

'And Ben thinks he's amazing, right?'

'He really does. He respects him, which is something he's never done with Phil.'

'Well that's not really a massive shock, is it?'

Hannah rolled her eyes. 'Not exactly, no.'

Hannah left Katie to get her things unpacked and headed for the kitchen to put some plates in the oven to warm. Ben was – as usual – out with his friends, but she'd save him some for later.

'I'm just going to nip out and get something from the Chinese takeaway. I'll ring and order and it'll be ready by the time I get there. Are you hungry?'

'Starving,' Katie called from the little spare room. 'I could eat a horse. Or at least a whole container of beef in black bean sauce and some noodles and maybe a helping of prawn toasts?'

'Done,' said Hannah, taking her phone out of her bag. 'I'll ring them from the car.'

It was funny how quickly she'd become accustomed to the patterns of village life – if someone had told her a year ago that she'd have to drive a ten-mile round trip to pick up a takeaway meal or visit a supermarket, she'd have laughed at them. Things had changed so much in such a short time. She drove out of the village and past the turning that led down to Greenhowes. Looking over the hedge, she could see the lights of the big house glowing in the trees. Jake was probably down there, pottering about, doing whatever he did on a Saturday night.

It was weird that he'd never talked about the woman who had collected him from Helen's dinner party. He'd mentioned a PA – maybe that's who she was? Maybe, though, it was someone who was something more. It didn't really matter, though, did it? It wasn't as if he was about to declare his undying love to Hannah. It was nice that they'd become friends, though. She'd never really had any male friends – Phil had always been weirdly possessive, and of course it wasn't as if she'd had much opportunity to meet new people while she'd been bringing up Ben. Now here she was, living in the tiniest little village, and somehow her social life had expanded in ways she'd never expected.

She parked in the car park by the canal and made her way up the narrow passageway to the Chinese restaurant. One of the streetlights was flickering ominously, and she felt a prickle of apprehension as she walked along the empty lane. Bletchingham was hardly an inner city, though – she shook her head, trying to convince herself not to feel uncomfortable. But when a huge, heavyset man came towards her she twisted the car keys she was holding, turning them so the point of the key was tucked between her fingers, in an almost instinctive motion. The man gave her a sideways look as he passed, then pulled out a mobile phone to make a call.

'Yeah, just trying to work out where she is. It can't be that hard.'

Hannah sped up, relieved to step out of the gloomy passage and onto the main street. The food was bagged up and waiting for her and she collected it with a smile of thanks, deciding this time to walk the longer way round to the car park past the old library.

When she got back to Little Maudley, there was a

familiar dark-coloured Range Rover parked outside the shop. She picked up the bag of food and headed inside, frowning in confusion. As soon as she opened the door she heard Katie shrieking with laughter, and a familiar voice talking.

'Ah,' Katie said, as she walked in, 'we've got a visitor.'

Jake stood up from the edge of the sofa where he'd been perched, chatting to Katie who was curled up on the armchair, looking quite at home.

'Hello.' Hannah put the bag down on the coffee table and looked at Jake.

'Hi.' He rubbed his jaw, looking suddenly awkward. 'Sorry, I should have thought you'd be eating.'

'It's fine.' Hannah looked over his shoulder at Katie, who was mouthing *oh my God* at her, eyes saucer-wide.

'Jake just wanted to ask you a favour,' Katie said, standing up. 'I tell you what, I'll go and get the plates and cutlery and he can tell you what's happening tomorrow.'

'Not *tell*,' Jake began, looking uncomfortable.

'Tell,' said Katie, with a note of finality in her voice. 'I'm not hearing any arguments.'

'What's going on?' Hannah sat down on the coffee table, knees pressed together. Jake hovered for a moment, as if he wasn't sure whether to stand or sit. Eventually he sat on the sofa, palms pressed down on his long thighs, leaning forward slightly.

'I've got a – thing – tomorrow night. To be honest, I was trying to get out of it, but a friend of mine's had to pull out, and I'm needed to present an award.'

'Okay . . .' Hannah's stomach churned – she wasn't sure whether it was with nerves or anticipation. Maybe both. She put a hand to her mouth and looked at him, not speaking.

'The thing is, I need someone to take.'

'A date?' Hannah squeaked the words out, flushing pink as soon as she did so. Oh, God, why couldn't she just be *cool* for once? Katie wouldn't have behaved like a fourteen-year-old in this situation.

'Um.' Jake made a face, 'Well, yeah. Sort of.'

'Okay.' Hannah inhaled carefully, trying to appear zen and calm. 'So who are you thinking of?'

'You, silly,' Jake said, and started to laugh. 'I mean – I'm just – well, I need someone to come along who won't take it all too seriously, and I just wondered if maybe you'd like a night away from village stuff – but then I discovered you've got Katie here, and—'

Katie reappeared with three plates and the food decanted from the bag and set out on a big metal tray. 'And *I* said that I would have absolutely no problem in staying here, keeping an eye on Ben, and holding the fort so you could go to London and hang out with the famous people.'

'Famous people?' Hannah looked at Jake, questioningly.

'Well, famous sports people. It's the Sports Personality of the Year awards.'

'Oh my God. Ben's going to die of envy.'

'He'll be there himself soon enough, if he carries on playing the way he has been.'

'You see,' Katie said, looking pleased with herself.

'But why do you want me to come?'

Katie shot Hannah a look of utter despair. 'God, Hannah, what you're supposed to say is *oh wow, thanks very much, Jake, I'd love to come.*'

'Oh –' Hannah pushed a lock of hair back behind her ears. 'Sorry. Yes, I would love to. But I don't have anything to wear.'

'You do,' said Katie, firmly. 'And I'll do your hair and make-up and stuff.'

'You'd be doing me a massive favour,' Jake said, pushing up his shirt sleeve and absent-mindedly rubbing his arm. Standing beside him at an awards ceremony, she was going to look like a very drab and unexciting plus-one. Maybe that was the idea. She knew how much Jake loathed press and publicity. If he had someone unremarkable on his arm, the photographers wouldn't take any notice.

'I'd love to,' she said decidedly.

'Seriously?' Jake looked relieved and smiled broadly. 'That's amazing.'

'Told you she would,' Katie said, with all the self-satisfaction of a born matchmaker. 'Now, I'm bloody starving. Jake, are you staying for some of this food?'

'I would,' he said, looking at it longingly, 'but I think you two probably have loads to catch up on. Hannah, I'll give you a shout tomorrow and tell you what time I'll be picking you up?'

'That's perfect.' She tried not to think about how petrified with nerves she already was at the prospect.

'Right, well, I'll get off.'

'You sure you don't want to stay?' Katie waggled a piece of sesame prawn toast at him.

'No,' he laughed. 'But thanks.'

'I'll see you out,' Hannah said, getting up.

As Hannah turned to close the door behind her, Katie's eyebrows were raised so far up that they were in danger of disappearing into her hairline. She gave Hannah a huge smile and a thumbs-up sign, then shoved the piece of prawn toast into her mouth.

'I've never been to anything like that before,' Hannah said, standing by the door of the cottage. Jake paused in the little porch. He was so tall and broad that he took up most of the space.

'It'll be nice to do it with someone I actually enjoy spending time with,' he said, looking at her directly. She felt her stomach flip over with excitement and anticipation.

'Okay, let me know what time you're coming in the morning. Do I need to get dressed here, or—' She didn't want to presume, but what did people usually do at things like this? Did they stay over, or get a taxi home? Or a chauffeured car? It was way, way out of her comfort zone.

'I'll pick you up. I'm not going to drink, so I'll take the car. You can have all the champagne you want, though.' He smiled at her and raised an eyebrow. 'I promise not to take advantage.'

Her heart gave an uneven thump and she felt herself colouring slightly at the flirtatious line. She walked back into the sitting room, closed the door, and collapsed back against it with an enormous sigh.

'Oh my actual God,' said Katie, fanning herself. 'Where do I start?'

'I have no idea.' Hannah slid down the door and onto the carpet, sitting there with a slightly dazed expression on her face. 'When I said I was moving to the countryside for a quiet life, this isn't quite what I was thinking of.'

Katie got up, walked across the room and held out her hands to pull Hannah upright. When she was standing, Katie wrapped her arms around her in a tight hug.

'I'm so bloody happy for you, Han. All that time I spent telling you you needed to do something in life that was for *you*. Well, you're bloody well doing it, aren't you?'

Hannah sat down on the sofa, ignoring the cooling take-away food. She wasn't even remotely hungry any more.

Katie flicked on the television and spooned some noodles and sweet-and-sour chicken onto a plate, passing it to her. 'You need to eat something, you look like you're on another planet.'

'I'm fine.' Hannah picked at a noodle, half-heartedly.

'You're not fine,' said Katie, looking at her beadily. 'You've got the major hots for him, and don't try and tell me otherwise.'

Hannah opened her mouth.

'I said don't.' Katie pointed a warning finger. 'And what's more –' she speared a piece of green pepper with a fork and waggled it in the air – 'he's got the raging hots for you right back.'

'Yeah, right.' Hannah rolled her eyes. 'Because million-aire England football players always go for frazzled-looking thirty-five-year-old women with teenage sons. He probably just feels sorry for me.' She thought about the comment he'd made about not taking advantage and felt a tiny, secretive flutter of excitement. Surely he wasn't actually interested in her?

'Hannah, you're gorgeous, you're a lovely person, you've come down here and finally come out of the shadow of effing Phil. You've set up a book group and a bookshop, and as far as I can gather, everyone in the village thinks you're the bee's knees. I think it's about bloody time you saw yourself the way other people do.'

'Well, that's me told,' Hannah said, laughing.

'Yes, it is.' Katie's voice was firm. 'And as soon as I've eaten all of this –' she motioned to the huge tray of food – 'I'm going to take you through to the bedroom and we're going to find you something lovely to wear.'

Hannah woke up the next morning feeling slightly sick with anticipation. She checked her phone straight away, just in case he'd messaged – not expecting him to be awake.

Morning – hope you're still on for tonight?

She tapped a reply straight back.

Of course.

That's a relief. Okay, I'll pick you up at three? Traffic might be a nightmare, and that'll give us a chance to get to the hotel and get organized.

Hotel? Hannah took a sharp intake of breath in surprise.

I thought you said we were driving back?

Of course ☺ They give me a room as a matter of course – just somewhere to get dressed and sorted before it all kicks off. I'm going to be ready to go, but you can bring your stuff and get dressed there if you like? It's a suite, so I won't get under your feet.

She had to admit that the prospect of getting ready in a fancy hotel suite had a certain appeal. If only she could bring Katie along to help out.

That sounds perfect. Can I bring anything?

As soon as she'd typed it, she realized how utterly naive it sounded. It was a massive sporting award ceremony, not the sixth form disco where they'd be sneaking in a bottle of cheap vodka and necking it when the teachers weren't watching.

Just yourself. x

Hannah looked at the kiss for a long moment before she replied.

Katie, meanwhile, was having the time of her life playing shops. Fortunately one of the village volunteers was on hand for the whole day and was in charge of cashing up and all the technical stuff, but she was determined to get her hands dirty. She'd already donned one of the 'The Old Post Office' aprons, tied her hair back in a jaunty ponytail, and was dusting the bookshelves with a feather duster and humming to herself.

'You having fun there?'

'Bloody loving it,' Katie beamed. 'I might give up work and come and do this full time.'

'I can't see that happening. The money's not good enough, for one thing.'

'Yeah, but my success rate at bagging a glamorous night out with a gorgeous footballer has been zero per cent so far, and you seem to be doing okay in that department.'

'Oh, shut up,' Hannah giggled.

'Right, let's have a look at your outfit for tonight, then.' She looked across at the counter. 'Just popping upstairs to sort Hannah out,' she explained to the woman who was serving, who looked slightly nonplussed. Hannah shook her head in mock despair as she followed Katie back into the cottage.

'I tell you what,' Katie said, holding up a long black dress scattered with sequins and scrunching up her face in thought. 'There's one thing we have to be grateful to Phil for. All those incredibly dull work nights out mean you've at least got some nice dresses in the wardrobe for a thing like this.'

'I still think it's a bit plain, though, don't you?'

'Classy, not plain. Classy with sparkles. That's a good look, I think.'

'I feel really bad that you've come down here to see me and now I'm swanning off to London.'

Katie made a snorting sound and shook her head. 'I'm bloody not. You deserve this, every bit of it.'

'You don't have to do anything in the shop, you know. Grace will be fine running it herself.'

'I know.' Katie rubbed her hands together. 'But I'm

secretly quite excited about playing shops and soaking up some of this village atmosphere.'

'You sound like Beth. Mind you, it wasn't atmosphere she liked, it was gossip.'

'Yeah, I'm up for that, too. If anything exciting happens, I'll let you know.'

Chapter Twenty-eight

Over in Greenhowes, Jake was hoovering the car seats. Despite having been valeted in the week they were somehow still covered in dog hairs, thanks to Meg and Mabel and their habit of leaping into any car door that happened to be open on the off chance they might be taken on an adventure. Pippa had taken the dogs off to hers for the weekend, so he didn't have to worry about what time he got back. He was buzzing with excitement – not at the thought of the awards, which he'd duck out of given half a chance, but at the prospect of a whole afternoon and evening spent with Hannah. As long as he didn't run out of things to talk about – except that didn't ever seem to be a problem for them. Whenever he went to the shop, they'd stand chatting for ages. And after football, Ben and the boys were happy to carry on kicking a ball about while they stood drinking coffee and talking. She was the easiest person to talk to he'd ever met – and it didn't harm things that she was incredibly pretty. He couldn't wait to see her all dressed up for the awards this evening.

He'd just locked up and was throwing a suit carrier onto the back seat when he heard the sound of a car coming down the drive. He waited a moment, wondering what it could be – he hadn't ordered anything online, and the post had already been delivered. As it drew closer, he realized it was a taxi. It pulled to a halt and after a moment Sarah climbed out, hefting her bags onto her shoulder.

'Hey,' he said, crossing the gravel drive and taking a bag from her. They weighed a ton – he wondered what on earth she'd got in there.

'Hi.' Sarah looked uncomfortable. 'I thought you'd have gone already.'

'Nope,' he said, following her back to the house. She opened the door with her key and dumped her bag in the hallway, switching on the lights. It was only half past two, but already almost dark. Thank goodness the shortest day was on its way and they'd be coming back to the light again. He hated the gloom of winter.

'I thought your course didn't finish until Monday?'

Sarah had only just headed off for the second part of her mindfulness course, disappearing with her bags laden with books and her meditation mat tucked under her arm.

'It didn't.'

He frowned. 'What happened?'

'I dunno.' She sighed. 'It was all a bit – intense this time. I found that every time we did mindfulness stuff, bad things would start going through my head and it made me feel like I was going to freak out.'

'That's why I've always found all that meditation stuff hard. If I want to get out of my head, I'll read a book. I don't really want to contemplate my inner thoughts, or whatever it is they do.'

'I think the idea is, you're not supposed to think about anything . . . But I just kept thinking about Mum, and what it was like growing up. And about Joe.'

'What about him?' His tone was careful. She hadn't mentioned her ex in ages.

'I dunno. It wasn't all bad, you know.'

'He hit you,' he said, bleakly. 'How bad does it have to get?'

'I know, I know. I just . . .' She tailed off. 'Anyway, I realized that the last thing I needed was to be sitting on a yoga mat thinking about all that stuff. That was sort of the point. So I decided that maybe the best thing I could do was get back here, chill out by the fire with the dogs, watch a film and think about what I'm going to do next.'

'You don't have to do anything.' He reached out, pulling her into a hug. 'You've had enough shit to deal with, Sarah. Maybe it's all right if you just do nothing for a bit.'

'Maybe.' She looked up at him and frowned thoughtfully. 'Yeah, maybe that's the answer. Where are the dogs, anyway?' She stepped back, looking down the hall.

'They've gone to Pippa for the night.'

'Oh.' She looked momentarily crestfallen. 'Oh well, I'll just flop on the sofa and watch crappy movies.'

'There's loads of stuff in the fridge if you're hungry – and there's champagne and wine if you want.'

He didn't like to say that a tiny, hopeful part of him

had stocked up the fridge with drinks and nibbles on the off chance that after the awards, he might persuade Hannah to come back and join him for a glass of champagne or something. He didn't want to admit to himself what the *something* might be, but he'd found himself thinking about her more and more over the last few weeks.

'Cool.' Sarah picked up her bag. 'I'll deal with this later. Where are you off to?'

'Oh, just some awards thing in London. Have a look, you might see us on the news later.'

'Us?' She cocked an eyebrow.

'I've asked Hannah to come along. It's got to be more fun with her there.' He tried to keep his tone light.

She looked unconvinced. 'Right, so you're just hanging out, casually.'

'Exactly.'

She rubbed her chin and raised both eyebrows, looking at him with a knowing expression.

'Well, I hope I haven't cramped your style, big bro.'

'You have not.' He shook his head, laughing. 'Now I'd better get going.'

There was no way he was ever going to admit to her that yes, she absolutely had.

Chapter Twenty-nine

'Don't do anything I wouldn't do,' called Katie, as Hannah climbed into the passenger seat of the car. She'd said goodbye to Ben in the house, but – studiously cool – he'd refused to come out and wave goodbye.

'Oh, shut up,' she said, laughing. Jake, who was putting her bags into the back of the car, didn't seem to have heard. He sat down in the driver's seat and turned on the engine.

'Right then. London?'

'London.' She nodded.

For the first five minutes or so they sat in silence. Hannah began to feel slightly awkward. What on earth had she been thinking, agreeing to do this? Last night, after they'd eaten, she and Katie had Googled Jake – she'd felt guilty, but she'd gone along with it.

'Let's have a look at the competition,' Katie had said, spinning round Hannah's laptop and scrolling through Google Images. 'He's got a different model-actress-whatever on his arm in every bloody one of these.'

'Is this supposed to help me?' Hannah had dropped her head into her hands and groaned.

'You're gorgeous,' Katie had said, trying to boost her confidence.

'Not supermodel gorgeous.'

'But it's you he's asked out, not them.'

'Probably because he feels sorry for me,' Hannah had said, shaking her head in horror.

Sitting in the car, she sneaked a sideways look at him as he drove down the country lanes towards the motorway. He'd had a haircut and the five-day beard he always wore looked as if it had been trimmed at the same time. He looked across at her, smiling.

'What?'

'Just wondering . . .'

'Wondering what?' He glanced left and right and pulled out onto the dual carriageway.

'It's a big house to live in on your own.' Oh God, she'd started now, so she'd just have to go with it. 'Don't you ever feel like you're rattling around in there?'

'I'm not actually on my own at the moment.'

Her stomach sank like a stone. This is precisely why you don't ask questions, Hannah, she told herself.

'Oh?'

He raised a hand, rubbing at the back of his neck. 'No.' A muscle jumped in his cheek. 'I've got someone staying with me right now.'

'I see.' She bit her lip, feeling stupid that she'd ever given credence to Katie's bonkers idea that he was interested in her. 'Does she not like award ceremonies?'

Jake gave a brief laugh. 'Sarah?' He shook his head. 'No – I don't know. It's complicated.'

Hannah didn't say anything. Next he'd be telling her she didn't understand him.

'She's – oh, look, I can trust you.' He stopped midway through his sentence and looked at her for a moment, taking his eyes off the road. She waited.

'She's my sister. Half-sister. She's staying with me just now because she was in an abusive relationship and she found me and – well, it was the least I could do. I wish there was more.'

'She found you?'

'I didn't know she existed. I grew up with my aunt and my cousin in Wythenshawe – we didn't have much, but I had a decent sort of childhood. I feel awful knowing how Sarah was dragged up by our mum.'

'You didn't know your mum?'

'Nope.' He looked bleak for a moment. 'In some ways, knowing what a hard time Sarah had, I feel – well, lots of things. Guilty I wasn't around. Sad she lived the way she did. It's complicated. Anyway, when she died, Sarah ended up having to fend for herself. Then she got involved with some arsehole who treated her like dirt.'

'God.' Hannah thought of the pale-faced girl she'd seen at the wheel of his car the night of Helen's dinner party. 'She's the one who picked you up from Helen's place?'

He nodded. 'Yeah. I hoped we'd get away without anyone noticing.'

'I don't think anyone else did.' She steepled her fingers, feeling her face turning pink. 'I just did because – well, because I thought she must be a girlfriend.'

'Absolutely not.'

The atmosphere in the car had shifted. It definitely

wasn't her imagination. Jake's hand sat on the gearstick, and she thought how easy it would be to reach across and cover it with her own. Maybe Katie wasn't completely off the mark.

'So there's . . . I mean, you don't have . . . ?'

'No, I do not.' He looked at her then, amused. 'If I did, do you think I'd be inviting you to an awards ceremony as my plus-one?'

She made an open-handed gesture. 'I don't know. I thought maybe you just wanted to – well, I thought perhaps you were feeling sorry for me, or something.'

'Hannah,' he said, his voice gentle, 'I might've taken in my sister because she was escaping from a shitty relationship. I might have two rescue dogs and spend all the hours I have working on a village football team. But I did not – absolutely not – invite you because I felt sorry for you.' He reached his hand across and touched the side of hers with the edge of his. 'I invited you because I wanted to spend time with you – and because you're the only person I know that could make something like this bearable. I hate all this stuff.'

She extended her little finger so it touched his, and then he covered her hand with his, holding it there on her thigh. She could hardly catch a breath, and her heart was crashing inside her ribs like it was trying to burst out.

'It's handy that we're on the bloody M40 having this conversation, isn't it?' He tightened his grip on her hand. 'Because there's absolutely nothing I can do right now.'

'Like what?' She looked at him, lifting an eyebrow, feeling a strange new sense of confidence.

'Like kiss you, for starters.' He exhaled slowly. 'This road is far too bloody long.'

The rest of the journey seemed to go past almost unbelievably slowly – but it was an exquisite sort of wait. They chatted about books, football, and growing up in Manchester; about places he'd visited as a player and countries they'd like to visit. They had so much to talk about and so much in common. She loved talking to him, but she was longing for the moment when he'd stop the car and – well, she couldn't quite believe that anything was going to happen.

The five-star hotel was on an expensive street in London. They drove into the underground car park, Jake pulling to a halt and then taking the keys out of the ignition and turning to look at her.

'So,' he said, taking one of her hands in his.

'So.' She laced her fingers through his.

'About that kiss I couldn't give you before.'

She nodded.

'Could I?'

'Please. Yes.'

He reached a hand up to her face, cupping her chin in his hand and running a thumb across her cheek gently. She closed her eyes for a moment, losing herself in the sensation. And then she opened them again, heart thumping in her chest, looking into his eyes. He looked down at her mouth and leaned towards her, twining his fingers into the soft curls at the nape of her neck. She put a hand to his cheek, feeling the softness of the dark stubble. He inhaled sharply, pulling her close – and kissed her gently at first, his lips just grazing hers, and then she was pressed against the hardness of his body, feeling his breath in her ear as he kissed her jaw, her cheek, her neck. Hannah ran a hand down his back, feeling the muscle beneath the soft cotton of his t-shirt, and he found her mouth again.

'We should probably go inside,' he said some time later, breathless, hands still caught in her hair.

'Probably.' Hannah smiled, realizing she likely looked like the cat that had got the cream.

'I've wanted to do that for so long,' he told her, pulling her close again for another kiss.

'Me too.' She traced her fingers along his. 'But I think maybe we should go in before that security guard gets the wrong idea.'

Jake turned, looking at the security guard dressed in high-vis gear who was frowning in their direction.

'Well, we'll have given him something to talk about over dinner later,' he said, laughing.

When they got out of the car he picked up her bags, leaving her with nothing to carry. She walked alongside him, feeling like she was floating on air. They took a lift from the car park that brought them straight up to the fifth floor and opened onto the corridor where their room was situated.

'But you haven't checked in.' Hannah was confused.

'It's all done online. Look.' He tapped in a keycode on

the pad outside the hotel room door, and it swung open. Inside was a room that was almost bigger than her cottage. There was a sitting room area, complete with huge television, and a massive, luxurious bathroom.

'This is amazing.'

'They always pull out all the stops,' Jake said, setting their bags down. She looked at him, feeling a sudden wave of nerves.

'I said I'd let you get dressed and just stay out of your way,' he said gently, putting his hands on her waist. 'But you might have to kiss me first.'

'I think I can do that,' she said, snaking her arms around his neck and reaching her mouth up to meet his.

'And then,' he promised, between kisses, 'I will leave you alone.'

Hannah made a tiny sound of regret, and she felt his lips curling into a smile against hers.

'For now, anyway.'

Katie had done Hannah's hair earlier, so all she had to do was relax in the huge bath with some deliciously scented bubbles and then climb out and put on make-up and get into her dress. Jake was as good as his word and stayed out of the way – she could hear the sound of the television from the sitting room of the suite, but he left her to get ready in peace. She was grateful for that – butterflies were gathering in her stomach and she was already having a wobble about the idea of making polite conversation at the table with a load of famous people she'd never met.

'You look utterly gorgeous,' Jake told her, pulling her into his arms and dropping a kiss on her temple as they waited for the lift to take them down to a waiting car.

'So do you.' She traced a finger down the lapel of his dinner jacket. He caught her hand, lifted it to his mouth, and kissed the inside of her wrist. Hannah thought she might actually faint from longing. So this was what it felt like to actually desire someone . . . no wonder she'd struggled all those years with Phil. She didn't just find Jake attractive, she actually liked him as a person. And the strangest thing – she stepped forward into the lift, catching a glimpse of their reflections – was that he seemed to feel the same way.

There were two other people in the lift. Hannah caught Jake's eye in the mirrored glass and they exchanged a glance that made her insides feel like they were melting.

The evening was more fun than she'd expected. They were seated at a table with Jake's agent and a couple of other sports stars she didn't recognize, and their wives. All of them were friendly and seemed far more down to earth than Hannah expected – she even popped to the loo with Grace, one of the wives, who confessed that she hated things like this and only came along out of a sense of duty.

'You and Jake seem to get on really well,' she added, leaning towards the mirror to apply some plum-coloured lipstick.

Hannah looked down at the sink for a moment, trying to compose herself. The little voice in her head had been trying to convince her that he was this charming and attentive with every single woman he met.

'I've never seen him look so into someone before,' Grace continued. 'Normally he's pretty reserved – stand-offish, even.'

'Jake?' Hannah frowned. 'He's one of the most friendly and open people I've met.'

'Proving my point, rather,' said Grace, cocking an eyebrow and smiling before she blotted her lips on a tissue. 'Whatever's going on between you two, he's clearly pretty smitten.'

They returned to the table and Jake got out of his chair, standing while they sat down. 'See what I mean?' Grace whispered, under her breath. 'Old-fashioned manners. I don't see any of the other men at the table bothering.'

Hannah shook her head, smiling. Jake leaned sideways towards her, talking in a low voice so only she could hear.

'You okay?'

Hannah nodded. His hand found hers under the table and he closed his fingers over hers for a moment.

'Not long now. Once I've done my bit we can sneak off, unless you're desperate to see it through to the bitter end?'

'Not particularly.' She wanted more than anything to be alone with him, somewhere she didn't have to worry about the press getting wind of anything or where people like Grace would be scanning their behaviour.

Chapter Thirty

'Finally.' The lift door closed and Jake pulled Hannah into his arms, burying his face in the soft cloud of her dark hair, inhaling her scent. He closed his eyes for a moment, realizing as he did so that his heart was thumping so loudly in his chest that she must be able to feel it through the crisp cotton of his shirt. He pulled back slightly, looking down at her. Her lips curved into a questioning smile.

'What?' She gazed up at him.

'Nothing.' He lifted a hand to her face, letting his fingers trace gently down her cheek. He closed his eyes for a second time. He could feel the softness of her body against his, his hand on the curve of her hip. It would be so easy to let desire take over – but if he did, what would it mean the next day?

The lift came to a stop, the *ting* of the door as it slid open bringing him back to his senses.

'It's a shame,' Hannah said, standing so close to him as he tapped in the keycode for the room that he could feel her body heat, 'that we have to go home, really, isn't it?'

The door swung open and, suddenly bold, she pulled him by the hand into the room, snaking her hands around his neck and kissing him. Her lips were tentative and gentle at first, but when he responded, she reacted with a passion that surprised him and only fuelled his need.

'We don't have to go home,' he said, his mouth on hers, 'if you don't want. We could stay here.'

'I don't want.' Her hands had found their way under his shirt and she was running them up his back. He pulled her close, bending to kiss a trail from beneath her ear, down her neck and along the pale, freckle-strewn skin of her shoulder.

'That's settled then.'

'Good.'

'Good.' He tipped up her chin with his finger, lifting it so he was looking directly into her eyes. 'As long as you're sure this is what you want.'

'It's what I want,' she said simply.

He inhaled sharply as he felt her thumb tracing a line along his stomach, following the edge of his belt. And then he stopped thinking about anything at all.

He woke early the next morning, automatically reaching for his phone to check the time, realizing as he did so that no, he wasn't at home and nor was he alone. Hannah was curled up against his back, still fast asleep, her hair a tangle of waves on the pillow. He moved carefully, not wanting to wake her.

'Oh,' she said, eyes snapping open. 'Um, hello.'

He felt his stomach tighten with a wave of apprehension. Had she woken up regretting what had happened?

'Hi.' He turned so he was facing her fully.

'That was nice,' she said, curling a hand around his neck. 'Last night, I mean.'

'Nice,' he said, starting to laugh, teasing her.

'All right, maybe that's not the best word.'

It felt strangely natural to wake up in bed with Hannah. For years, he'd been happy to keep the women he'd met at arm's length – it had seemed easier that way. He'd loved Diana, but the way he felt about her was nothing compared to this. And yet here he was, lying in bed with someone he actually liked – not just lusted after, but actually admired and wanted to spend time with. Maybe he could open up to the possibility of—

His phone buzzed three times in quick succession.

'Sorry.' He turned back towards the bedside table and reached across again, picking it up. 'I'd better check what this is.'

'I must go to the loo,' Hannah said.

I don't want you to worry, the first message said, *but Joe's turned up.*

Before you say anything, I'm safe, he's fine, and I think actually he's – well, he seems different. Let me know when you get this and tell me when you'll be back.

Jake looked at his phone in disbelief. Hannah returned from the bathroom a moment later, wrapped in one of the thick white towelling dressing gowns that were hanging on the bathroom door. She climbed onto the bed and sat, legs curled underneath her, looking suddenly much younger and vulnerable. His heart squeezed as he spoke.

'I'm sorry,' he said, still holding his phone. 'I really need to get back.'

'Oh,' she said. She put a hand to her mouth for a moment as if trying to compose herself. 'That's okay. It's fine.'

'No,' he reached out a hand. 'It's not you, it's – I need to get back. Something's going on with Sarah.'

'Shit.' Her brow furrowed. 'What's happened?'

'The ex I told you about? He's turned up.'

'Oh my God.'

'I know.'

Chapter Thirty-one

They drove home in a slightly uncomfortable silence, punctuated by fleeting conversations about nothing in particular. It was clear to Hannah that Jake was preoccupied by thoughts of his sister, and she didn't know him well enough to know how best to respond or to help. When they turned into Little Maudley she actually felt a sense of relief that she'd soon be home and drinking tea in the kitchen with Katie, who at least would be able to share the burden of her growing sense of guilt that she'd managed to mess up a perfectly good friendship with the aid of a bottle of champagne and a sense of being miles away from all the usual responsibilities she felt.

'I'm sorry,' Jake said, as they pulled up outside the post office. Christmas lights were sparkling at the windows and it looked warm and welcoming on a drab, grey December morning. She could see Katie inside chatting to Ben, the two of them laughing about something together.

'It's fine,' she said, scooping up her coat.

Jake took her bag from the boot and made to go into the shop with it.

'Don't worry.' Hannah took it out of his hands. 'I'll take it. You get off and find out what's happening.'

He looked relieved at that. She was almost surprised when he brushed the hair back from her face and leaned over, giving her a gentle kiss on the cheek.

'I had a really good time last night,' he said, stepping back and looking at her with his intent, blue-green eyes.

'Me too.' Why did she feel like this was the *thanks very much but no thanks* conversation? She gave him what she hoped was a brave, I-do-this-all-the-time smile.

'Right, I'd better get inside and find out what they've done to the shop in my absence. Knowing Ben, he's probably spray-painted the walls and told Katie I've given him permission.'

Jake's face broke into a smile. For a moment, the anxious expression he'd been wearing all the way home was gone and he looked more like his old self.

'Good luck. I'll give you a shout later, let you know what's happening.'

'Please do.' She put a hand on his forearm, feeling the muscle beneath his shirt, and squeezed it gently in a gesture of affection and support. 'I'll be thinking of you.'

His eyebrows lifted slightly. 'I appreciate that.'

'Well hello, dirty stop-out,' Katie said, the moment she walked into the shop.

'*Katie,*' Hannah hissed, looking around for Ben. Fortunately he'd disappeared into the cafe and was standing at the counter chatting to one of the girls he knew from school who worked there at the weekends.

'I want all the gory details,' Katie said, rubbing her hands together. 'And I mean *all* of them.'

'Let me just stick this bag upstairs.' Hannah shouldered it and headed for the connecting door.

'I'll be two minutes. Ursula here,' Katie motioned to an older woman who was reorganizing tins of soup on the shelves, 'has been keeping me on the straight and narrow.'

'She's been very helpful,' Ursula said, chuckling. 'Although you might not be so happy with what she's done to your bookshelves . . .'

Hannah spun round. Katie had rearranged all of the books so they were shelved in rainbow order. It looked stunning, but Hannah could only wonder what on earth the villagers were going to make of it.

'You've got to admit that looks good,' Katie said, looking pleased with herself.

Hannah moved closer. Katie had shifted the little armchair in the corner and added a colourful striped blanket and a squashy pillow, and hung some of Ben's paintings on the walls.

'You've put price tags on Ben's paintings?'

'Yep.' Katie nodded. Ben appeared from the cafe, holding a bacon roll he'd wheedled out of his friend.

'Katie reckons I can sell these,' he said with his mouth full. 'So if I don't make it as a player, I can always become a graffiti artist.'

'Like Banksy,' Katie added, looking pleased with herself.

'Exactly,' said Ben.

'Well, as long as it keeps you out of trouble,' Hannah said, raising an eyebrow. 'Has he been behaving himself in my absence?'

'Good as gold,' Katie said, winking at Ben stagily.

'Oh God,' she sighed, laughing, 'What's been going on?'

'Nothing.'

'What kind of nothing?'

'We saw you on TV,' Ben said, and Hannah was astounded to see that he actually looked impressed. 'You were sitting with Kian Burrows and Jordan Hall. Did you get their autographs?'

It hadn't even occurred to her. 'God, sorry.'

'It's fine.' Ben shrugged. 'We saw Jake doing his bit. He looked really cool. Did you feel weird being there and just being an ordinary person?'

Katie snorted with laughter. 'Your mother isn't just an ordinary person,' she said, elbowing Ben in the ribs. 'She's bloody marvellous. She's come down here, set up a bookshop, sorted this place out, kept you from going off the rails . . .'

'Yeah, yeah,' said Ben, shaking his head. 'Whatever.' He strolled back towards the cafe, laughing.

'He bloody adores you,' Katie said, as they headed back into the cottage.

'You think so?'

'Absolutely. I mean, he's always been more your son than Phil's anyway, but moving down here – well, it's made your bond really strong. Is he seeing much of his dad at all?'

'Nothing, really. I think they chat on WhatsApp. Phil keeps promising he's going to come down and then making excuses for why he's not.'

'That's a bit shit.'

'I know.' Hannah took a packet of make-up wipes out of her bag and started removing the mascara and tinted moisturizer she'd put on that morning before they headed home. She just wanted to climb into bed and sleep until morning – partly because she felt a nagging sense of unease, and also because she'd had barely any sleep the previous night.

As if reading her mind, Katie crossed her arms and looked at her sternly. 'So . . . are you going to tell me what happened to make you decide to *just stay over after all*?'

Hannah put her hands over her face for a moment, aware she was going distinctly pink.

'Oh my God,' Katie said, eyes like saucers. 'You did *not*?'

Hannah pressed her lips together, removing her hands from her face and looking directly at her best friend. 'I . . .'

'I *knew* it,' Katie exclaimed, clapping her hands together in delight. 'I was watching you two every time the camera panned across your table and I was like *he has totally got the hots for her* – and I was right!'

'Yeah, but . . .' Hannah sighed.

'Oh don't start with the "oh but" nonsense – he gave you a lift home, didn't he? You're not going to try and tell me you think he's given you the elbow already?'

Hannah sagged back into the cushions of the sofa. 'He couldn't *not* give me a lift home, could he? We live in the depths of beyond.'

'Yeah, but – what on earth makes you think he's not interested?'

Hannah rubbed her chin thoughtfully. Jake had talked to her about Sarah in confidence, and somehow – despite the fact that she'd always told Katie everything – she felt honour bound to stay quiet.

'Oh, I don't know.' She wondered what was happening up at Greenhowes, and turned over her phone to check just in case he'd sent a message – but of course he'd only just be home. And anyway, realistically, texting her was hardly the first thing he would do under the circumstances.

She needed to get a grip and focus on what was in front of her. There was an email from a journalist who was calling her from the local newspaper tomorrow to talk about the ways bookshops were changing in a world where online shopping was taking over. That was what she needed to focus on – not whether or not Jake was planning on taking things any further.

'You're entitled to be happy,' Katie said, assertively.

'What?'

'I mean, it's okay for you to have had a nice night with him, and it's okay if it leads to something else. If you want it to, that is. I mean, you can always just have it as a one-night thing, although that might be awkward with the whole standing at football every weekend situation, but I'm sure you'd work it out . . .'

'I did have a nice night.' Hannah closed her eyes for a moment as an aftershock of overwhelming desire washed over her, making her feel as if she'd been struck by a particularly violent bolt of lightning. She shook her head. 'I mean – all right, it was more than nice. But he's got – *stuff.*'

'Stuff?'

'Family stuff.'

'That doesn't mean you can't have a thing with him. You've got *family stuff.*' Katie pointed to a framed photograph of Hannah and a much younger Ben.

'I do,' she said, nodding. 'I dunno. It's complicated.'

'It doesn't have to be,' said Katie.

'I suppose you're right.' Hannah wasn't convinced.

Later that night, with Katie having headed back to Manchester and the shop locked up, Hannah sank into a hot bath. She was sore all over – she felt herself blushing at the realization that the reason was a night of . . . well, the sort of exercise she hadn't had in a bloody long time. And she was antsy, even though she didn't want to admit it to herself. Jake hadn't called or texted. She'd allowed herself to check WhatsApp but he hadn't been online, and she'd left her phone in the bedroom, resolving not to be the sort of person who spends all night checking. She was, of course, lying in the bath desperately wondering if he'd been in touch. She sank back into the bubbles, closed her eyes and told herself that she should focus on the interview tomorrow. There was a photographer coming too, and she needed to decide if she should re-organize the books back from Katie's rainbow into a more traditional – if less photogenic – order.

Chapter Thirty-two

Jake pulled into the drive, his stomach in a knot of anxiety. He had no idea what to expect from Joe and his basic, brotherly instinct was to walk inside, grab him by the scruff of the neck and sling him out. But he knew he couldn't do that without risking alienating Sarah. He needed to be strategic, like he'd been for all those years on the pitch. He looked at his phone. He wanted more than anything to ring Hannah and ask her for her advice – what the hell was he supposed to do? If he pushed, Sarah might just leave with Joe, and God only knew if he'd ever see her again. As he stared at it, lost in thought, the phone rang out, making him start with surprise.

'Jake.' It was Max, his agent.

'You all right?'

'Yep, great. Was good to see you last night. And Hannah's a peach, isn't she?'

Max always made Jake smile. He was such a rough and ready Cockney bloke, but underneath he was a real softie with a heart of gold. He'd been married to Steph, his wife, since they were eighteen, and he absolutely adored her.

'She's lovely, isn't she?' He thought about how gorgeous she'd looked when she'd walked – uncertain and clearly uncomfortable – out of the bathroom in the hotel, her black sequinned dress sparkling in the light, hair a mass of shining dark waves. His mind took him somewhere else then, remembering how she'd looked when she was lying naked on the white sheets, hair tangled and spilling over the pillow, hand under her cheek as she slept – before the bloody phone had gone off. God, he should just get rid of phones altogether. All they did was bring him trouble.

'Yeah, she's gorgeous. You looked great together. Just wanted to say we've had another offer for you to do some presenting work, and—'

'Nope,' he said, shaking his head in mild amusement. It didn't seem to matter how many times he said no, Max was like a dog with a bone.

'You'd be bloody brilliant at it,' Max said, trying another tack.

'Maybe,' Jake said. 'But it's not me. I've spent my whole career trying to avoid the bloody press. The last thing I want to do is start courting it by shoving my ugly mug on the telly every weekend. Plus I'm a player, not a pundit.'

'You're a stubborn bugger,' Max said, laughing. 'I can't persuade you at all, can I?'

'You can't.' Jake thought for a moment. If there was one person he could rely on for straight-talking advice, though, it was Max. 'There's something you could help me with, though.'

'What's that?'

'It's awkward. And it's a long story.'

Fifteen minutes later, Jake headed into the house, having offloaded to Max and talked through what to do next. He was going to play it cool, just try and keep things calm. And then he was going to get the toxic, abusive arsehole out of her life forever. He just had to stay calm enough to do it.

Sarah and Joe were in the sitting room, by the log burner. Jake was relieved to see that she was in one armchair and he was in another. The dogs were sitting close by her feet, not looking particularly happy. They'd always been pretty good judges of character and it was clear that they didn't think a lot of Joe.

'Hi,' Sarah said, giving him a little wave. She looked haunted again, the old shadows beneath her eyes having somehow reappeared. Joe looked at Jake for a moment and stood up, extending a hand.

'Nice to meet you, man,' said Joe. 'Nice place you've got here.'

'Thanks.' Jake looked at him, trying not to give anything away. 'So . . . how did you find it?'

'Easy enough,' Joe said, looking pleased with himself. 'I found out from a friend of a friend.'

Sarah snorted slightly at that, muttering, 'She's not that much of a friend,' under her breath.

'Anyway,' Joe said, pinning her with a fleeting but intense stare, as if to tell her to shut up, 'this friend happened to mention that Sarah was staying with her newfound half-brother, and it wasn't that hard to work out where you were. Then I went to the village shop and some bird behind the counter told me exactly where to find you.'

Jake clenched his teeth. So someone in the village had blabbed and now here Joe was, sitting in Jake's house as if he had every right to be there. He fisted his hands and then released them, remembering what Max had said.

'I was thinking we could do some dinner, if you fancy it?'

Sarah looked at him with a puzzled expression.

'That sounds good.'

'I've got some steaks and stuff,' Jake said, moving so he was standing behind Joe. 'Sar, do you fancy giving me a hand?'

Her eyes widened almost imperceptibly. 'Course,' she said, making to get out of the chair.

Joe didn't miss a trick. He stood up at exactly the same time, rubbing his hands down the side of slightly ill-fitting jeans. 'I'll give you a hand too.'

He didn't leave Sarah's side the whole time they were cooking, or when they were eating. It was clear he'd worked out that Jake wanted to get her alone, and Jake was just as determined that he'd succeed. It was just like the old days, playing with an opposition team member dogging his footsteps all the way into the penalty box as he tried to score. Eventually, though, having downed enough red wine and expensive malt whisky to sink a battleship, Joe passed out snoring on the sofa, and Jake motioned for Sarah to follow him into the kitchen.

He looked at her, eyebrows lifted in query, and raised his hands in a gesture of confusion.

'What the . . . ?'

Sarah shook her head. 'I – it just – I thought maybe he'd changed.'

'People like that don't change.'

'But he said he was sorry, and that he'd messed up, and that he wanted us to start again.'

'Of course he did.' Jake exhaled a puff of breath, trying his best to stay level-headed. 'And how long d'you think it would be before he hit you again? Abusers follow a pattern, Sarah – we've talked about this – we've read about it.'

'I know.' She sagged. 'I just – he turned up, all charming, and I thought . . . but then today we were going to take the dogs out and he changed his mind at the last minute. It's stupid – he got angry because Mabel was growling at him, and he said they could eff off.'

'Dogs are a pretty good judge of character, usually.'

'I know.' She hitched herself up onto the kitchen worktop and sat there, cross-legged. She looked tiny and fragile, and he felt a wave of brotherly protectiveness. He had to do whatever the hell he could to get her away from that man.

A loud snore emitted from the sitting room.

'I've had an idea.' He pushed a hand through his hair, screwing up his face in thought. 'You have your passport with you, don't you?' It was one of the handful of essential documents that had been in her almost-empty rucksack when she arrived.

'Yeah, it's upstairs in my room. Why?'

'Right. You get off upstairs and have an early night. I'll stay down here and keep an eye on knobhead, make sure he doesn't try wandering if he wakes up. Although after the amount of red wine he put away, I'd be surprised.'

'Thanks.' She hopped down from the counter. 'Why are you asking about my passport?'

'Just an idea. Leave it with me.'

He waited until she'd gone upstairs and there was silence, and then he picked up his phone.

Chapter Thirty-three

Hannah decided the best thing to do was leave the rainbow book display exactly the way it was. The photographer would just have to take them as they found them – and it would at least give the readers something to talk about. If there was one thing she'd learned since taking over, it was that people had a *lot* of opinions about books, and bookshops, and just how things should be.

She woke early, creeping downstairs to let Pinky out, and was surprised to discover that the village was sparkling with a layer of frost. The grass was shimmering white and the leaves of the hedge outside the cottage looked as if each one had been carefully and individually rimed. It was absolutely beautiful, with the lights of the village Christmas tree twinkling in the early morning darkness.

She dressed in a knee-length woollen sweater dress and tights, with a pair of chunky brown biker boots finishing off the outfit. Hopefully they wouldn't want her in the photo, but if they did, at least she'd look halfway decent.

The shop was busy when the photographer turned up – almost an hour late, at lunchtime – and she had to juggle customers and deal with him at the same time. Just to top it off, her phone rang and she missed it, cursing under her breath when she saw it was a call from Jake. Her stomach tightened with nervous tension.

It only took a few moments for the photographer to get the shots he wanted and then he whisked off in his bashed-up old Kia, skidding slightly on the still-icy road. The journalist was calling to do the interview at some point, as well. Hannah looked at the phone – should she ring Jake back? He hadn't left a message, which seemed like – well, maybe whatever he had to say wouldn't work in a text.

She decided that she'd just leave him to it and hope he got in touch. Meanwhile, she had Christmas to prepare for and Ben had one last match to play. At least there – for better or worse – she'd see Jake and find out what was going on. All she had to do, meanwhile, was get organized for the return of Beth and Lauren, who were coming to spend the holiday with them. It would be strange to welcome her cousin back into the cottage where she'd lived for so long, and Hannah was determined to make it a Christmas to remember for all of them.

She and Ben sat in the car in silence on the way to his next training session. There was still no word from Jake, and Hannah was trying her hardest not to feel upset. But by now she had convinced herself that she was just another notch on his football player's goalpost, and that their burgeoning friendship hadn't meant as much to him as it had to her.

'I'll just have to chalk it down to experience,' she'd told Katie the night before, trying to sound brave.

'Or you could ring him and find out what the fuck is going on?' Katie was her usual straight-talking self.

'No.' Hannah was resolute. 'I'm not chasing him. And I've got other stuff to deal with, anyway.'

'What stuff?'

'Oh, God. Phil.' Hannah shook her head. 'Apparently he's moved this new woman into the house, and the chances of him actually bothering to get down here to see Ben before Christmas are looking even slimmer now.'

'I wonder if she knows what a div he is?' Katie said, scathingly.

'I dunno.' Hannah shook her head. 'To be honest, I'm just relieved he's not my problem anymore. Is that bad?'

'No, it's quite the opposite. You spent all those years holding stuff together and washing his sodding underpants. At least they're not your responsibility anymore.'

Hannah grimaced. The thought of Phil – not to mention his underpants – filled her with a vague sense of discomfort. Whatever happened between her and Jake, the one thing she had resolved was that she'd never settle for *just good enough* ever again.

'Another gorgeous morning,' said one of the dads, joining her at the side of the pitch as a gust of rain blew into their faces.

She shook her head and laughed. 'Someone said the forecast was for winter sunshine and showers. I think they must've forgotten to order the sunshine.'

'He's settled in well, hasn't he?' He nodded in Ben's direction, watching as he jogged towards the group of boys starting to warm up on the other side of the pitch. 'He's certainly made a difference. We've never had someone play up front who can actually aim the ball at the net and get it in.'

She was used to the dry humour of football parents by now. Most of them would make fun of their team when the boys weren't listening, but their self-deprecating humour gave way to positive and encouraging support when the after-match team talk took place. It helped that the Little Maudley team had Jake at the helm. He was firm but positive and had a way of getting the best out of everyone, coaxing better playing out of them than anyone had ever done before.

'Not many Saturday league teams can say they've got an England player as coach,' the man went on with a nod of approval. 'We're doing pretty well, all things considered. We thought the team was going to have to fold last spring when Gary got sick.'

'No Jake today, though, I see?' Hannah kept her tone casual.

He shook his head. 'No, Gary's covering for him. I guess he's busy or something.'

She bit her lip and tried to disguise her concern. As far as she knew, this was the first time since he'd taken over that Jake hadn't shown up for training.

'I thought it was just a training session today,' she commented, nodding towards where another team of boys was warming up across the pitch.

'Nope.' One of the other mums – hood up and scarf

covering half her face against the weather – shook her head. 'Apparently they set up a friendly.'

The first half dragged by. Neither team seemed at their best, and the heavy driving rain wasn't helping. It was a while before Hannah realized that the figure making its way along the sidelines towards her had a familiar gait, head tucked into a hood against the rain.

'Hello, stranger.'

She peered at him, not quite believing what she was seeing. *'Phil?'*

They stepped away from the two parents she'd been standing chatting with. 'What the hell are you doing here?' Hannah asked him. 'You didn't say you were coming.'

'I know. I thought maybe we could have lunch and talk, only I forgot you'd be at football.'

She pursed her lips momentarily. Of course he'd forgotten – not once in all the time Ben had been playing had he ever gone to a game, claiming that he had a violent aversion to the sport. She bit back a sharp comment, deciding to be the bigger person.

'Every weekend, yes.' She tucked a limp strand of wet hair behind her ear and adjusted her hood, which was doing nothing much to keep the rain out. 'There are a couple of Saturday staff who cover the shop, so it works perfectly. I'm on hand if there are any problems, because it's not far.'

'Bloody far enough in the pissing rain,' Phil said, shaking his head. 'Anyway, look. We need to talk about stuff.'

'What stuff?'

'Us stuff. I mean the thing is, we're splitting up, right?'

She frowned at him. On the pitch, the half-time whistle had just blown and she could see Gary beckoning the boys into a huddle, where they were gulping down energy drinks and listening to what he had to say. She could tell by his body language that it was along the lines of *if you're going to get up on a Saturday morning and play, you need to actually put some effort in* – which seemed reasonable, given how they were faring.

'Who's that?' Phil screwed up his eyes, trying to see through the rain, which had settled to a misty sort of drizzle.

'Gary,' she said patiently. 'The coach.'

'Oh, right.' He shrugged. 'You know me and football. Is that the famous one Ben's been going on about every time we've spoken?'

'No,' she said. 'And, well, the usual coach, Jake, *was* famous. Now he's just a perfectly normal person living in the village.'

'Bet he's got an attitude, though. You can't be that famous without getting a massive big head and an ego problem.'

'He does not,' she said. 'He's lovely, and he'd do anything for the boys. He's given up two evenings a week to training them, and he's—'

'All right, all right, enough about your new football boyfriend.'

'He's not my *football boyfriend*. He's been an amazing influence on Ben, that's all.'

'And I haven't?' Phil looked injured.

She looked at him sideways. It was the weirdest thing, distance. They'd been together all those years and she'd never really questioned it, just assuming that what they had was love and that they were happy together. And now she looked at him and felt – nothing. Nothing apart from a vague fondness, and a nagging sense that she'd spent sixteen years of her life not really feeling much. Maybe that was unfair.

'Of course you are,' she said, over-generously. 'I bet he'll be delighted to see you here.'

'Oh, I wasn't planning on staying for the whole thing,' he said, looking up at the sky. 'It's pissing down, for one thing, and I've got – well, I've got dinner plans.'

'You have?' She spun round to face him, realizing as the other parents looked up in alarm that she'd almost shouted that, rather than saying it.

'Yeah. Well. It's – well. Look, the thing is, I wanted to do the right thing, Han.'

She swallowed.

'I met Gemma through work. Nothing happened,' he said, quickly, in response to her eyebrows shooting skywards. 'Nothing happened until you and I were over.'

'I didn't say it did?'

'I know, it's just – well, with her having moved in and everything, I don't want you getting the wrong idea.'

'I haven't. I mean –' She tried to find a nice way to say that she really didn't care, and couldn't think of the words. 'It's fine. Honestly.'

Phil stood, grumbling about the cold, until the game was over. 'I don't know why you don't wait in the car,' he said, hands thrust deep into his pockets.

'Because I like watching him play,' she said, trying not to roll her eyes like a teenager. 'And because—'

'Because what?'

She wanted to say, *Because one of us had to be the kind of parent who pulls their weight*. But she bit her tongue again. There was no point in trying to change who he was now. Phil was Phil, and that was that.

To give him his due, he did take Ben out for lunch to the village pub, which gave her the chance to go home and sink into a hot bath to try and defrost after two hours standing in freezing rain. She picked up her phone and idly checked her Facebook account, almost dropping it in shock when she realized there were hundreds of notifications.

'This Village Bookshop is A Dream', said the article she was being tagged in. She clicked on the link. The newspaper had led with the rainbow shelves of the bookshop on their piece about the different ways that books were finding their way into the hands of shoppers these days, and it seemed to have caught the imagination of book lovers online. The journalist had written about how the bookshop had been an offshoot of the telephone box library, and there were hundreds of comments. She'd been tagged, it had been shared all over the place, and the village Facebook group was going absolutely bonkers.

Well, this will put Little Maudley on the map, Helen had written in a private message. *That was a piece of clever thinking.*

The next few days were a whirlwind. The Christmas holidays had begun, and there was a steady increase in the number of visitors to the bookshop. Helen was delighted to announce that the takings were making a real difference to the fundraiser for the village hall kitchen, and shared the good news on the Facebook group.

'Well,' Beth said, arriving on Christmas Eve, 'you seem to be a complete hit here in Little Maudley, doesn't she, Lauren?'

Hannah flushed pink. She didn't want her cousin to feel as if she was treading on her toes, but Beth seemed genuinely delighted for her.

'You're so much better at the whole village thing than me,' Beth said, standing in the shop taking in the changes. 'This place looks amazing.'

Christmas was strange, but fun. Hannah had always found something oddly intense about spending time just the three of them, but with Beth and Lauren it was far more enjoyable. They spent the day eating until they were stuffed, watching terrible television shows and snoozing on the sofa. It was exactly what they all needed, Hannah decided, climbing into bed that night.

Boxing Day flew past, and the next morning Hannah was downstairs at the crack of dawn, getting things ready and preparing for the villagers to descend as if they'd been deprived of shopping for a month instead of two days. Lovely as it had been to see Beth and Lauren, she was looking forward to it being just herself and Ben in the cottage again – and not having to listen to constant reminders of the way Beth had done things when she was running the shop.

Phil had been expected to come down on Christmas Eve to see Ben, but nobody was the slightest bit surprised when he cancelled, asking if he could see Ben the following weekend instead. Beth was now upstairs packing her things in the cottage, and Hannah tidying up the shelves of the bookshop, which had been busy all morning. They'd even sold several of Ben's paintings, so he was completely over the moon and already planning the expensive new trainers he was going to buy with the proceeds. He was catching a lift into Oxford with Beth and Lauren that morning, and Hannah was looking forward to catching up with Katie for a chat.

'Hello,' she said, picking up the phone. 'Thought you were calling at two?'

'I was,' Katie said, 'But I had to get out of the house before any more of the Christmas chocolate fell into my face. I'm on the cross trainer. Can you hear me okay?'

'Of course.' Hannah propped the phone up on the counter. 'I'm in the shop, though, so I might need to hang up if it gets busy. You know how it is after Christmas, everyone's popping in for bread and milk.'

'And wine?'

'Oh yeah, and wine. All the essentials.'

'So,' Katie said, diving straight in on the attack. 'Phil.'

'I can't believe he's ducked out again. He's barely seen Ben since we split up.'

'I'm just surprised you're surprised,' Katie said, with the distant bass thud of the gym in the background. Hannah felt tired just thinking about it.

'He just seems to have done that thing where he's gone out of sight, out of mind. He wasn't that shit a parent when I was living with him, was he?'

'Yes he was. You just made excuses for him constantly, and now he's not part of your life you're seeing what the rest of us could see.'

Hannah groaned. 'Well, cheers for that, now I feel like a complete idiot.'

'Not an idiot,' Katie said cheerfully. 'Just a bit of a mug.'

'That whole straight-talking friend thing can go a bit too far,' Hannah retorted.

'Fair enough.' She could imagine Katie's shrug. 'But the truth is you've done all the spadework bringing Ben up, and now—'

'And now Phil's dumped him the second he has some new woman on the scene, and hasn't even bothered to tell him himself? Apparently she's moved her *kids* in with him, did I tell you that?'

The door closed quietly behind her and Hannah spun around. Ben was standing there, a blank expression on his face, eyebrows lifted a fraction. He was dressed for his trip to Oxford, a rucksack on his back.

'Got to go,' Hannah said quickly to Katie. 'Speak to you later.'

Ben was standing, arms by his sides, hands fisted. His jaw was rigid. Hannah moved towards him, reaching out a hand to him, and when she touched his arm it felt tense as a coiled spring.

'You ready, hun?' Beth crashed through the door with her bag over her shoulder, Lauren following up the rear with her expensive-looking trolley case and her hair and make-up immaculate.

'Oh God, sweetheart,' Hannah moved towards Ben, her voice a whisper. 'You weren't meant to hear it like that.'

'But I did.' A muscle jumped in his cheek.

'Ben – you know what Dad's like, he doesn't mean any harm, he's just—'

'Well, that's bull and you know it. I don't suppose he's giving you any child maintenance, either, is he?'

She looked at him with surprise. 'That doesn't matter,' she began. She'd realized the other day that Phil hadn't sorted anything out. All the Christmas present shopping had come from her own money.

'Really? So he messes around working the whole time I'm growing up, then dumps you for some other woman the moment we move down here?'

'That's not what happened, Ben.'

'Right.' He shook his head. 'Snakey behaviour. It makes me sick.'

And with that, he turned and stalked out of the shop.

Beth, who had forgotten something and rushed back to pick it up, reappeared. Her gossip antennae were activated.

'What's happening?'

Hannah shook her head. 'Just Phil being a dick, and Ben overhearing stuff he shouldn't.'

'Oh God.' Beth hugged her cousin. 'I'll have a word with him on the drive down.'

'Thanks.'

They said their goodbyes – Ben still angry and pre-occupied – and Hannah went back inside. Hopefully a day of shopping with Lauren would cheer him up. Meanwhile, she was going to phone Phil and tell him exactly what his pathetic attempts at parenting were doing to their son.

She was composing a message when the shop door opened.

'I'll just be a moment,' she said, not looking up.

'That's okay,' said a familiar voice.

Hannah's heart leapt. She put down her phone and looked into the eyes of Jake, who was standing across the counter from her, holding a bunch of white roses.

'These are for you.' He handed them to her. 'I'm sorry, I didn't mean to vanish off the face of the earth.'

'It's fine.' She bent her head to smell the roses.

'They don't seem to smell of anything.'

'They're beautiful, though.' She laughed.

'Look, if you're not busy later, can I take you for a drink and explain everything?'

'You don't have to.' She sort of felt like she should

play it cool. Half of her wanted to say *what the hell were you doing?* and the other half – the more rational half – recognized that there must be a logical explanation for everything. 'How's Sarah? Is she okay?'

'She's fine. She'll be fine. I got back, dealt with her ex, and got her on a flight to Malaga. That's where I've been.'

'Malaga?' She frowned.

'My aunt and her husband live there – the ones who brought me up. Of course, they've never met Sarah, but I figured that family was family. And it was the safest thing to do, just getting her out of the country.'

She nodded. 'That makes sense.'

'Anyway, I've literally just got off the flight back. If you fancy it, we can grab some food and talk later?'

'I'd like that.'

'I would, too.'

She watched him leave, then got back to work.

Three o'clock came, and it was one of those winter afternoons when the sky had never quite seemed to get light. The lights were glowing softly in the village as Hannah walked across the green to swap a couple of copies of books in the telephone box library. She located the battered, worn-out ones and slipped the newer ones in to replace them, then hurried back across the road. Hopefully Ben would be back before she went out – after all, the shops would be shut soon.

Just checking what time Lauren's coming back? Still no sign of Ben.

She tapped out a message to Beth.

Lauren? She was back here by two. She dropped Ben at the station at one.

Shit. He's not home.

I'm sure he's fine, Beth typed. *Probably bumped into a mate at the station or when he got off the bus in Bletchingham.*

Ben wasn't back by four, and he wasn't answering his phone. Hannah gnawed at a thumbnail anxiously. Normally he'd pick up or reply to a text, but on the odd occasion when he went AWOL she always had a pretty good idea where he was. She went upstairs to his bedroom, hoping she might find something that would give her a clue.

His bed was unmade – which wasn't a surprise – but his wardrobe door was hanging open and the contents tipped on the carpet beside his chest of drawers. She scanned the desk – nothing to indicate – well, what? Maybe he'd just gone to a friend's place. Her stomach clenched uncomfortably. She had a feeling something more than that was going on.

Hi all, she wrote on the football team parents' group chat, trying to keep it casual as much for herself as anything. *Just trying to locate Ben before his dinner ends up in the dog, ha ha. Anyone seen him?*

Not here ☹

Nope

Haven't seen him today, I've checked with Finn

The replies came back quickly but none of them said what she hoped they would. Her phone pinged again.

What's happened?

It was Jake. She let out a sigh of relief.

No idea where he is

Her phone rang straight away.

'I'm coming down, give me five minutes.'

She tried to sound unconcerned. 'It's fine, honestly.' But as she exhaled a shaky breath, she was utterly relieved that she wasn't doing this on her own.

He was as good as his word. Hair standing up on one side as if he'd been snoozing on the sofa, Jake strode in through the little front door of the cottage and into the sitting room.

'When did you see him last?'

'This morning. He went to Oxford with Beth. He was supposed to be shopping with her daughter, but apparently she dropped him at the station at one. Where the hell is he?'

'I'm guessing this has something to do with his father?' Jake's expression was disapproving.

'He overheard me on the phone this morning.' She nodded. 'I'd been trying to work out the best way to tell him that Phil has moved in with Gemma and her kids, but he heard me talking to Katie. I can't believe I was so stupid.'

'You're not stupid.' He reached out and put his arm around her shoulder, pulling her in for a hug. 'Okay, so where d'you think he's likely to go?'

She shrugged. 'I can't think. Back to Manchester? To see his friends? I can't think of anywhere else he'd think to go, to be honest.'

'That makes sense to me.' Jake picked up his car keys. 'Give me some addresses. You stay here, I'm going to check Bletchingham just in case he's mooching around there feeling sorry for himself, and then I'm going to head up the motorway.'

'To Manchester?' It came out as a sort of strangled squeak.

'Yep.'

'You don't have to—' she began.

'Don't. Just stay here, keep an eye out. Message me the addresses of his mates back home.' In his urgency, his accent had thickened and he sounded more Northern than she'd heard him before. 'And give me the address of your old place. Just in case.'

'Okay.' She picked up her phone and started scrolling through her contacts. 'I'll copy them over now.'

He put a hand on her arm, and she found herself pausing for a split second and looking up into his eyes. They seemed darker than normal, the sea green fanned with spiky black lashes. A breath caught in her throat and he gazed at her intensely for a moment, neither of them saying a word. She looked down at the floor, feeling her heart banging against her ribs, and was taken completely by surprise when he tightened his grip around her arm and dropped a kiss on her temple.

'Try not to worry. We'll sort it.'

And with that, he was gone.

*

What the hell was he thinking? He sped along the road to Bletchingham in the gathering dark, shaking his head at his own idiocy. Hannah was completely wrapped up in what was going on with Ben, and he'd allowed himself a moment of self-indulgence where he put his own desire for her before everything. He turned left and followed the road down the hill and into town. But it wasn't just that – he'd realized the moment something went wrong that he wanted to fix it for her. She was hurting and worried, and he wanted – needed – to be the one by her side.

His fingers tightened on the steering wheel as he crossed the bridge and curled up the narrow streets, scanning the pavements. The shops were closed now and town was almost empty, only a handful of people wandering home after Sunday lunch or a walk. None of them were Ben. The little bus station was empty apart from a couple of teenagers kissing in one of the shelters. He turned the car round and headed out of town, hitting the call button on his steering wheel as he did so.

'Hello?'

'No sign of him in town,' he said, putting his foot down as he reached the main road.

'Nobody's heard anything here, either.'

'I don't suppose you've heard anything from his father?'

'No reply,' she said, flatly.

'Of course there bloody isn't,' he said, under his breath.

'Sorry?' Hannah hadn't caught it, thank God.

'Oh nothing, just thinking out loud. Keep me posted – let me know if you hear from him. And send those addresses through, don't forget.'

'I will.'

He flicked through the radio stations, trying to find something to take his mind off things, but nothing seemed to fit the bill. In the end, he listened to Radio 5 and found himself muttering with irritation at the post-match commentary as he headed up the motorway, thankful that for once it wasn't jammed with traffic cones and roadworks. The time passed surprisingly quickly.

'Just heading to your old place now,' he said, ringing Hannah as he navigated the streets of Salford. God, it was weird being back.

Chapter Thirty-four

There was a glow of light from the hallway that spilled out onto the narrow path outside. Jake rapped on the door, ignoring the bell, swaying on the balls of his feet like a boxer. He told himself it was apprehensiveness, but the truth was that he wanted to lamp Hannah's ex one as soon as he opened the door. It was lucky he didn't, given that when the door opened it was a blonde woman, her hair tied back in a ponytail, wrapped in a green fluffy dressing gown. She stood looking at him, her mouth hanging open.

'Is Ben here?'

She didn't say anything, just carried on staring at him, her mouth agape.

'Who is it, babe?' A voice carried through from the sitting room, where he could hear the vague noise of a comedy show on TV. There was a burst of laughter from the audience.

'Um,' she said, after what felt like about thirty seconds. 'I'll just – I mean no, Ben's not here – he doesn't live here, he lives with his mum. Is he in trouble?'

'What's going on?' Phil appeared in the doorway in a pair of boxers and a t-shirt. His hair was standing up on end and he looked like he was hung over. Bruised dark shadows sat under his eyes.

'I'm looking for Ben. Your son?' Jake was trying very hard to stay calm.

'Ben?'

These two seemed to be sharing one brain cell between them. Jake shook his head and focused very hard on not losing his temper.

'He's disappeared. Hannah's going out of her mind. He's not answering calls, and he's not with any of his mates in the village.'

'What makes you think he'd come up here?' Phil scratched his head.

'You mean *oh shit, I hope he's okay*?' said Jake, icily.

'Yeah, of course. What the hell?'

'Oh my God,' said the woman, as if she'd just come back to life. 'Jake Lovatt! I knew I recognized your face from somewhere.'

'I've got a list of his old mates from Hannah. Do you want to split up and we can check them out? It'd be much quicker that way.'

'Yeah, sure,' said Phil, going up at least a point in his estimation. 'Give me two secs.'

'What about me?' said the woman.

'You stay here,' the two men said in unison.

It took Phil a couple of minutes to get into some clothes and locate his car keys. Jake took a moment to put the address of the first house in his satnav and gave a brief nod to Phil when he came out.

'Here's the addresses I've got.'

He copied them over to Phil's phone, and they divided them up between them.

'If you hear anything, Gem, give me a shout, okay?'

Gemma nodded. She was clearly still processing the fact that she'd worked out who Jake was. He shook his head slightly, marvelling at how strange people could be about stuff like that.

Back in the village, Hannah was going mad with worry. The parents from the football group had gathered in the shop and were heading out in the dark to see if they could find any sign of Ben. It all felt far too much like being in a horrible Sunday night TV drama. She'd bitten her nails down to the quick and was pacing back and forth in the shop, repeatedly checking that she had the phone on full volume and hadn't accidentally put it on silent.

'You okay?' Nicola put an arm round her. She'd come over the moment Hannah had texted, which was the sweetest thing. Somehow saying it out loud to her made the fact that right now her son was missing a reality, rather than just . . . she exhaled a long, shaky breath.

'Do you think we should call the police?'

Nicola nodded. 'I don't think it'll do any harm.'

'And what if he turns up in ten minutes? I'll be in trouble for time-wasting.'

'This isn't exactly in character for him, is it?'

Hannah bit her lip. The only person who knew about

Ben's past behaviour was Jake. As far as everyone in the village was concerned, he was a perfectly amenable, well-behaved teenager. The trouble was – if she called the police, would they automatically assume he was up to his old tricks?

Her phone buzzed, making her jump.

Tried two friends – no luck so far.

What Jake hadn't added was that at one of the doors, he'd been told where to go in no uncertain terms – the parent adding that 'Kian wasn't living there any more, mate, and if he'd done anything wrong it wasn't anything to do with him'. At the other he'd been received with a vague shrug, and then a request for an autograph. Neither of which had filled him with hope.

What would he have done in the same circumstances at sixteen? He furrowed his forehead in thought, sitting with his elbows resting on the steering wheel, looking down the darkened street. The bins were out for tomorrow morning and the pavement jammed with parked cars. He could see televisions blaring through windows where the curtains hadn't yet been drawn. A man walked past, talking insistently into a mobile phone, his hoody pulled tight against his face.

Something had triggered this in Ben – something had pulled him back to where he'd come from and away from the new life Hannah had provided for him. What was it about finding out about Phil that had done it? He shook his head.

Putting the car into reverse, he drove round the streets, scanning the pavements, until he reached the dilapidated shopping arcade. There was a little huddle of teenage lads there, messing about on a BMX bike, a cloud of smoke from an illicit vape hanging above their heads. He got out of the car.

'All right?'

'Watch out, we've got a nonce on the prowl,' said one, making the others laugh.

'You haven't seen a lad called Ben? I'm trying to find him.'

'Ben Reynolds?'

'That's the one.' Jake let out a breath and tried not to build up his hopes. 'You seen him today?'

'He was down the park half an hour ago. Haven't seen him in ages, like.'

'Which park?'

'Don't be telling him that,' one of the other boys said, 'You don't know who this bloke is.'

The bright white of a mobile phone light dazzled Jake as it shone directly in his face.

'I do,' said another. 'That's Jake Lovatt. What you doing round here?'

'Looking for Ben.'

'What's he got to do with you?'

'He's a – he's my friend's son.'

'Oh yeah?' The cheekier of the boys made a jeering noise. 'Friend,' he said, in a singsong voice.

'Which park?' He wasn't going to be wound up by them.

'Greenbank. Down the end of Harroway Road.'

'Thanks.'

'No sweat,' said one of the boys. As he turned away, he heard the click of a photo being taken on a phone.

Greenbank Park wasn't floodlit, and he trudged across the wet grass looking around, eyes scanning in the darkness – but there was nothing.

His phone rang.

'Any luck?'

'Nothing.'

'I'm going to try the last two houses,' he said to Phil. 'Then we can meet back at yours?'

'Sounds like a plan.'

Neither of the two houses brought any positive news. One was empty, the other door was answered by a teenage girl in a pair of Snoopy pyjamas who said that no, her brother wasn't in, and she hadn't seen Ben in months.

'He moved down south, didn't he? To some posh place.'

'Thanks,' Jake said, jumping back in the car.

He was just turning the corner onto Hannah's old street when he saw a familiar tall, loping figure making his way up the path. His heart leapt. Slamming on the brakes, he jumped out of the car and locked it as he sprinted up the road.

'Ben!'

Ben turned, looking at him with unfocused eyes, as if he couldn't quite remember who he was. It took Jake a moment to realize that he was absolutely plastered. Ben swayed as he leaned towards the front door to bash it with his fist.

'Gon' tell him what I think of him. He's always been shit.'

'Let's get you inside,' said Jake, as the door swung open and Gemma, still wide-eyed and clearly not a person to rely on in a crisis, stood there looking at them both.

'Can we get in?' He was impatient.

'Oh! Sorry, yes.' She stepped back.

'Who're you?' Ben looked confused for a moment. 'Oh—'

Jake put an arm around him to steady him, and led him forward to the stairs where he slumped down, tried to put his head in his hands and missed, flopping like a rag doll.

'Where's Dad? I wanna tell him what I think of him.'

'I'm here.'

'Shall we get him a cup of tea?' Jake glanced at Gemma. 'Give them a chance to talk?'

She nodded, leading him through to the kitchen. There was a pile of small school uniforms folded on the table.

'How many children do you have?'

'Two. Connor and Kelsey.'

'Right.' He nodded to the uniforms. 'They have a good Christmas?'

Gemma filled the kettle and switched it on. 'Lovely, thanks.'

'You didn't think maybe it might've been nice if Phil had come down to see Ben?'

She took out mugs, put teabags in each one, found the milk. He waited for an answer.

'I did, yes.' She leaned against the kitchen counter. 'I just . . . I wanted to have him to myself for a bit before we got caught up in the whole blended family thing.'

'Seriously?'

She looked down at the floor, scuffing the kitchen tiles with her sock. 'I know. It probably sounds selfish, doesn't it?'

'You're not joking.' He shook his head in despair. 'You didn't think how it might feel to Ben? He's a good lad, you know.'

'I know. I just . . .' She paused for a moment. 'I've had a really shitty time. My ex disappeared when the twins were only toddlers. Phil and I met and I just wanted . . .'

'. . . someone all to yourself?'

'Exactly.'

He wanted to yell at her, point out how bloody hard Hannah was working, tell her how Phil's behaviour impacted on Ben. But there didn't seem much point. She wasn't a bad person, just thinking of herself first, before anyone else. There was a lot of it about.

They waited in the kitchen for a few moments, then Gemma went through with tea for Ben and Phil. He hovered, updating Hannah on what was going on. He wanted nothing more than to grab Ben, chuck him in the passenger seat and belt down the motorway to Little Maudley.

'Jake?' He stood up from the kitchen table, hearing Ben calling for him.

'Coming. Two secs.' He shoved his phone in his pocket.

'I've made a complete hash of this,' Phil said, rubbing at the top of his head, looking rueful.

'It's not your fault,' Gemma said, putting an arm round his shoulders. Jake suppressed the impulse to point out that treating people like they were expendable, then refusing to acknowledge you'd done so, wasn't exactly stellar parenting. What the hell did he know? He didn't have kids. He took a breath and steadied himself.

'All right, well, if it's okay with you, I think we should be thinking of heading back?'

Ben nodded.

'And maybe you can come up and see us before you go back to school?' Phil suggested.

'Maybe.' Ben didn't look convinced.

In the car, Jake put the radio on and let Ben sit in silence for a good while before he spoke.

'You okay?'

Ben nodded.

'Think you gave your mother a fright.'

'Yeah.' Ben put his hand to his head. 'I know, I didn't really think it through. I just sort of saw red.'

'I get it.' Jake indicated left, making the decision that a burger would probably help. 'You've got a big year coming up. The thing is, you need to decide if you're going to step up and actually be ready to take on a career in football, or if you're going to mess about doing crap like this.' It was harsh, but he knew Ben could take it on the chin. He needed to.

'I do want a career in football.' Ben looked determined.

'Right. Well, there'll be less of this –' Jake pointed to the McDonald's sign as they pulled up to a halt – 'and more treating your body like a temple.'

'Ugh,' Ben groaned.

'With days off now and then,' Jake added, laughing. 'I'm not a monster.'

Chapter Thirty-five

Hannah waited at the door of the cottage for the lights of Jake's car to show themselves in the midwinter dark. It felt like an eternity had passed since Ben had left in the morning, and she was beyond relieved that he was home safely.

'One errant teenager,' Jake said, bringing Ben to the front door. Hannah enveloped him in a hug, which he accepted with good grace.

'I've had a word and pointed out that it's probably a good idea if he doesn't disappear every time he gets stressed out about stuff.'

'Can I go in now?' Ben shifted from foot to foot.

'Of course you can.'

He loped off, not looking back.

'Your ex is a knob, if you don't mind me saying so.'

Hannah snorted with laughter. 'That's why he's an ex.'

'Good call.' Jake shivered slightly.

'God, you must be freezing. It's a bit late for our dinner, but do you want to come in for a drink?'

'A quick one.'

She sent him into the sitting room where he sat, looking tall and long-limbed, on the sofa beside Pinky. The cat stood up, rubbed her head against his hand for a moment, then climbed onto his knee.

'That's the seal of approval,' she said, smiling at him sitting there looking quite at home.

'That has to be a good sign.'

'I think so.'

His eyes met hers and he smiled back.

In the kitchen, though, Hannah felt torn. It was glaringly obvious that Ben needed her right now, and the last thing she should be doing was putting her own needs first. She popped open a bottle of beer and tipped it into two glasses.

'Here you are.'

'Thanks.' He took it from her.

She sat at the opposite end of the sofa, the distance between them feeling enormous.

'I—' she began.

'D'you—' Jake said, at the same time. And then he added, 'You go on.'

She felt sick, but she knew what she had to say. Just in case, she told herself, even if it meant that she was humiliating herself because he wasn't even interested.

'I think right now I need to focus on Ben,' the words tumbled out.

'I think you're right.' He stretched his arm across to her and she inched hers towards him. Their fingers touched. 'I mean, it's not what I want, but I think it's the right thing to do.'

'I do, too.' She looked at him over the top of her glass.

'I want Ben to feel like he can rely on me. He's a good kid.'

'You're a good person.' She took a long breath, trying to find the strength to step away from the nicest man she'd ever met because she was doing the right thing for her son.

'Takes one to know one, and all that.' Jake made a face. 'Seriously though, I'm glad we met.'

'Me too.' She extended a finger so her pinky curled over the top of his and he turned his hand palm upward, pulling her gently towards him. She leaned across to the coffee table, putting her glass down, leaning in. She could feel the warmth of his body. Almost without thinking, she lifted a hand to his cheek, sensing the tension in his jaw.

'We can be friends,' Hannah said, trying desperately not to kiss him. If she moved one inch closer . . .

'Definitely.' Jake took the initiative and moved where she hadn't. He pressed his lips to her forehead, curling a hand around so his fingers were caught in the curls at the nape of her neck.

Hannah lifted her head and her lips found his. For a brief moment, they kissed with an intensity that left them both breathless. He pulled away.

'I'm not sure friends do that.'

'I don't think so.'

'It's fine,' she said. 'I'm very good at self-restraint.'

'Me too.' He took a drink of his beer and sat back against the chair. Pinky, who had hopped off his knee in protest, leapt up and started meowing at him, looking for attention.

'Well, that's that sorted then.'

'Good.' His eyes met hers, and all she could see was desire.

'Good.'

'Mum,' said Ben, crashing through the door into the sitting room. 'Have you seen my Adidas bag?'

They shot apart, Hannah leaping to her feet and Jake sitting bolt upright. If he hadn't been a teenager, Hannah reflected later, Ben might well have realized there was something going on. But fortunately he was sixteen and completely wrapped up in himself and his own life, so he sailed through the room, oblivious, only stopping to comment: 'Oh, are you still here?' to Jake, who laughed.

'Yep, just going.'

'I'll see you out,' Hannah said, leaving Ben collapsing on the sofa to watch something on television.

In the darkness of the cottage doorway, Jake put a hand to Hannah's waist and pulled her close, pressing her against the solid muscle of his chest.

'This is not friendly,' Hannah said into his t-shirt.

'On the contrary, it's very friendly indeed.' Jake's other hand trailed down the outside of her arm, catching her hand and lifting it to his mouth. He kissed each fingertip, one by one, and then dropped his head to kiss her again, tenderly at first, and then as if it was the last time he would ever do so.

'Friends, then,' he said, stepping back. He looked at her and raised an eyebrow.

'Yes.' Hannah put a finger to her lips.

'Right. We can do this.'

Three Months Later

Hannah stood at the side of the pitch, thanking the gods of weather that for once Saturday had brought sunshine and a hint of spring warmth in the air.

'Gorgeous day,' said Helen, who'd been out walking her dogs. She kissed Hannah hello, tucking a strand of her neatly highlighted blonde hair back behind her ear.

'Lovely, isn't it?' Hannah was peering across the field at the man who was talking to Jake. He'd been standing there the whole time, watching the game, occasionally talking into his phone. The boys had done brilliantly, easily beating their rivals at the top of the league with a 4–0 victory. As the final whistle was blown they high-fived each other, shaking hands with the other team. Jake called them all over for an end-of-game talk, and Hannah excused herself.

'I just want to hear what he's got to say,' she explained to Helen. The other parents who'd been watching had already climbed over the rope barrier and were heading across the field.

'Excellent job, lads.' Jake passed out water bottles. 'They're not an easy team, and you made it look like you were playing a team of twelve-year-olds.'

'I nearly let that goal in just after half time,' said the keeper, shaking his head.

'But you didn't.' Jake held a finger to his lips, hushing him. 'The whole thing about football is what actually happens on the pitch is what matters, not what could have or might have been.'

He looked across at Hannah briefly, his eyes meeting hers, and her heart squeezed. She'd tried so hard for the last three months to keep her distance, and so had Jake. They'd been polite and professional every week at football, and she'd put all her energies into coming up with ideas to make the bookshop a success. They'd started selling some new books as well – walking guides, and a biography of Bunty and the work she'd done during the Second World War, written by Lucy. She'd had a book launch party a week before and it had seemed as if the whole village turned out – dressed in 1940s clothes, no less – to celebrate.

Ben was settled and happy, and he'd achieved surprisingly decent grades for his mock exams. If he carried on as he was, he'd be on course to get into sixth form college and study sports science. He'd turned down the offer of a sports scholarship place at the Grammar, saying that he didn't want to hang out with a load of rich kids, which Jake had been secretly delighted to hear.

Sarah had settled in Spain, and was training as a beauty therapist at a salon in Malaga. Her ex had been caught with a carful of stolen goods and was up on a charge of theft, so it looked like karma was going to get him in the end. Even Phil had started making an effort to be less hopeless – he'd come down with Gemma and her twins, and they'd all had a slightly awkward lunch together at the village pub. But Ben seemed happy with the set-up, and Hannah had been surprised but glad to find he wanted to go and spend part of February half-term back in Manchester. She'd spent the whole time biting her nails, worrying that he was going to go back to his old ways and start getting into trouble, but nothing of the sort happened. He'd come home – dressed head to toe in new sports gear, bought for him by Phil – and told her that he'd ended up hanging round with some of the friends he'd been close to at primary school.

'Right, that's it,' Jake said, dismissing them all. 'You can get off.'

The man who'd been hovering on the sidelines was still standing off to one side. Maybe he was a parent she didn't recognize? She smiled at him politely.

'Ben,' Jake said, putting a hand out and catching his arm. 'Can you just hang on a sec?'

Ben nodded briefly.

'Hannah, I need you for this bit, too.' Jake looked at her and she felt a wave of regret. Everything else seemed to be falling into place, but the only thing that she wanted she couldn't have.

'This is Rob,' Jake said, beckoning the man over. 'He's a scout for Oxford United.'

Ben looked as if he might pass out. She'd never seen him so quiet, or so still.

'Hello,' said Hannah, shaking his hand. She gave an

almost imperceptible nod of the head and Ben, coming back to life, did the same.

'Rob's been to see a couple of games.'

'I have.' Rob nodded. 'And I'd like to – well, we'd like to – offer you a place at the Academy, Ben, if you're interested?'

'Seriously?'

Rob laughed. 'Seriously.'

'Oh my God.'

'I love this bit of my job,' Rob said, chuckling. 'It never gets old.'

'You're talking serious training, Ben, and you'll have to be up at the crack of dawn to get to Oxford on time in the mornings.'

'I can do that.' Ben was nodding vigorously.

'I tell you what,' Rob said, 'I've got the paperwork in the car over there at the car park. If you come over, you can have a look, and we can get your mum to sign it as well.'

'Yes, please,' said Ben, suddenly sounding much younger. He looked lit up from inside. Hannah turned to Jake, who was smiling broadly.

'Told you he had it in him.'

'Come on, lad,' said Rob. 'These two can follow us up.'

Hannah stood with Jake, watching as Ben made his way across the playing field, chatting animatedly to Rob.

'Not bad for a lad you thought was going off the rails,' Jake said.

'You made all the difference,' Hannah replied, turning

to look at him. She'd kept her distance as much as possible, but standing this close, she realized that her feelings hadn't changed one bit.

'You've done this, Hannah. You've put him first, done everything you can – and I think it's time.'

'Time for what?' She looked at him, not daring to breathe.

'Time for you.' He closed the distance between them, looking briefly over his shoulder to make sure Ben and Rob were still heading in the opposite direction. 'Time for us.'

She gave the ghost of a nod. 'What about—'

'We can deal with that in time. But it's time to put your needs first.' He pulled her into his arms, kissing her for a brief moment. 'Well, yours and mine,' he said, laughing. 'I can't carry on being this restrained for much longer. I think we deserve this, don't you?'

'Yes.' His mouth was almost on hers as she said it. 'I do.'

They made their way across the field to Rob's car, and stood chatting for half an hour about the practicalities of Ben's new footballing career. They made plans to travel down to the Oxford United ground that week to see what he'd be doing and meet some of the coaches, and Rob headed back with a cheerful wave, leaving the three of them standing in the car park.

'So,' said Ben, looking at them both and trying not to smirk.

'So?' Hannah crossed her arms and stood looking at her son.

'Are you two going to stop messing around?'

'What d'you mean?' Jake glanced at Hannah, a smile tugging at the corners of his mouth.

'Oh, come on,' Ben said, shaking his head. 'It's pretty obvious what's going on.'

'Nothing's going on,' Hannah and Jake said in unison. 'We're just—'

'Yeah, right,' scoffed Ben. 'Just friends.'

'We are,' Hannah tried to protest.

'Uh-huh.' Ben nodded.

Hannah waved hello as in the distance Nicola and her husband wandered past, out for a Saturday afternoon stroll. The sky was blue and full of the promise of spring, and her heart soared suddenly at the idea that maybe, just maybe, things were all going to work out.

'Well,' said Ben, speaking very slowly as if trying to explain something to small children, 'if you happen to decide that maybe you're more than *just friends* –' he made air quotes – 'I'm just saying that it's okay with me.'

'Fair enough,' said Jake, laughing.

'We'll bear it in mind,' Hannah added.

'Right.' Ben shook his head. 'But if you can keep the public snogging to a minimum, that would be great. Because *that* –' he gestured in the direction of the field where they'd stood kissing half an hour before, thinking he'd been too preoccupied with his chat with Rob to notice – 'was beyond gross. Honestly.'

And with that, laughing, he jumped on his bike and

cycled away, leaving them open-mouthed and shaking their heads in amusement.

'Well,' Jake said, a moment later. 'I think that as we've been given permission, we'd better start again. Officially.'

'I think,' she said, as he bent to kiss her, 'you're right.'

Acknowledgements

Writing a book has been an unusual experience this time around. However, there are two people in particular who made it happen – huge thanks to Amanda Preston, my agent, who is there for me day and night, always knows the right thing to say, makes me laugh, and is a general wonder. And more huge thanks to Caroline Hogg, my editor, who met me (in one of the brief times when we were allowed to see other people), took me for brunch, and walked with me round a Buckinghamshire park while we worked out the story I had tangled in my head. Thanks also to the brilliant team at Pan Macmillan who work so hard behind the scenes to make all the bookish magic happen.

To the amazing, inspiring and brilliant Book Camp gang and the Word Racers – I love you lot. Particular love and thanks to Cathy Bramley, Alice Broadway, Miranda Dickinson, Josie George, Caroline Smailes, Keris Stainton and Hayley Webster, all of whom have kept me (relatively) sane this weird year.

Huge love (and potatoes) to Melanie Clegg and to Violet Fenn (for highly inappropriate gossip). To Jax and Elise, enormous love and thanks for always being there.

To Verity, Rosie, Archie, Jude and Rory – thanks for

being the loveliest, funniest people with whom to spend a pandemic. (There's a sentence I thought I'd never write.)

And to James, who thanks to lockdown was by my side for lots of the writing of this book – thank you for the love, and the inspiration. You are the best thing.

The Telephone Box Library

The Cotswolds: the perfect retreat for a stressed-out teacher. And Lucy has found just the right cottage for a bargain rent. All she has to do is keep an eye on Bunty, her extremely feisty ninety-something neighbour . . .

With her West Highland terrier Hamish at her side, Lucy plans to relax and read up on the women of nearby Bletchley Park. But the villagers of Little Maudley have other ideas, and she finds herself caught up in the campaign to turn a dilapidated telephone box into a volunteer-run library.

Along the way, she makes friends with treehouse designer Sam, and finds herself falling for the charms of village life. And it seems Bunty has a special connection to Bletchley and the telephone box, one that she's kept secret for decades . . .